MAYFAIR MISFIT

The Castleburys
Book 1

By Jennifer Seasons

ARE YOU SIGNED UP FOR DRAGONBLADE'S BLOG?

You'll get the latest news and information on exclusive giveaways, exclusive excerpts, coming releases, sales, free books, cover reveals and more.

Check out our complete list of authors, too!

No spam, no junk. That's a promise!

Sign Up Here

www.dragonbladepublishing.com

Dearest Reader;

Thank you for your support of a small press. At Dragonblade Publishing, we strive to bring you the highest quality Historical Romance from some of the best authors in the business. Without your support, there is no 'us', so we sincerely hope you adore these stories and find some new favorite authors along the way.

Happy Reading!

CEO, Dragonblade Publishing

CHAPTER ONE

May 1832
Mayfair, London

I T WAS A truth universally unacknowledged that Lady Carenza Castlebury possessed the habit of running away from home. No woman, gently bred or not, wished to marry a spineless toad of a man. In fact, she would quite likely prefer an actual toad rather than be forced to cast her lot and fortune into the hands of one of the most useless, repulsive men to ever have lived.

"I would rather throw myself into broiling flames than consider *that man* for a husband."

"Oh, for the love of—Why ever not?" Carenza's father, the Earl of Castlebury, exclaimed in clear exasperation, his wits and composure rapidly deserting him. "We've been at this for an hour and forty-five minutes, with me offering up suitable gentlemen for you to consider as marriage prospects like pastries on a platter. You have rejected every single one out of hand. This young viscount makes the twelfth!"

That was because she *knew* things about him.

The viscount. Not her father. Certainly not. Sometimes she wondered if she knew her sire, Lord Winslow Castlebury, at all. As it stood, after years of dogged observance, Carenza only really knew the earl as strict, distant, and often domineering.

Hence the reason for the running away.

Well, that, and because society deemed a woman's position in life well below that of man, money, and often beast. Blame her radical constitution, but she refused to settle for an existence of mediocrity determined and laid out for her by a man for whom she became property. Literal property. To be treated however said man wished. No, she was not for that. Not made for a life of servitude and powerlessness.

Yet, *as a woman*, she must not dare make her rebellion obvious, lest the consequences be dire. Ever clever and never transparent—that was what she was. If one wished at all for the chance at some dominion over one's very own life, a woman developed craft and wit, deceit and manipulation. The necessities. How she then chose to employ such lessons learned was entirely up to the lady.

Carenza chose to utilize them *all*.

The woman's weapons.

"I have heard it told that Lord Farnsley is a debaucher and a cheat." She said the shocking words demurely and softened, smoothing her defiant posture as she looked at her father through a flutter of lashes and settled on the arm of the deep green chaise arranged before the fireplace in his study.

The earl speared her with a glance, his blue eyes glacial and sharp beneath thick white eyebrows. "How would you know of such indelicate things?"

As if she would confess the truth to him.

Carenza waved a hand, a motion resembling the brushing off a gnat too close to her shoulder. "That is not important. What *is* of consequence is that you should not wish me connected to such a person, should you? One with even the slightest hint of scandal associated with his name? Why, think of what it could do to this family!" She finished with a tug at her lace-rimmed sleeve, rather pleased with herself, all the while schooling her features into a perfect mask of innocent concern. "It could tarnish even the formidable Castlebury name!"

Her father stared at her for a good, long while, deadly silent and still.

"You would try a saint, child," Lord Castlebury finally ground out between even white teeth, before regaining animation and downing the last of the amber liquid in his glass and slapping it unceremoniously on the table.

I am not a child. Angry rebellion sparked hot and hard in Carenza's chest, but she held her tongue. At three and twenty, she most certainly was not a child. And if she could but hold out on marriage for one more year, then she could pass thankfully and quietly into spinsterhood and simply live her life. On her terms. That was all she wished.

Wasn't that all any woman truly wished?

"I weary of this conversation, your stubbornness, and am acquiring a headache," her father said with a tightening of his lips, a move that compressed the weathered skin about his face and accentuated the deep grooves around his dour mouth. "See yourself out, but consider this matter unfinished. As the eldest daughter of the Castlebury line, it is your duty to marry a gentleman of the peerage. Crawford accepts his responsibility and position as heir to this family. Even Catamount understood that, as the youngest Castlebury male, he must attend the military. There are roles within this family, and we all must fill them— including you. And as I am your father, I will brook no refusal. You *will* accept marriage, Carenza. It is the way of things." His cold gaze swept over her, from her flyaway, messy bun, down to her most comfortable, tattered slippers, and he dismissed her with obvious disapproval. "It will be good for you. Now go, while I am still feeling charitable."

Wishing she could tell him exactly what he could do with his charitable feelings, Carenza inhaled deeply and rose from the arm of the chaise, her heart beating strong and purposeful in her chest. Anger bubbled just under her surface, yet she calmly smoothed her skirts and inclined her head in her father's direction. "Thank you, Father. Good evening."

She held her emotions together until her feet hit the wood planks of the hallway and the door to her father's study smacked soundly closed behind her. Then the tears fell. Hot, raging tears of injustice that fueled her with purpose and burned with agony all at the same time. They landed in fat smatters across the bodice of her dress and ran in thick rivulets down her throat, leaving wet trails that glistened in the candlelight lighting the walls.

Lit to her left and right, the candelabra guided her through the halls of Tipton House safely back to her room. The Castleburys' London house was many things, but modest was not one of them. The largest and grandest of them all on the square, Mayfair's darling. Mayfair's gem.

Carenza detested it with all her being.

"Mayfair's prison, more like," she muttered as she navigated her way to her quarters on the second floor. Slowly and casually at first, lest her father hear her hustle and become suspicious, and then faster as she ascended the stairs, her father's study far below. Faster and faster she went until she reached the threshold of her room, hand on the ornately painted doorknob, breathing rapidly from exertion. With a flick of her wrist, she turned the knob and slipped inside, her breath coming out in a rush of relief once the door shut quietly behind her. Briefly, she leaned back against the door, her head falling back and her eyes closing. She inhaled deeply again, both to calm her racing heart and to console the anger humming ardently through her veins.

"Father at it again?"

Carenza's eyes darted across the room, pegging her intruder with a hard, tear-filled stare. "When is he not *at it?*"

"I'm sorry he was so impassioned this time, Car." Nora, her younger sister by two years, slid off the slick satin coverlet draping the bed, her voice uncharacteristically soft and compassionate. "You did not deserve his anger."

"What is so wrong with wishing to have autonomy over my very own life?" With a long-suffering sigh, Carenza flung across the bed her sister had so recently vacated. "Men are perfectly accepted for remaining unmarried. I simply want the same consideration."

"But you're a *woman,* Carenza." The steely undernote of frustration in Nora's tone was impossible to miss.

"Quite. How silly of me to wish such outlandish things." The pang around Carenza's heart hurt. Oh, how the truth of it scored deep. Men held one set of rules for themselves and dictated an entire other set for women, and never would the two be equal.

It left a woman no choice but to run away.

Wiping furiously at the hot track of tears staining her cheeks, Carenza allowed herself the luxury of wallowing in the futility of it all for exactly ten very long, unsteady breaths before she shoved herself up from the bed and clambered off.

"What are you doing?" Nora asked, suspicion lacing her tone as Carenza dropped to her knees at the side of her bed.

"Well, I am getting something, if you must know," she answered without glancing over her shoulder at her sister, her fingers busy working the wooden floor planks under her bed. She counted in toward the center three rows, the notch she sought suddenly dipped beneath her fingers, and Carenza grunted with effort as she raised the old wooden slat, slipping her fingers under it and quietly setting it aside.

Nora marched across the room and stopped directly behind her, accusing, "I know what you're about, Carenza." Her sister's hands were undoubtedly clenched in fists at her hips. Such passion in that one.

Shaking her head, ever thankful for and always exasperated with her sibling, Carenza grinned with a jolt of satisfaction when her hand clasped the items stashed under the boards. After pulling out the small satchel and cloak, she quickly replaced the floorboard before returning her attention to the bag. No, not a bag. *Freedom.*

Tap, tap, tap, her sister's booted foot went, an irritated staccato that rang sharp and clear in the quiet room. "You're planning to leave again this evening."

"Always." Alarm darted through Carenza at her secret being voiced for the first time, yet her quiet tone rang with unwavering conviction. She ignored the censure in Nora's clipped accusation. They were not the same, and she did not expect her sister to understand. But she did entirely expect not to be dissuaded from her path by a stubborn, temperamental redhead. "I will not be stopped."

Silence. For several moments it stretched until finally a long, resigned sigh. "Where do you go?"

"We cannot discuss this, Nora. And I cannot tell you." Moving now, Carenza began riffling through the bag for the items she needed, always double-checking they were there, her mind already turning to the logistics required to obtain her precious tidbit of freedom tonight.

"You know Father will eventually catch you."

She did, she most absolutely did. Good God, she did. Each day brought that near-certain reality one step closer.

Which meant she hadn't a moment left to spare.

Carenza stood up, flung the dark, nondescript cloak around her, and shoved the little bag into an inside pocket for safekeeping. "Until he does, I am going to keep living this one life I am given—and I am going to do it *my* way."

With that, she marched to her tiny window balcony and slid the latch open, quietly pushed it aside. Cool evening air brushed across her cheeks, soothing the chafing feeling that anger always left along her skin.

Taking in a deep, calming breath, she set one foot on the small balcony and was instantly wrapped in a fierce hug from behind. "Be safe," Nora choked out, her voice thick with emotion.

"Always. I love you." Leaning into her sister for a moment, Carenza hugged her back before pulling away. "I must go now." Time didn't wait.

With a quick glance over her shoulder and a dazzling smile full of anticipation for the night ahead, Carenza winked at her favorite sibling and slipped silently out the window into the dark cover of night.

And it began.

CHAPTER TWO

D AMON CROWE NOTED the shadowy figure dashing through the back gardens of Tipton House without so much as a twitch of his dark brows, revealing not even the slightest indication that such a thing might be considered odd or out of place.

"You don't say?" he murmured in response to the soft-bellied toff sitting across the ornately carved desk from him. For the money he was about to be paid, pretending interest in the man's abominably boring shipping affairs was a very small inconvenience. "Sounds terribly important."

"Oh, it is. If you've not thrown your hand in with East India Company, obtaining quality silks from Zhongguo is damn difficult. And I shan't even start on about Canadian deal."

"Hmm," he offered, hiding his true thoughts about the lord's trading endeavors behind lowered lashes as he sipped expensive brandy from a handcrafted, ornately cut crystal glass.

Aristocracy. So damned overwrought, all the bloody time.

It was no wonder he derived so much satisfaction from taking their dusty, tarnished ancestral money. They hadn't earned it; they didn't deserve to keep it. That had been his deeply held personal belief ever since he was a lad. Early on, life had revealed that truth to him.

"Tell me, Mr. Demon—"

"It's just Demon." A grin tugged at his lips. He was ever

amused at the use of the *ton*'s melodramatic nickname for him. From his first moment of interaction with the peerage when he was a tender lad of fourteen, he'd scared them and fascinated them—and he wasn't entirely sure they didn't simply adore the fear, since they had saddled him with such a ridiculous moniker and then kept coming to him. Still, he admitted he'd leaned into the name upon occasion and earned himself a reputation over the years befitting the title.

For only a demon could learn the secrets he uncovered.

Dark and brutal, buried beneath ice and dirt, lies and blood and betrayal, way deep down where the devil resided. That was where one found him.

And that was where he found *them*.

Not an occupation for the faint of heart, but quite a lucrative business it had become, finding and retrieving, learning and keeping the secrets of the rich and titled. Sometimes the payment came for the discovery or retrieval—and sometimes the payment came for his silence. And sometimes it came from a mixture of both, such as it was with this particular assignment.

Reluctant to shift his midnight gaze from the window beyond the earl's padded shoulder, he felt a dash of disappointment zip through him when the escaping figure fell into the cover of nighttime foliage and disappeared from his view. Shame. Such a shapely, comely figure it had been.

"Let me venture a guess," Damon said, finally turning his attention and steepling his fingers together in front of him as he continued to lounge in what appeared to be total relaxation and nonchalance, his muscular legs stretched casually in front of him, elbows resting on chair arms. Truth was, at any moment he could react, his muscles ever alert and ready. It had been that way ever since childhood. Relaxing was an activity other people did.

Damon kept guard. "I believe you have asked me here this evening to assist you in a small family issue and you would very much appreciate my discretion around the matter, yes?"

The earl's mouth went slack, and he seemed taken aback by

Damon's candor and forthrightness. "Well, ahem, why yes," the aristocrat finally sputtered, "that is exactly right. How did you know?" He cleared his throat and shifted in his overly stuffed leather desk chair, the buttons on his waistcoat straining across his middle. Clearly, he was well fed. Like a grain-fattened steer.

Damon smirked. "Because I've found that the peerage has more familial secrets than a rookery tenement has rats, my lord." He had considered being less blunt—but then he would not be him. For better or worse—mostly worse, undoubtedly—Damon held true to himself.

"I had heard you were a real salty son of a bitch." Mumbling behind his white mustache, the Earl of Castlebury reached for his own glass of liquor and took a long, thorough drink, his hand not quite steady. Yet the scowl he directed Damon's way held a wealth of privilege and arrogance and resentment for his having dared spoken such distasteful truth aloud.

And instantly Damon was quite eager to take the earl's money, and to discover why a female within his household should feel the need to sneak out at night. Because that was the thing about secrets. They revealed so much more than they concealed.

Suddenly, he was smiling—a fully executed, devil-infused grin that twisted his sculpted lips and bared his crooked incisor, transforming him from dark and brooding into something far more dangerous. Into a wolf with razor-sharp fangs.

Or a demon.

"I am what I am, your lordship," Damon replied. "Which is precisely why you've sent for me."

"True, true." The white-haired earl puffed weakly, waving a hand in a rather anxious gesture in front of him, his countenance paling measurably.

Damon's smile always had that effect on people.

"Unless, of course," he continued, "you've changed your mind and no longer have need of my services." He arched his dark brow in clear challenge, his gaze steady and unyielding. Given that he had witnessed a person's escape from this very house mere moments ago, he rather doubted the earl had suddenly dispensed of need for him.

His flippant response to the nobleman was little more than a control tactic. He simply had no patience for the posturing and lukewarm insults the peerage was so fond of tossing about. If he was a bastard, proclaim it. Call it out loud.

"In which case, I will be off."

Damon made a show of unfolding his long body and preparing to rise, prompting the exact response he already knew he would receive. "No, no!" the earl cried. "It's quite imperative I obtain your aid, Mr. Demon."

"Just Demon," Damon reiterated.

"Right. My apologies, Mr. Demon."

"It's *just* Demon."

"So sorry. You see, I'm aggrieved by this delicate and private situation I find myself forced into, and I am not at my personal best. If this situation was to be discovered by my brethren in the House of Lords or any of the peerage, well, there's no telling how far my status could drop. I do not wish the scandal, Mr. Demon."

"*Just. Demon.*"

Bloody bollocks.

Agitated and annoyed, Damon pushed out of his chair and stretched to his full, impressive height. Which was noteworthy, true. Yet more impressive than that was how a man such as him, who stood over six feet tall and possessed shoulders strong and tough as granite, could move through a crowd light-footed and fleet as a child. Yet he did now as he spun on his heel, standing behind Castlebury before the lord had summoned a full intake of breath.

"Good God, man!" the earl exclaimed, clapping a beefy hand hard to his chest. "Pray, do not sneak up on me like that! It is unnatural."

Loving this part of the game, Damon leaned over the old aristocrat until his midnight hair brushed Castlebury's cravat, and let his Covent Garden upbringing seep into his voice as he whispered in the earl's ear, dark and intimate and full of wicked glee, "Well, you all do call me Demon, don't you, poppet?"

Castlebury launched from his overstuffed chair on a shrill, ear-piercing squeal more fit for an adolescent girl than a man. "Fucking bloody hell!" he wailed. "Cease that immediately!"

Sliding like water into the earl's vacated chair, Damon felt the hem of his steel-gray coat flap satisfyingly around his thighs as he settled in with another disturbing grin twisting his lips. "Do you wish my assistance, my lord, or not?"

Wiping sweaty palms down the front of his straining silk waistcoat, Castlebury blanched considerably. Distaste, anger, outrage, and fear all battled behind his icy blue gaze for several heartbeats before the nobleman took a decidedly deep intake of air and released it with a rather ungentlemanly *"Ooof,"* his shoulders rounded and slumped.

Damon's grin turned sharp. The earl was his.

Nobles were so pathetically easy.

"Tell me what I need to know." He reached for a letter opener lying on the earl's desk and picked it up, testing the point for sharpness with the pad of a finger. "Do not skimp on facts, or I will not help." Castlebury opened his mouth to speak, and Damon pointed the letter opener at him, arching a warning brow. "Facts. Not your opinion or beliefs. *Facts.*"

With resentment oozing off him, the earl began to explain why he had called Damon to him. "One of my children has been deceitful, I have recently come to discover, and I want the truth of what she is doing. I want her stopped."

A daughter. So that was the figure he had seen escaping through the gardens. Interesting.

"Continue," he said.

"My eldest girl, Carenza, has been participating in nighttime debauchery of some kind, I'm certain. Or so my staff tell me after much examination, though they pretend to know infuriatingly little, and I should fire them all." The lord's face contorted with barely concealed fury. "The insubordination of this child!" One fist slammed into the palm of his other hand, making a harsh smacking sound that would have made a weaker man flinch, but Damon continued to calmly watch and listen. "I want her tracked down and brought back. I want to know where she goes, and I want to know whom she meets. I will deal with those people accordingly. *Her*, as well."

Damon thought about reminding the earl that whomever his daughter met, they were not to blame for, or the cause of, his current situation. Alas, it would be wasted breath. Instead, he asked, "Do you have her likeness? I must know what she looks like if I am to find her. Describe her to me."

Already fumbling with the small pocket of his waistcoat, Castlebury retrieved a gilded-framed miniature, clearly relieved to finally be ridding himself of this problem. That his child, disobedient or not, could be such a heavy burden to him made Damon's stomach curl in disgust. He would never understand how some valued social station and reputation over another human being. A whole *person*. Yet he witnessed it firsthand, time and time again.

This time was no different.

Sighing somewhere deep inside where his spirit stood weary and battle-scarred, Damon reached for the miniature, trying not to notice the warmth it still carried from the earl's body. Such men should be as cold on the outside as their hearts were on the inside.

"There is not much to describe about Carenza that is of note, I must say." The earl shrugged dismissively. "An unremarkable girl of average height and build, with light hair and eyes. Always unkempt, to my great dismay." He circled a hand around his head. "Her coiffure is often a disheveled mess."

"How old is she?"

A beat. Two.

"Three and twenty," Castlebury finally admitted. "Far too old to remain unmarried."

Damon prepared to leave and placed the miniature into his

pocket without sparing it a glance. Truth be told, he had no need of the likeness. With his skills, he could track her without it. "I will find her and bring her back."

"Thank you, Mr. Demon."

Blasted hell.

"I am counting on you."

Damon shot him a piercing look. "I'm quite certain you are."

Enjoying how the color drained from the earl's countenance, he stood up and strode to the study door, his body beginning to hum like a tuning fork as his mind turned to this new assignment, the tracker in him awakening. Feeling the heightening of senses and sharpness of focus settle over him, Damon reached for the doorknob and said, "We have our deal. I will return."

With that, he opened the study door, inhaled deeply the scents lingering within Tipton House, and brushed past the waiting butler. He headed directly to the foyer and outside into the fresh night air, reaching into his coat pocket for a smoke. The air was fragrant with the scent of spring roses and lush Mayfair gardens, and Damon breathed in the richness of the evening air and closed his eyes. The breeze washed gently over him, and he stilled his mind, listened to what the wind whispered, catching the slightest hint of scent that may have been her. When he opened his eyes again, he lit his cigarette and took a long, contemplative drag before turning left and beginning to walk, knowing without knowing the direction in which the Earl of Castlebury's daughter had gone.

Damon left the pompous, deceptively perfect grandeur of Mayfair, following instinct and a vague *something*, and made several more turns before he found himself under a street lamp in the heart of London on a bustling stretch of cobblestone pavement that housed several taverns, and not a few doxies hooting and hollering and seeking payment for a good time. Stopping, he disregarded it all and returned to the tepid description the earl had made of his child. He retrieved the miniature from his pocket and held it up to the light, narrowed his eyes until they focused on the image.

Lady Carenza Castlebury.

His heart stopped.

It seized tight in his chest and simply stopped functioning at the sight before him.

Anything but unremarkable, the woman in the miniature was radiant sunlight and sky, all golden hair and big blue eyes, with a smile that glowed like the stars. She was perfection.

Damon's heart began thumping again, low and thick and purposeful, and he released a long, steadying breath as he returned the miniature to his pocket.

Oh yes, he would find her.

Women like her could not hide for long, even when they tried.

CHAPTER THREE

S HE WAS FREE.

If only for a short while, Carenza was her own person. Free to choose her actions, her words. To possess a voice and utilize it.

To have *fun* in her life.

"Almost curtain call, Meadowlark!" came a muffled, deep, American-accented male voice through the thick wooden door that separated them, followed by a sharp rapping of knuckles. "Ten minutes."

"Thank you, West!" she replied to the tavern owner, a young Boston businessman with a mysterious past, whom, after more than a year of routine interaction, she knew little more about than when they had first met.

Yet she trusted West. For this long he had sheltered her secret and provided a place for her. Granted, fiscal reward was quite the motivator for such an allegiance, and Carenza drew patrons to the Meadowlark Tavern like flies to berry pie left forgotten in the sun.

"Packed house tonight!" West hollered as he retreated, his voice fainter behind the door now. "Best get ready!"

Excitement fluttered in the pit of her stomach. Packed taverns were her absolute favorite. She adored the energy and unrestrained expression of emotions she experienced from the pub's patrons when she stood on her tiny stage and performed. To be a part of it—to *lead* it—oh, it was utterly worth the risk. Every precious moment of it.

Because it was *life*.

Pulsing, beating life. Inside this dark and smoky tavern, when she sang, she was the heart of it. For it, to *feel* it, she would risk everything. Did.

"Get a move on, Meadowlark!" West called one last time from the end of the hall before returning to the main room to tend bar.

Right. Where was she again?

"*Psst!* Meadowlark, are you in there? It's me. Hurry, open up."

Instantly recognizing the voice, Carenza rushed to the dressing room door and swung it wide, just long enough for her good friend, Sadie Crisp, to hustle through. "I wondered if I would see you tonight, with Father's new shipment having just arrived at the docks."

"Wasn't a lumber shipment," the petite, dark-haired woman replied with a shrug by way of explanation, moving into the room with an agility and grace that Carenza terribly envied. "Wood shipment from the Baltic is set to arrive tomorrow. I'll be working then."

"Look at you, carrying deal quayside rather like a man."

"Rather *exactly* like a man to most of the world," Sadie corrected her with a boastful grin.

Carenza smiled back at her friend. "You lead an interesting life."

"Ha!" Sadie snorted, her green eyes flashing with amusement. "Says the woman leading a double life."

"Says the *other* woman leading a double life," Carenza retorted cheekily, laughing with her friend. "I overheard two dockworkers last week discussing the young male deal porter with moves and acrobatic skills like a monkey who's making quite a name for himself down at the docklands. A Thomas Baker, I believe was the name."

"Oh stop, you'll make me blush." The words were humble, but the expression upon her friend's countenance was much the opposite.

"You love it, confess."

"I really do," Sadie admitted around a laugh. "I've always loved climbing trees, and it's satisfying now performing the adult version."

"But it's men's work, you know," Carenza mock scolded in a stern voice.

"Eh." Sadie waved her off. "Bugger that. Work gets done better and more efficiently with a woman."

"Shame, though, that we have to hide that fact."

"As women, there is much we have to hide so as not to upset man's delicate ego." Sadie gestured to her outfit, a plain dress of soft green, most befitting a woman of modest means. "I would greatly prefer my trousers, loose shirt, and waistcoat, yet I wear this when not moving deal to assuage the male temperament, knowing full well they would not stomach a young woman in men's clothing. Society forbids it!"

"Just as society forbids a woman of the peerage from public singing beyond her parlor tricks during parties." And that was simply bollocks—to proclaim that a woman of class could not pursue a passion for singing, should she have one. Or that any dreams of standing on stage at the Royal Opera House were simply that: dreams. Never to be touched, ever ephemeral.

"Society is foolish, so we make our own rules." Sadie waved a hand back and forth, gesturing between them. "The two of us."

They grinned at each other in a moment of shared rebellious sisterhood. "I'm thankful we met here that first night I arrived."

"Me too, though I still think I should have broken that man's arm for harassing you."

"You broke his nose, which is nearly as excellent."

"Meadowlark, you've got three minutes!" cut in West's gruff Yankee voice from the end of the hall. "Move your satin!"

Carenza chuckled and smoothed her hands down the front of

her luxurious, emerald-colored satin dress. "Keep your boots on!" she hollered back, and then turned her attention to Sadie. "How's the crowd out there?"

"That's what I came to tell you." Suddenly serious, her friend pointed at the door. "There's a man at the bar chatting up West. New bloke. Seems to be asking a lot of questions."

"New?" Carenza stilled, her stomach clenching. One of Father's lackeys? A Masked Meadowlark admirer? Simply an innocent nobody?

"Indeed." Animated now, Sadie began to move as she paced around the small back storage-room-turned-dressing-room. "Good-looking fellow. Tall, dark, very brooding."

"Well, that doesn't sound so worrisome." Carenza let out her breath. Quite unlikely her father's errand boy, then. His men were ugly brutes.

"That's not the troublesome bit. It's that he feels like a Runner, yet not a Runner. And decidedly not a Peeler. Nor a thug. I'm not certain how to place him."

Unease pooled in Carenza's gut. Maybe it was indeed her father's man. A hired hand or investigator. "You don't think he's Bow Street?"

A pause. "I don't, no." Sadie made a face, uncertain. "Yet he's something, so you should be aware. I don't trust him."

Carenza relaxed then, and said with one last primp of her golden hair in the oval mirror above the scarred wood desk, the top of which was littered with powder jars, rouges, and eye coals, "To be fair, you trust no one."

"There's no one worth trusting." A shadow crossed behind her friend's eyes briefly, vanishing as quickly as it arrived, and she smiled. "Save you, of course."

"We are a unique duo, are we not?" Carenza reached out and gave Sadie's hand a quick, reassuring squeeze. "Now, how is my appearance?"

"Beautiful as always." Sadie turned toward the door and paused, turned back. "Speaking of which, I nearly forgot. Horrid

A is in attendance this evening."

Carenza groaned. "Truly?" At her friend's nod, she pulled a face. Lord Horace Arnold was quite possibly her least favorite person in the whole of England. Far more so than even the disgusting Lord Farnsley her father had placed upon her "marriageable bachelor" list. "Why will he not leave me alone? I gave him an answer months ago, quite clearly. I will never give him what he seeks, as he's a terrible human being."

"Doesn't mean he will stop trying."

"It will be an icy day in Hades before I agree to sing in that man's theatre. I detest the way he tries to touch me at every imagined provocation."

"Understood, which is why I am going to do you the favor of distracting him after your performance so that you may slip out of here without enduring his hollow, over-effusive compliments, bribery, and general salaciousness."

"You are the best person in the world." Carenza went to her friend in a rustle of satin and shimmering curls and gave her a fierce hug.

"As said best person, I must additionally disclaim that Rainville is also here."

"Goodness, I am quite the popular one tonight! Though Rainville is not unwelcomed, for I may be persuaded to perform in *his* new theatre."

"Indeed?" Sadie raised a surprised brow.

"No." Carenza laughed. "But it is quite amusing watching the duke try. Although I confess I do appreciate that he asks in a completely different way than the awful Horrid A."

"Isn't it amazing the difference it makes when someone is a decent human being?"

"Quite."

"And handsome."

"Is he?" Laughter tumbled from her lips. As if she hadn't noticed. His Grace Joss Rainville's lion-esque beauty was renowned amongst the *ton*. Since her debut into Society years ago, she had witnessed him prowl around the edges of social events like a beast, caged and restless. Men such as him were impossible *not* to notice.

"Are you not worried that he'll recognize you—the *real* you?"

"Absolutely not." She waved the concern off. "Though we are peers of the realm, we are of very different circles. Believe me when I say he would not know me from a garden statue."

"*Meadowlark!*" West's gruff voice broke in, carrying strongly down the hall. "Get your ass moving!"

Carenza rolled her eyes, unconcerned. "Such surliness."

"That man needs a woman in the worst way."

While she wholeheartedly agreed, she also knew he was right. It was time. "Thank you for your assistance with Horrid A, and the warning about the new man. I will be certain to locate him."

"Do." Sadie rested a hand on the doorknob. "He is easy to spot. Gorgeous bloke. Rugged. There is quite a forceful air about him."

"Forceful bad, or forceful good?" Carenza asked as she grabbed her jewel- and feather-encrusted mask from the wall hook by the door, put it on, and secured the satin bindings.

"Depends on context." Sadie twisted the knob until it clicked open. "If you're on his bad side, I wouldn't want it. But if I was under him? That's a whole different story." She winked and set off down the hall, her fit body quick and efficient.

Just as Carenza began to follow, an image flashed across her mind of a large, dark, and brooding man above her, naked and glowing like amber against her pale alabaster skin, his lovemaking a thunderstorm of desire. "Oh my," she breathed.

"*Meadowlark!*"

Right.

With a final smoothing of her skirts, Carenza pushed the titillating image from her mind, drew back her shoulders, raised her head high, and began walking.

She was in a fit mood tonight. Whoever was out there was

about to receive quite the performance.

DAMON STOOD AT the back of the tavern next to the bar, one hand holding a half-finished cigarette, the other wrapped around a plain glass tumbler of whisky. Not bourbon or brandy or a fancy cup to put it in. Just whisky in a glass. Simple. The way he liked it.

"Thank you for the drink, O'Connell," he said before taking a lazy, disinterested sip, his mind far away on the gilded-framed miniature in his pocket and the image it held.

Unremarkable?

How utterly wrong a statement.

"Most people around here call me West," said the tavern owner from behind the bar, where he continued to pour drinks as the orders arrived, the pub bustling, a plain white towel tossed over his burly shoulder. "How come after three years of us knowing each other you still don't? You got a thing against first names?"

"Using it would imply that we're friends." Damon slid the bartender a glance, the small gleam in his eye the only indication that he was joking.

"Merely acquaintances," West shot back, pouring an ale for a thirsty-looking bugger who slid into a spot four stools down, hand limp-wristed in signal.

Damon smirked and took a slow drag of his cigarette, the scent of tobacco surrounding him as he wondered for about the hundredth time that evening why he was there. Absolutely nothing conflicted with tracking Castlebury's daughter the next evening, so why had he not pursued her then? Why now? This was an easy assignment. He could have taken the night off for a change. Hell, he had informed Castlebury earlier that he would start tomorrow. He could have been home enjoying his own scotch and the latest volume of Byron's poems recently released by John Murray publishers. In the quiet. Alone. The way he preferred it.

Yet he was here.

He shifted uncomfortably and surveyed the large, welcoming tavern with its worn wood floors and low, thick-beamed ceiling, noting that not a single table or stool sat unoccupied or unused. In fact, several men stood about without seats, ale glasses in hand and tales on their tongues. "Busy establishment you have tonight," he commented.

"Usually is when the Masked Meadowlark makes an appearance and decides to sing."

Damon's instincts were alerted, and he took one last pull on his cigarette and crushed it out on the small glass tray on the bar top before him, slowly exhaling. "A popular item, this Masked Meadowlark."

"Wait till you see her. You'll understand why," the American replied as he wiped down the glossy bar top. A few polishing swipes more of the cloth and he stopped, narrowed his gray eyes on Damon. "Hold it a minute. You don't come in here unless you're after something." He stepped back from the bar, crossed his thickly muscled arms, frowned. "Is she it? Is that what you're here for tonight? Meadowlark?"

Raking a hand through his mass of tousled waves, Damon shrugged his broad shoulders in nonchalance and reached once again for his whisky glass, leaned an elbow on the bar. "I honestly have no idea." Which was quite literally the truth. Though he was certain the lovely Lady Carenza Castlebury was currently within the confines of Meadowlark Tavern, he was yet undecided as to the matter of who she was. He only knew that if the likeness of her was even halfway accurate, then he had not yet set sight on her, for he had not seen the light of the sun's rays, had not felt its dazzling warmth upon his skin.

More importantly, he hadn't smelled her intoxicatingly female scent.

Damon jerked upright and mentally shook himself, scowled. What was that over-romantic nonsense? He was no Byron, that was for certain. What had possessed him to think such thoughts?

"If it is in fact the Masked Meadowlark that I am here for, will you try to stop me?" he asked West, shaking off the momentary, odd expression of poetic romanticism.

The mysterious tavern singer with a voice to rival every star at the Royal Opera House was not unfamiliar to him. He'd heard the gossip, knew West profited heavily from the attendance he gained when she performed in his tavern. Knew she was valuable to the American.

Damon also knew that if they came to physical blows over her, of the two of them, even though they both were pugilists, West O'Connell had the muscle. However, Damon was meaner. And far more dangerous.

West knew it, too. "I could," the bartender replied after several moments with a contemplative scratch of his beard-covered chin. "But I won't."

"How magnanimous of you," Damon drawled.

"*I* won't," West reiterated. "But *they* might." The pub owner tipped his chin in the direction of the crowd. "These folks have a special fondness for her. You try to take her away, they might object."

As if to prove his point, motion came from across the large, hazy room near an alcove, and suddenly everyone in the room began to clap and holler as all conversation ceased and attention turned to the impossible vision that stepped from behind the plush velvet alcove curtain. He saw her.

It hurt, the punch of her. Like an iron fist in the gut. Not even fair—the Masked Meadowlark took him down in an instant, complete knockout. Never in his life had Damon been so ill-prepared for the power of another human being, for the physical response he would experience. He gasped and sucked in air like a gutted, wounded beast.

Unremarkable? his brain screamed, utterly outraged.

Try *extraordinary.*

Lady Carenza Castlebury stood center stage before him, shining bright as the sun, commanding attention with her very presence. Glorious as Aphrodite herself. Underneath her sinfully styled dress, makeup, and masquerade mask, Damon recognized the woman from the miniature. The almond shape of her blue eyes, the plumpness of her mouth—especially her top lip—and the saturated gold of her hair.

And her body…

Christ.

The miniature had not shown him what a wonder it would be. How untamed her curves, how lusciously ripe and perfect her shape. His cock stirred in his trousers, waking. "Fuck me," he swore under his breath, and snatched up the last of his whisky, tossed it back. Slapping the glass on the bar top, Damon scowled and swiped the back of his coat sleeve across his mouth. "I knew I should have gone home." Would. Now. Lady Carenza Castlebury could have her enjoyment tonight.

"Yet you didn't go home," West commented from a few feet away, his hands busy drying pint glasses.

"I did not," Damon agreed, his lips compressing into a tight, tense line, his gaze locked on the Masked Meadowlark, his senses assaulted by her on every level. He was still reeling from the shock of it. From the shock of *her.*

He had followed the faintest scent of a woman across half of London, and she was a goddess. It was the very last thing he needed.

"Might as well stay and listen to her, then," West encouraged him with a tip of his chin toward the stage.

"Might as well," Damon reluctantly agreed, though in truth he wasn't sure his feet would have carried him away even if he had tried to leave. They were rooted to the floorboards.

"It just might change your life."

He stared at the vision in green, transfixed as she opened her beautiful mouth and a voice as intoxicating as ten Greek sirens flowed out, surrounded him, and held him spellbound.

In that moment, he silently confessed to a sneaking suspicion: it might already have.

CHAPTER FOUR

"I WILL HAVE you know that I remained awake until nearly dawn ensuring that no one disturbed your chamber, aiding in your secret while I awaited your arrival back home. You are indebted to me, and if you do not tell me the details of your escapade last night, I shall scream. I mean it."

Nora appeared ready to do exactly that, inhaling an enormous stock of breath, her chest rising beneath her soft, lilac-colored Spencer jacket.

"Shh, keep it down!" Carenza latched on to her sister's forearm with gloved hands and steered her away from their mother and other sister, Lottie, as they perused the newest fabrics and chatted happily with the head seamstress at Madame Toussaint's, Mayfair's chicest new modiste on Bond Street. "You've a voice loud as a brass bugle, Ceranora Castlebury, and I've no wish for my personal affairs to be broadcast all over London."

"Then you had best tell me what I wish to know," Nora hissed back through a victorious smile, then picked up a ready-made bonnet of plush purple velvet and delicate silk roses and held it aloft for inspection, clearly quite pleased with her persuasive abilities, if her smug countenance was qualification for such judgment.

"I had rather we not discuss it here at the modiste with Mother and our sister and Madame Toussaint nearby, as you know as well as I that they all have extremely excellent hearing.

Like owls."

"Oh, dears! Do share what you are discussing most ardently over there by the stocking selection. It appears to be quite enrapturing." Lady Castlebury smiled sweetly, her blue eyes wide and innocent and finely lined, though her daughters knew the truth of what she was about. The countess had undoubtedly heard herself mentioned. The more hushed the tone, the more one could consider her to have overheard.

Madame Toussaint merely flashed them a knowing smile, the young, stylish Frenchwoman quite obviously used to fervent whispers in her shop. Carenza could only imagine the daily gossip the seamstress pretended not to hear.

"It is nothing, Mother!" she called over her shawl-covered shoulder before shooting Nora a warning look. "Merely a sisterly disagreement upon the appropriate level of decorative embellishment. I prefer minimal, and Nora prefers a great abundance."

"Too little is too little. Just enough to be elegant, but not so much as to be gaudy, my dearests!" Mother replied before her attention was quickly gained by the youngest Castlebury female, Lottie, who at nineteen years of age was the least enthusiastic of all the siblings toward fashion. "Absolutely not!" their mother admonished Lottie, her interest in her eldest daughters' affairs instantly forgotten. "You simply cannot wear that hue with your coloring—it's atrocious."

"But I like it, Mama," protested Lottie as she held a swatch of fabric against her front, smoothing it with the flat of a hand.

"Well, unlike it," the countess countered, tone growing brittle and terse.

Noting it, Lottie sighed heavily and set the fabric back on the table with one last longing caress across the deep gold-toned velvet. "Yes, Mama."

"Where did you set off to last night?" Nora whispered from behind a curtain of blue French silk she held up as a privacy screen and pretended to consider.

"Must we do this now?" Carenza asked. Of all the places and

times for such an intimate and potentially ruinous conversation! "I promise I will confess the truth in full once we are returned to Tipton House and ensconced in privacy."

Nora narrowed skeptical green eyes on her. "If you do not, *I* promise *you* that I will follow you to your rendezvous and learn of your secret myself." She finished the threat with a hitch of her stubborn chin.

"You do realize that if you follow me, you risk your safety, reputation, and exposure—as well as the entire family's ancient royal roots and legacy?"

"I do." Her sister did not even flinch. "Same as you do each time you abscond out the terrace window."

"Damnation, why do you have to be so vicious?"

"Because I love you."

"*Pfft,*" was Carenza's unladylike retort.

"I do love you," Nora said more firmly, replacing the silk upon the glossy embellished tabletop, her expression troubled. "And it worries me greatly, everything that you are doing."

"It's fine," Carenza protested. It really was. It had to be. She was not yet ready for her freedom to be over.

"Father met with a man last evening in his study."

"That is not unusual. Our father meets with several men in his study each week. He has business affairs to attend." All the same, unease skittered up her spine. Ignoring it in favor of some fine German lace, she forced the feeling away and arranged her expression into a mask of serenity. Unbothered and unaffected, that was she.

"This was not a business associate. At least not anyone that I have ever seen before."

Now she *was* affected. Blast it all. "That too is not cause for concern, dearest." If she stated it emphatically enough, perhaps it would become true. Nothing. Of. Concern.

Why, then, was she so jumpy?

Nerves. Clearly, she hadn't had enough sleep last evening, and that was the cause of her anxious state. As liberating as her nighttime adventures were, they boded very ill for a full, restful night's sleep and next-day spritely demeanor.

"I'm quite certain you are right, however," her sister conceded, combing through a drawer of spooled ribbons, her red-gold curls shining under her cheerful bonnet. "It is merely that this man was most startling in appearance, all dark and serious, with an air of danger about him. Nothing at all such as the men Father usually tends business with."

Dark and dangerous.

Oh no. Oh no no no. Her mind went reeling.

It's him.

Carenza's stomach plummeted to her practical brown leather half-boots, and she simply left it there, too frozen with shock to even bother picking it up. It had to be the same man from the tavern last eve, for that was the only way one could have described him—dark and dangerous.

Moments after she stepped on stage and started singing, she'd spotted him at the back of the crowd. Exactly as Sadie had reported, he was at the bar in conversation with West, and such a feeling swept through her that singing had become nearly impossible. Air rushed from her lungs, and for several beats she had been unable to breathe, all because of him. This dark and dangerous-looking man.

He was just so…so…*compelling.* Truly the most fascinating-looking person she had ever beheld. His broad-shouldered and fit frame had held more than a hint of restrained physicality—a sense, rather, of near savagery and a ravenous appetite constrained in a neatly knotted cravat and the subtle, masculine hues of finely tailored fabrics. His hair, a chaotic mess of rich coffee-brown waves tumbling sensually to above his shoulders, was the only aspect of him that appeared soft. Yielding. Everything else was honed toughness.

The bell above the entrance to the modiste's chimed, alerting all of new shop arrivals, yet Carenza paid it little notice as she continued to think upon the stranger's worldly appearance. For, quite obviously, he had been a man of experience. It was etched on his rugged face, present in his darkly intense and too-knowing eyes.

When his gaze locked with hers from across the tavern, there had been a spark. It could only be described as such, a spark of something she knew not, only that the jolt of it had left her half-witted, breathless, and tingling from her golden hair to her stocking-covered toes.

"I—" she began to say to Nora, her voice coming out embarrassingly thin and high-pitched as she recalled his dusky gold skin tone, his intriguing facial stubble. After clearing her throat with a discreet cough, Carenza tried again. "I am thankful for your observations, truly."

Important information, that which Nora had provided. For if it was indeed the same man, Carenza had quite a problem. An *issue*, if thy will. A grand, Father-sized one.

Nora waved her off and silenced her with a gloved finger to her lips. Then she tipped her head ever so slightly aloft, and Carenza understood her sister's gesture. She scanned the decadent dress shop until her gaze settled on the store's newcomers, a small group of ladies in animated discussion, feather-adorned heads together like a flock of hens. Of course she recognized them all. It was the duty of every gentleman's daughter to familiarize themselves with Ladies of Importance.

"Pray tell it is not so!" exclaimed Lady Ashcroft, an elderly marchioness renowned for her rather vast collection of waterfowl oil paintings and penchant for tawdry gossip.

"It mustn't be true!" her granddaughter, Miss Eloisa Faddington, dramatically wailed, lace-gloved hands aflutter at her breast.

"I tell you it was in the *Gazette*, reported right and proper," the matronly Lady Bramblewood declared, her expression most earnest. "The Revivalists have struck again!"

Carenza gasped and spun to her sister. "It can't be!" she whispered, alarm darting through her. "They have not attacked in almost two years! It is believed they had disbanded or been shot or killed or some such thing."

Nora merely shrugged her linen-clad shoulders. "Apparently we've been misinformed on the matter." Snatching up another swath of silk for cover, she added, "Let us listen."

Their mother ruined their entire attempt at discreet eaves-dropping by crying out, "Those vile, unholy monsters? Tell me it isn't so, Lady Bramblewood! Tell me it isn't so!" And off she rushed to join the others in their compact huddle, leaving the youngest Castlebury free to choose whichever fabric she truly liked without admonishment or censure.

"The Revivalists, you say?" Madame Toussaint stepped back into the front of the shop with an exquisite hat adorned in ostrich feathers in her hands and worry marring her normally serene countenance. *"Oui?* It is true they are returned?"

Lady Bramblewood nodded so enthusiastically that Carenza had a moment of genuine concern for the safety of her neck. "It is! They struck again last night in St. Giles, attacking and slaying nearly a half-dozen poor folk before melting like phantoms back into the night as they were always wont to do. The Peelers have no leads."

Carenza's blood went icy. The Revivalists were a London nightmare, a terror group of upper-class scoundrels who had rampaged through the city's streets two years before, determined to re-enact the atrocious crimes of another, century-old gang of upper-class scoundrels called the Mohocks. And exactly like their deadly, elitist, and boorish predecessors, the Revivalists' horrendous misdeeds had been sensationalized in all the circulating papers, Fleet Street alight with constantly churning steam presses. News of their brutality was splashed in bold lettering across the front pages of every print rag, freezing London in fear. No person had felt safe on London's streets after dark.

City dwellers had been warned by the newly formed Metro-politan Police and through a declaration from King William himself to stay indoors. Stay safe. Stay *alive*.

It had been an awful spring.

Scarring.

Shocking.

Then the Revivalists had simply disappeared.

All the chaotic destruction of property, all the raping and beating and murdering…stopped.

Overnight.

It had left a collective London reeling.

"I truly hope it is not *them!*" Lady Ashcroft thumped her cane on the glossy hardwood floor, the rapping sharp and jarring. "For all our sakes."

"Would you rather it be a new group of miscreants attacking us?" Carenza blurted out, inserting herself boldly into the conversation, unable to help herself. Sometimes—well, oft times-people's lack of rationale bordered on the ridiculous, and it genuinely irritated her. And today, well, today it *grated.* "How would that be better, pray tell?"

"I am quite certain I do not understand your meaning," replied the gray-haired marchioness, her back snapping straight.

Reckless anger rose in Carenza, spurring her to say, "Slaughter is slaughter, regardless of who is committing the crime. If indeed it is not the Revivalists, then that means there is still a group of miscreants loosed upon London, menacing all of us and making us unsafe. Hurting us. *Killing* us."

"Carenza!" Lady Castlebury cut in, voice sharp as splintered glass. "That is quite enough!" To Lady Ashcroft she rushed to add, "I don't know what has come over her! My daughter is not herself today. I do apologize."

"Humph," was the single, condemning reply.

Falling silent, bosom heaving with barely leashed emotion, Carenza dropped her eyes to the floor in a display of submissive apology and curtsied, loathing the movement. Ever aware of her *duties* and *role* and all the bloody *rules* and how decidedly she had stepped wrong just now, she inwardly screamed. The lecturing from her mother she'd receive should she not correct this egregious social blunder immediately would be intolerable. As it was, she would barely hear the end of it.

"I beg your forgiveness, my lady, I meant no offense," she said to Lady Ashcroft with practiced humility. She had, though. She absolutely had meant it. "This terrible news of horror once again upon us is so very upsetting that I quite forgot myself." To appear sincere, she made her eyes round and apologetic and a little tearful before she raised them and connected her gaze with Lady Ashcroft's, knowing exactly how to appear contrite. The woman's weapons, ever at the ready. "My speech and manners were most atrocious. Please let me offer my sincerest apologies."

Inside she regretted none of her words. Not in the least. Speaking her mind had felt *good*. Liberating, even.

"Thank you, though that is rather understandable, my dear," replied the marchioness after an intentionally long pause, her demeanor and tone softening in such a way that Carenza understood the magnitude of her forgiveness. "I daresay it is shocking news to us all, and none of us are at our best just now."

"Yes, quite true," Carenza agreed, gritting her teeth. That she should have to assuage the old marchioness's ego by tucking her tail between her legs like a bad puppy and begging for scraps of forgiveness, all simply for having an opinion, was so much more infuriating these days than it ever had been in the past. Carenza wanted to stamp her feet and fling her hands high and point accusing fingers at every person who demanded her meekness, her silence. Somehow, she had reached the point in her life when it had become too much to blindly and silently follow any longer. When had she grown intolerant? Impatient? She knew not.

Maybe the true answer was the first night she had snuck out of Tipton House determined to have an adventure.

"Sister!" Nora hissed under her breath, snapping Carenza out of her thoughts. "Have you gone mad?"

"Quite, apparently." Smiling apologetically at Lady Ashcroft one last time for good measure, Carenza let her sister tug her by the arm down the aisle until they were squeezed between two standing dress displays up at the front of the shop near the window.

"Come now, ladies, let us discuss the latest fashion over biscuits and tea!" Lady Castlebury declared, and ushered the tittering flock toward a long table at the back of the store that held a beautifully arranged collection of delicately embellished sweets.

"Oh!" cried Lady Bramblewood, clearly delighted. "How marvelous!"

"What a lovely display!"

"Those macarons do look delectable, I must admit." This from the ever-disapproving Lady Ashcroft.

"*Merci,*" replied Madame Toussaint with a smile that didn't quite reach her hazel eyes. "I am pleased you enjoy them."

Watching until the ladies melted into conversation and an eager sampling of treats, Carenza broke free of her sister's grip and waited.

It did not take long. "What were you thinking, insulting Lady Ashcroft in such manner?" her sister demanded to know.

"I wasn't." She shrugged and adjusted her favorite summer shawl, a soft yellow silk of exactly the right weight that perfectly complemented her cream and yellow dress.

"Beg pardon?" Nora said, scrunching her pert nose in confusion. "You weren't?"

"Correct. I was not."

"You were not thinking?" her sibling reiterated, her green eyes wide and disbelieving.

"Correct again—I was not thinking."

"But...but you're *always* thinking!" Nora burst out, incredulous.

"Shh! Keep it down!" Carenza whispered around a silent chuckle, loving her sister in that moment for her unguarded response. She rather liked that someone considered her a thinker.

"What's that, dears?" Lady Bramblewood called out from across the modiste shop between bites of shortbread. "Did you say something?"

Carenza thought fast. "Merely exclaiming over the stitching

on this gown, my lady!" She snatched the hem of the nearest freestanding dress and shoved it in her face, examining it closely. "The stitching is impossibly small and tight!"

"What has come over you?" Nora asked as soon as the ladies returned their interest to the dessert table. "You sneak out at night and won't say where you disappear to, and now you're being rude to aging marchionesses!" She crossed her arms. "Quite frankly, I'm concerned about you."

When it was spoken out loud that way, Carenza could perhaps understand the concern. What *had* come over her? "Don't you tire of always biting your tongue, of always doing exactly as you're told? Of watching life pass you by in this lackluster, apathetic haze while men live exactly as they choose?"

"Yes!" Nora snapped, darting quick glances over her shoulder toward the group dining upon sweets. "I confess it, yes. Sometimes I do tire of it all." Then she also pretended to examine the same dress hem, creating a close distance in which to whisper fiercely into Carenza's ear, "I do not, however, act out in such ways as to get myself caught!"

"Why, I am the very soul of discretion!" For more than a year, Carenza's secret had remained entombed in silence.

"Do not start quoting Jane Austen on me." Nora leaned back and glared at her. "You are no Fanny Dashwood."

"Of course not—I'm much nicer than she." How rude of her to even suggest such a comparison.

Outside the front window, a carriage had rolled to a stop, its driver on the ground settling a handsome pair of bays stamping their hooves irritably as a tiny, ratlike dog barked incessantly at them from nearby. Its owner, a matron in an oversized hat with enough feathers on it to down a goose, appeared quite useless as she wiggled her fingers and cooed at the mongrel to come back to her, doing nothing to effectively mitigate the situation. Poor horses.

"Do you see this woman?" Carenza quietly asked her sister, for surely she could not be the only person noticing how spectacularly foolish the lady appeared. "She should have the good sense to leash her dog if she cannot control it." A simple line of leather, a tether, and those horses and that harried driver could have been saved the headache. "If that team spooks because of that ill-mannered dog, the potential harm it could cause is profound. All those pedestrians, all those hacks and carriages strolling along. This over-plumed lady is oblivious."

"So long as it is not her carriage, I'm afraid I believe she cares not," Nora observed through the window with a scowl.

The two of them stood there, frowning at the scene unfolding beyond the modiste's front window, when a blur of motion off to the left snagged Carenza's attention. Her breath caught. Unease slithered up her spine. She reached out and grabbed her sister's hand, squeezing hard. "Did you see that?"

"No, what is it?" Nora returned the squeeze, instantly protective.

"I thought—" Carenza started, scanning the busy street scene beyond the window. "I thought I saw someone." Fleeting it had been, just a flicker of a moment. Yet she was almost certain.

"Whom did you see?"

"*Him*." She stretched as she forgot her manners once again, craning her neck and furtively looking left and right down the bustling street for another glimpse.

"Him?" Nora questioned in confusion.

Carenza nodded. "The dark and dangerous one."

Her sister inhaled sharply as the meaning registered. "Oh, *him*."

"There!" Aha! Carenza had him. Well, only a blur of darkness and strength and well-tailored velvet jacket to her left beyond the restless team of horses and the flower costermonger. Still, it was enough. "I'm going after him."

"What? Wait, *why*?" Nora gripped Carenza's hand and kept her anchored to her side, refusing to let her rush off. "Why on earth would you do such a thing?"

"Because he is clearly following me, and I want to know

why." Carenza yanked her hand free and called over her shoulder, "I need some fresh air, Mother!"

"What do you mean he's following you? How do you even *know* him?" Nora tried to bodily pull her back. "Don't do it!" Clearly such an action was difficult to be discreet about, so she gave up before she had really started, and the result appeared to be a quick, affectionate embrace between sisters.

"Oh, I'm doing it." Carenza marched out the door, with the bell above it signaling her departure before any person could utter one more comment about her choices, her life. Somehow time had ticked out on her Obedient Good Girl clock.

Outside the modiste's shop, the little brown dog continued to bark in an alarmingly high-pitched tenor, and the lady continued to take up unnecessary space on the sidewalk, slapping her thighs and cooing in a similarly alarming, high-pitched manner for her *smoochy-woochy puppy-wuppy* to come back to her. A footman had joined the driver in managing the increasingly agitated pair of horses after trying unsuccessfully to retrieve the dog himself (the mongrel growled and snapped at him!). The men's low, calming, reassuring voices were a stark pitch difference from the barking and cooing.

Setting her jaw, Carenza forcefully ignored the chaos and raked her gaze over the street until she caught a flash of navy-blue topcoat and dark, unruly hair up ahead on her left. She took two steps forward, coming directly behind the dog lady, who was in near hysterics now as she called to her yapping little beast.

"Pardon me," Carenza said as she brushed by, gaze locked on the sidewalk ahead.

The matron threw up her hands and cried out, "Oh my!" She was clearly startled by Carenza's closeness, and her parasol swung in an arc through the air and came down, cracking Carenza across her upper back as she passed by, sending her careening out of control toward the bustling street.

That was when the horses quite lost it. Who could blame them?

"Excuse me!" she cried as she flailed her hands about, searching for precious balance—or, failing that, something solid with which to stop her tumble toward stomping horse hooves and hard carriage siding. "Incoming!"

"Mind yer step!" hollered one of the groomsmen toward her before shouting, "Somebody get that bloody dog!"

"How dare you speak of my Wilton in that manner?" exclaimed the lady, highly offended. "He is a particular type of handsome! Someone such as you would never understand."

"Don't care, neither!" shouted the driver as he grappled with the reins on the bay nearest him.

"I can't stop!" Carenza tripped over her feet as she spun once more, helplessly pivoting dangerously close to the unsettled horses, her shawl flapping wildly around her, the hem of her dress tangling about her ankles.

"Whoa, Clementine!" one of the men shouted as the bay nearest her whinnied and reared up, its hooves shockingly close to her head.

Screaming in alarm, her stomach leaping into her throat, Carenza tried to fling her arms up for protection but tripped again and went soaring through the air.

Preparing for impact, she closed her eyes and braced for the fall. The hard, unforgiving ground.

It never came.

Instead, warm bands of steel wrapped around her waist and began hauling her out of hooves' reach and back to the relative safety of the sidewalk.

"Oomph!" she said as she slammed against a rather solid chest covered in navy-blue velvet.

"Easy there," growled a very deep, very male voice from above her left ear. "I've got you."

"Mmmph," was all she managed to say, as the foreign yet alluring scents of earthy spice, wood smoke, and tobacco filled her nostrils. *How masculine,* a part of her noted. With her nose firmly buried in warm, sumptuous velvet, she flung up her hands and fought for purchase. Finding it, Carenza dug her fingers into the fabric covering broad, tightly muscled shoulders and clamped down.

"Are you hurt?" came the voice again, and she couldn't stop the shiver that darted down her spine at the roughness of the tone. It was unlike any other she had heard before. Darker. Edgier. *Grittier.*

Swallowing, Carenza found her own voice, shaky and hesitant. "I-I don't believe so."

"So, you are unharmed?"

The shiver intensified and pooled hot at the base of her spine in response to the utter *maleness* of the voice. "I am unharmed." The words were muffled incoherently against the man's chest. Wanting to thank her rescuer clearly and with at least a modicum of dignity, she slowly raised her head and prepared to try again, eyes still closed from the shock of impact.

"I'm afraid I failed to understand that. Are you certain you're not injured?" that deep voice asked. "Perhaps all that spinning about rattled your head?"

"Not at"—a large, hard hand cupped her chin and tipped her face skyward—"all," she finished lamely before she opened her eyes. "You!" she gasped.

"Me?"

Him.

The dark and dangerous one.

"Yes, *you.*" Intense molten chocolate eyes, firmly sculpted lips, wild, dark tumble of hair. It could only be him.

He stared at her, his gaze unreadable yet somehow knowing, intimate in its appraisal of her. Carenza's skin prickled, goosebumps breaking out along her arms, and she went taut, her muscles tense with awareness of this…this *man.* Her nostrils flared, and once again the scent of him invaded her senses, intriguing and excitingly unfamiliar. Before she had her wits about her, she leaned the tiniest fraction toward him and breathed in.

A rumble began in his firm, muscled chest, low and deep, before rising on a growl so full of message and warning in its single, powerful note that Carenza felt it resonate in the pit of her stomach, quivering there.

Her body went rather hot and cold, all at once. Inhaling sharply, Carenza dropped her hands from his shoulders as if singed by fire—and felt the abrupt absence as he released his. Her heart skipped a beat and began pounding furiously; blood rushed to her cheeks and flooded her ears, crashing like ocean waves inside her head.

"Miss!" someone called from behind her shoulder. "Miss! Are ye unharmed?"

Through the pounding in her ears, she recognized the voice of the carriage driver and turned her head toward him to respond, wetting lips gone suddenly quite desperately dry. "I am safe, good sir," she croaked. "Thank you for inquiring." Offering a wobbly smile, she swung her head back around to *him*.

And discovered herself alone.

Like a ghost, he had disappeared.

Damnation.

Bloody hell.

How was she to discover his reason for following her now?

"Who the blazes are you?" she asked the breeze, knowing full well it would never divulge his secret. *Why do you smell so good?*

The door to the modiste shop burst open with a ring of the bell, and a bundle of pastel fabric and worried female voices rushed through, loud and discordant as clanging kitchen pots.

"Carenza, my dear, my darling!" her mother exclaimed with a flutter of hands and swirl of muslin as she hurried to assess the damage, her age-faded red hair loosing from its pins in her haste. "Are you hurt? Oh, I could not live if you were!"

"I am fine, Mother." All thanks to *him*.

As the swarm of concerned ladies descended upon her, tittering and fussing and creating quite a commotion, Carenza glanced over her shoulder and swept her gaze from one side of the street to the other, searching for a hint of navy-blue velvet. But nothing.

He was gone.

Yet his scent, so exotically male, lingered.

Carenza inhaled slowly, savoring, knowing it was one she was quite unlikely to ever forget.

CHAPTER FIVE

H E HADN'T MEANT to touch her.

Strictly observe—that had been the mission of the outing. Go, see, and record only. The mission had not been to wrap his arms around the shapeliest waist he had ever encountered and to practically bury his nose in sumptuous sunshine hair, fragrant with a hint of lemon.

Damon shifted his weight, his trousers snugging a bit across the front flap as the memory of her stirred his senses, warmed his blood. Cursing softly, he glanced around the Meadowlark Tavern to distract his thoughts, noting all the people in attendance, the overflowing pints, the veritable cheer in the air. Their eagerness for the Masked Meadowlark's talented vocals permeated the atmosphere. After what he had witnessed, he blamed them not at all.

Her voice had haunted his dreams.

Her voice, her scent.

He'd woken *smelling* her. Lilacs and lemons.

On his way to Mayfair that morning after breaking his fast, he had encountered a large purple shrub in full bloom smelling sweet as her, and he had snapped one clean off and buried his nose in its tiny and delicate petals before he knew what he was about. Bloody disconcerting, that. Quite especially for a man who considered such foolishness a personal character flaw. Of which he had many, no mistake. Simply not that particular one. Or he

41

had not *had* that particular one.

Now…

Damon shook his head, vaguely mortified. For a man who made his living sifting through darkness and greed and lies—who knew the darkness within *him*—the fact that he'd dreamt about her voice and scent and woke hungry with yearning was wholly troublesome. Perhaps he should go a few rounds in the ring with his boxing partner Aaron and let him knock some sense back into him. For clearly sense had up and deserted him.

"Frown any deeper and it will melt your whole countenance clean off. What has you scowling so fiercely?"

"Life." Sliding a glance toward the arrived company, Damon shrugged an ill-tempered shoulder, the motion jerky. "Rainville," he acknowledged the new arrival with a barely perceptible tip of his chin.

"Ah, so you do know of me," the blond aristocrat said, an air of entitlement and wealth about him. "I say, that's rather excellent, as I know exactly who *you* are, Demon."

Pulling his lips back in a snarl masquerading as a smile, Damon felt his nerves spike and wished suddenly for a cigarette. He roamed through his pockets until he found one, lighting it with a match, which he also kept in his pocket—prepared as always, since his nerves had a way of creeping in. Smoking was a way to handle the fidgetiness, the pent-upness.

"Everyone knows who I am," Damon growled around his cigarette as he cupped a hand at its end and struck the match, lit the tip until it glowed red.

"You're not a *ton* favorite."

"Their fault, not mine." Damon took a deep, slow drag.

"I concur," Rainville replied, amusement in his strange golden eyes. "Elites fear and dislike what can topple them."

"Which tack are you trying here, Rainville?" Damon said, cutting to the chase. "Buttering me up so that I'll help you, or befriending me so that I won't retrieve your own skeletons, should such a thing be asked?" He smirked and shook his head. "I can assure you that for the right price, I am nobody's friend."

"No loyalty, then?"

"Only to the highest bidder, Your Grace." Thinking that the insult would stave off the suddenly chummy duke, Damon made to leave. "Should you ever be in need, you can find me."

"Not so hasty." A long, jacket-covered arm cut across him, blocking his exit. "I'm not quite done."

"I am." Annoyed at the duke's high-handedness and never one to tolerate another's ego well, regardless of social status, Damon flashed him a warning look, his dark eyes smoldering. "Drop your arm before I break it."

Rainville must have seen the truth behind the threat, for he lowered his arm and raked a hand through his crop of tawny hair. "Apologies."

"Mmm," was all Damon replied.

"It's simply… I mean, I—" The duke broke off, cursing under his breath. "There may be something I need from you."

"When you figure it out, find me." Damon took another drag of his cigarette. "Until then, your presence is unappreciated." Craning his neck, he pointedly looked around the nobleman to the crowd. "I've things to do."

"I say, are you on an assignment?"

Bloody hell. Why were nobles always so damned nosy?

"Yes," he said between his teeth.

"Excellent!" Rainville's eyes lit up like a campfire, dancing with interest. "How does that work?"

Had Damon wanted a chum? A friend? Had he asked this oversized duke to play the part?

No.

Crushing out his cigarette on the tray atop the nearby bar, Damon tamped down the annoyance. No one had ever taken an interest in his affairs before, especially not a peer of the realm. Irritation aside, the question that begged to be answered was why. What was Rainville after?

"What is a person such as yourself doing here in the middle of

Covent Garden, in this dim and smoke-filled tavern? There are gambling hells aplenty closer to your neighborhood. What is your aim?" Damon asked, his tone gruff and to the point.

"Perhaps we should have a drink and discuss?" The duke signaled down the bar toward West. "Two single malts."

The tavern owner nodded his receipt of the order, white bar towel perpetually resting over his shoulder. "Coming up." He gathered two glasses and began to pour. "You here for Meadowlark's performance?"

"Always," the duke replied with a small smile. "I've plans."

Alert to that, Damon narrowed his eyes on the blond nobleman, protectiveness for Lady Carenza rising inside, shocking him. Protective? Of her? Since when?

More importantly, *why?*

And what bloody *plans* did Rainville think he had with Carenza?

"She's mine," tore from his throat on a low growl.

"What was that?" Rainville raised a bronze brow quizzically, retrieving their drinks with a languidness reserved for men of high-society leisure.

"Do you ever work?" Damon said. Unwilling to repeat the idiocy that had just escaped his mouth, he turned the topic of conversation. "And by 'work,' I mean do anything of worth or substance?"

"Ouch." Rainville frowned. "Do you ever do anything besides be a twat?"

"Not generally," Damon replied, biting back amusement and a dash of appreciation for the duke's pithy retort. He failed, and a grin turned his lips. "Touché." Raising the glass tumbler Rainville handed him, he added, "Well-done insult."

The aristocrat chuckled. "I was inspired."

"All right, duke." Damon rarely, if ever, found amusement with the aristocracy, and so this nobleman with the quick wit had his attention. "Tell me what you're after."

"Will you first tell me what your assignment is?"

Damon snorted. "Absolutely not."

"It was worth a shot," the duke replied with a grin, clapping him on the shoulder like they were Eton chums.

Damon glanced at his shoulder and quirked an eyebrow at Rainville. "Are we friends?"

"I hope to be, as I've no wish to be on your bad side, and I've a few items of import that could very much use your brand of talent."

"Such as?" Damon pressed, swirling his tumbler as his curiosity stirred. Knowing the duke's pedigree and reputation, it had to be good.

"Lord Horace Arnold," the aristocrat began, "is the first order of business." He pointed his glass across the crowded tavern. "See there? Over by the fireplace? The gentleman with the enormous sideburns."

"You mean the dandy?" Damon snorted, noting the huge and fuzzy sideburns, an unfortunate choice. "What has that ill-styled sod to do with anything?"

"That *sod* is a viscount, and he's currently conducting a business venture that clashes with my own interests." Rainville cut him a hard look. "Yes, even entitled dukes do, in fact, *work*."

"Impressive," Damon drawled, not even a little impressed. "I stand corrected."

"Are you always this disrespectful of your betters?" Rainville suddenly demanded, a scowl pulling his eyebrows together over his nose.

"Every chance I get," Damon replied with relish. Before the duke could respond, he added, "It's what makes me so good at what I do."

"Fair enough," Rainville acquiesced after a few moments, his frown easing. "What do you know about the theatre?"

"Not a bloody thing," Damon replied. "Attended an opera once, but only to fuck the soprano backstage. Never saw one from the audience seats." Why had he just shared that? What the blazes?

Damon promptly clapped his mouth shut, dove for his pack of cigarettes, and lit another one. Who the devil was he turning into, willingly sharing personal details about himself? With nerves leaping in his belly like restless frogs, he scowled and took a drag. His nerves refused to settle, so he repeated the action, taking another puff.

"Forget I said that," he grumbled.

"Not a chance," Rainville returned around a laugh, his eyes bright with mirth.

Damon glared at the nobleman. "Share that and I will pummel you, duke or not."

"Noted." The bastard chuckled.

Gritting his teeth, Damon turned his attention back to the fop with the overambitious sideburns. "You wish me to uncover something unsavory on the dandy to hurt his new business," he said quietly, cutting right to it, preferring to state things plainly, as it put everyone on the same page, with less chance of misunderstanding.

"Don't be so hasty." Rainville held up his palms, looking innocent. "I have no intention—" He broke off and gave a harsh laugh, dropping his hands. "Fine. In truth, I do wish to know if there is anything of ill note about the viscount. He is encroaching on my business and endeavoring to take what is mine."

"And what is that?" Damon asked softly, his instincts telling him that he already knew—and he didn't like it. Not one bit.

"The Masked Meadowlark."

"The hell you say!" exploded from Damon, and he shoved his cigarette between his lips, trying to pretend the outburst hadn't happened. Inside he fumed at the idea of her belonging to anyone…except maybe to *him*?

Christ, what the—?

"Is she your assignment?" Rainville sliced into Damon's thoughts and shot him a look, strange golden eyes narrowing on him in suspicion.

"No," Damon lied, irritated as hell with perceptive, nosy

dukes. In his experience, the lot were generally overbred, vain, and slowtopped. This one had proven at least to not be the last. "What is this other issue of yours that you wish me to inquire into?" He once again spun the conversation away from anything personal and glanced, a bit desperately, at the clock on the wall opposite him. Meadowlark needed to sing already and save him from further unwanted discussions. His monthly quota had hit full yesterday, and it was still the first week of May.

"Ah," Rainville replied, and leaned toward him. "That is a more delicate matter. One I should not wish to discuss in public."

Damon nodded. "A secret to keep. Understood. Find me when you're ready."

Feeling every moment of the interaction like a physical weight, Damon was nearing the end of his patience when he smelled her.

Lilacs and lemon.

His gut clenched and the memory of her flooded his senses. Her body flush against him, her voice so feminine and sweet against his ear, the way she leaned into him, seeking his scent.

His *scent*.

"Damn it," he swore, his body clenching with sudden tension. Good Christ, she'd wanted his scent. *His.* Like a she-wolf sniffing a potential mate. How could he not be affected? It was one of the sexiest things he'd ever seen.

"Something amiss?" Rainville inquired, an annoyingly regal eyebrow raised in question.

Bloody everything, Damon thought, Lady Carenza's feather-light scent bombarding him like a battering ram. "I don't even *like* her," he muttered. "She's aristocracy." The word tasted foul upon his tongue. Yet he heatedly scanned the tavern from one end and back, including the dim corners, all in search of the sun.

Sudden movement caught his gaze, and he noted Lord Horace Arnold with his hawkish nose and weak dandy chin making his way across the pub. In two seconds, Damon sized up the viscount and understood exactly who he was and how he ticked.

From the overt smugness he wore like a prized cloak to the predatorial glint in his eyes, Damon knew him instantly to be the worst form of coward and bully.

And this shit-sack wanted Lady Carenza?

Not on his watch.

Timing it just so, Damon waited as the viscount came closer, keeping a casual eye on his progress. "I'll help you with the dandy," he blurted suddenly, surprising himself.

"You will?" Rainville replied.

Damon hesitated for several breaths. "I suppose I will, yes."

"You suppose you will," the duke parroted flatly, sounding disappointed.

"What, do you want a proclamation? An announcement in the *Gazette*?"

"No, no, your agreement is good enough, reluctant as it is. Capital news!" Rainville cheered, clapping him on the shoulder. It was becoming a habit, that. "I'm thrilled I convinced you."

Damon rolled his shoulder, and the duke's hand slid off. "You didn't. *He* did." With a quick tip of his head, he gestured to the weak-chinned viscount moving steadily closer. "I don't like the feel of him. *Mala energia*," he added quietly in his mother's native tongue—*his* first, his home language.

"How does that work? *Feeling* people?"

"It's similar to determining their basic, vital personality. Who they truly are deep down inside when no one is watching," Damon explained, offering the truth up freely. He figured he was already in it with the duke, so why stop now? Besides, the nobleman genuinely seemed interested. For some reason, that almost pleased him. Not really. But a little. Maybe.

"Fascinating. Where did you learn this unique skill?"

"Here and there." Damon cursed his forgotten cigarette as it burned down and singed him between his fingers. "Bollocks!" After quickly crushing it out in a tray, he shook the sting out of his digits and noticed an empty pint glass on the pub floor nearby, spinning lazily.

Glancing over to Lord Arnold, he gauged the distance and decided he could do it.

"Damn, but those things can sting." Waving his singed fingers in the air for distraction, Damon discreetly snagged the glass with a boot and rolled it to himself.

"You could always quit and save your fingers," Rainville pointed out.

"I could," Damon agreed, knowing he wouldn't.

Shifting his foot and readying the pint glass, he held steady until just the right moment. It presented itself beautifully when the Masked Meadowlark stepped into the main tavern room and the viscount spotted her, his eyes turning overbright and unfocused. Cheering flooded the pub as she took the stage, this time in a frock and matching mask of sinful scarlet.

Though his brain and body tensed at her appearance, Damon kept his wits enough about him and took aim. With a flick of his booted foot, he sent the glass scuttling across the floor, timing the kick so that it was certain to be in Lord Arnold's path.

The viscount took a distracted step, his greedy gaze on the front stage, and cried out in surprise. His foot slipped on the empty glass, and the fop went flying, looking most undignified, across the tavern, crashing unceremoniously into a table full of ale mugs and people, toppling them all down upon him.

Damon smirked, enjoying the scene unfolding as the viscount sputtered and cursed and squealed and tried to untangle himself from the pile of limbs. "Get off me, you unsavory beasts!"

"I saw that," Rainville murmured, leaning toward him.

"Saw what?" Damon replied innocently, fighting a smile as the viscount continued to scramble on the floor with the "unsavory" common folk, making quite a scene. "I did nothing."

"Ah. So, I won't thank you, then."

"Nothing to thank me for," Damon asserted, his lips twitching.

"Well then…" Rainville trailed off, his gaze drifting to the stage, where the Masked Meadowlark held court.

Damon's amusement died, and the urge to plant his fist in the duke's pretty face for looking at Lady Carenza took him by surprise, had him swearing under his breath. How could he possibly feel so protective over a woman he hadn't even met yet?

He knew the answer had to do with the *feel* of her, and he didn't like what it said about him. He had no business appreciating a highborn lady, or her *alma*. But by Christ, how she shone. For a man accustomed to the dark, her light was nearly blinding.

When she sang she was completely mesmerizing.

"What the devil? What is *she* doing here?" Rainville's voice rose in alarm as he stared across the rambunctious crowd, his attention quite turned from the front stage. Damon couldn't help noticing the duke's frown and the stiffening of his posture.

Intrigued at the nobleman's response, he followed Rainville's gaze to the tavern entrance, and swallowed a grin at the sight that greeted him. "You know her?" he asked the duke.

Of course, Damon knew who she was. It was his business to know—quite literally. And Lady Carenza's sister was most definitely someone he should know. For if she, say, decided to don peasant garb and sneak into a questionable public house in the shady portion of the city, he should know enough to recognize her.

The interesting question was, why did Rainville?

"I know her," the nobleman begrudgingly admitted. "Or, I should say more correctly, I am acquainted with her family. She shouldn't be here. If she's revealed, the scandal would topple her family." He reached beside him and set his glass tumbler on the bar top, mumbling in a tone not meant for Damon's ears, "I may need them." Then stronger, clearer, "Excuse me."

With that, Rainville strode across the pub, his attention no longer on the Masked Meadowlark but rather her younger sister, Lady Ceranora Castlebury. Very intriguing. Why did the duke care she was there? It seemed to follow logic to Damon that if one daughter would sneak out, so too would another. However, the duke seemed not to be privy to the connection between the two—that the Masked Meadowlark and Lady Ceranora Castle-bury were related.

Therefore, his response was especially curious.

What interested Damon most was whether the sisters were aware of the other's clandestine activities or if this meeting at the pub was merely coincidental. Quickly glancing at the Masked Meadowlark, he surmised by the shocked expression she desperately attempted to hide that she had not been expecting her younger sibling's arrival. He chuckled quietly, thinking of the webs a person wove and the inevitable resulting tangle. People went to great lengths to avoid honesty.

As Meadowlark struggled for composure and calm on stage, Damon turned his attention, catching the younger Castlebury female apparently giving Rainville hell with a rather heated dressing-down. Her countenance was alight with displeasure as she waved her arms animatedly and shook her head, loosening a few strands of reddish hair from her bonnet. Each time the duke reached for her elbow, she yanked it away and scowled at him.

Damon's chuckle turned into a short burst of laughter at the clear affront the duke was experiencing; his expression of utter consternation was priceless. Served Rainville right, sparring with a feisty female. Still grinning, Damon slid his gaze back to the stage and jerked upright, smile disappearing when he caught the tail end of red satin as the Masked Meadowlark finished her song and melted from the stage into the crowd, out of sight.

Patrons applauded and murmured in confusion at her early departure, some calling for Meadowlark to return to the stage. When she didn't, discontent rose among the crowd, and West consoled them all by shouting out an offer for a free round of ale, already pouring them from behind the bar. With all suddenly at ease, laughter and chatter resumed throughout the tavern while pints were distributed.

"Let me go, you oaf!" caught Damon's attention, and he spun his head toward the entrance door just in time to see Rainville toss an incredibly displeased Castlebury female over his shoulder, his face unflinching and stony as she assaulted his back with little, angry gloved fists, her brown rough tweed cloak bunching over her face, blinding her. "I can't see!"

"Should have stayed home, then," Rainville growled, wrenching the pub door open. "My carriage is conveying you back to your residence immediately."

"Why do you even *care*?" the younger Castlebury wailed angrily in departure, her words lingering behind them as the duke adjusted her on his shoulder and stalked through the tavern door into the dark, moonless night.

Not exactly a subtle exit, that.

Eyes narrowed on the scene and with speculation cranking the gears in his mind, Damon smirked and watched on until the heavy wooden door closed once again behind the pair.

"I say, where did the Masked Meadowlark go?" Lord Arnold bellowed in outraged confusion, having only just regained his feet and composure. "She must speak with me!" The cream of his linen waistcoat was littered with footprints and dirt smudges, and his carefully styled hair was in wild disarray, long, wayward strands of it tangled with the overabundant fuzz of his sideburns. And was that a dusty boot print on the side of the viscount's cheek?

Damon choked back a bark of laughter and almost failed, coughing roughly instead, already moving toward the back of the tavern and the hallway there. *He* had something to say to Meadowlark.

Noticing the pint glass once again rolling slowly on the floor nearby, Damon detoured slightly toward it and sent it scurrying with a subtle flick of his boot just as Lord Arnold made his own move toward the back rooms where the Masked Meadowlark had retired. The viscount stepped on the glass again and shrieked as he slipped and floundered into a rather buxom barmaid, tumbling them both to the ground.

She rolled on top of the protesting toff and laughed heartily, smooshing his face between her bubbies. "Sugar, all you had to do was ask!"

"Get off, get off, *get off!*" Lord Arnold screeched.

Damon smiled and just kept walking.

Damn, it was satisfying.

CHAPTER SIX

B LAST IT ALL, what a disaster!
Carenza peeled off her gloves and tossed them carelessly on the desk in her dressing room, followed immediately by her red sequin and feather mask. *"Nora,"* she growled, frustration burning her cheeks. "She promised she would stay at home."

Was she truly surprised her sister had disobeyed?

No.

Well, actually, yes. Yes, she was. After their talk that afternoon upon returning to Tipton House and her robust explanation regarding her escapes, Carenza was rather surprised to see her sibling there.

Had she just thought of her nights out as escapes? She'd meant escapades, rather. Though, truth be told, they were quite like little escapes when she thought upon it. Tiny, hours-long escapes away from the stifling, smothering *nothingness* that was her existence while society dictated that she wait for a man to choose her as breeding stock—while she waited for her "opportunity" to fulfill her life's purpose of ripening her womb with some man's seed.

"Stuff that." Carenza picked up a comb and tossed it angrily back upon the desktop. "No, to *hell* with that!"

She was so, *so* much more.

A hard knock rattled the door, and Carenza marched to it, thinking it to be Nora, and yanked it open. "You have some explaining to do," she snapped, anger marching up her spine until she noticed the figure standing there. Then it sparked and popped like hot oil in a frying pan. "*You!*"

"That's the second time today you've said that."

"That's the second time today you've appeared where you're unwanted. Why are you following me?" Carenza demanded, her cheeks flushing hot from the sudden memory of his strong embrace. "Who are you?"

"So many questions," the man responded, his rough-edged voice resonating in the pit of her stomach, heating her there. "I'm afraid I must disappoint you with my lack of answers."

"Then I shall bid you good eve, sirrah." Carenza latched on to the door and gave it a sound shove closed.

"Damon Crowe." A strong arm shot out between the rapidly shutting door and the frame, stopping its closure. "My name is Damon Crowe."

Carenza stopped forcing the door closed on his elbow and eased it back a smidge. "Well, that was decidedly easy. Mr. Damon Crowe, is it?"

"Yes, my lady."

She froze. "Why did you just address me thus?"

He took advantage of her shocked immobility and slipped under her arm and into the disorganized dressing room. "Because you are a lady, my lady."

"Did my father send you?" Instead of fear flooding her body, as she had expected such a dreaded question to cause, fury bloomed, hot and unrestrained, infusing her limbs with crackling energy. "He sent you, didn't he? *Didn't he?*" She whipped her hand up and poked her trespasser hard in the chest with a stiff, indignant finger. "Answer me true right this moment, or I declare I will shout for West. He doesn't take kindly to men harassing me."

"Does that often occur?" He looked down at her, his dark eyes penetrating. "Men harassing you?"

"*Once* is too often, Mr. Crowe. By blazes, I'll never understand how it is that you men believe us women were put here on this earth singularly for your entertainment instead of entirely for our own person. Our own choice. Our. Own. *Experience,*" she said between gritted teeth, punctuating each word with another livid poke of her finger into his torso.

It mattered not that this man was a stranger. It mattered not that he was big and strong and so masculine that a part of her wanted to pool into a puddle of feelings right there in the middle of her dressing room floor, regardless of her higher intellect and objections to such sentiments of weakness. It also mattered not that he could harm her if he so chose and that she would be unconscious or dead before West even arrived at her door.

All that mattered in that moment was the rage building inside her over the injustice all women suffered at the hands of society. And that for all that this man was a stranger, something about him felt trustworthy. Solid. Reliable. As if she could be honest with him, even if he appeared dark and dangerous. Even if he worked for her father.

And that just made her all the madder.

"The restrictions placed upon a woman's life are a chokehold, a death sentence." Carenza stabbed him with her finger once again, completely oblivious to the discomfort the joints of her digit would suffer later from such harsh treatment. "Something you, awful man, would know nothing about, being a *man.*"

"Would you prefer me to be something else?" His deep voice reverberated in his chest—the one currently being assaulted by her furious appendage. "Something more suitable to your refined and delicate taste, perhaps?"

Though she heard the mocking note in his tone, Carenza ignored it. Too much momentum of emotion accumulated behind her ribcage, pushing against its barrier, seeking release. "I would *prefer* to be left alone to pursue the life of my choice on my own terms!" Oh, her head and heart were in it now. "Without censure! Without judgment or consequence!" Each word spat from her lips earned another hard jab of her finger, although now

Carenza was blind to the motion. Too many emotions, too much injustice.

"*Enough*," Mr. Crowe growled, pinning her hand flat to his chest and anchoring her close. "No more poking."

"Let go!" she cried, tears threatening her eyes and stinging her throat as she yanked against him to no avail. "Let go of me now!"

He tipped his head to the side, his gorgeous tumble of midnight waves brushing against his broad shoulder as he assessed her quietly, thoroughly. "Or what?" His soft-spoken words surprised her, taunted and propelled her, held her as captive as her hand under his large, strong palm.

"Or I will scream," she immediately promised, the unfairness of life lodging like a smoldering cannonball in the center of her chest. She made the mistake of looking into his dark, intense eyes as she defiantly boasted, "I am quite loud." The flicker of heat that sparked there shortened her breath, quickened her pulse, distracted her momentarily from her anger.

"Try it, milady," Mr. Crowe purred as his vowels reshaped, grew sharper with a baseborn accent previously imperceptible to her ears. His gaze dropped to her mouth. "Let me hear you scream."

His words slid over her body like fine silk, cooling one fire and lighting another, more elusive one, barely touching yet setting her skin alight with sensation after rolling, delicious sensation. "Why," she started breathlessly but stopped, swallowing back a jangle of excited nerves that standing so near him caused. "Why," she began again, "must you say it in that manner?"

"What manner is that?" he murmured, his gaze never leaving her lips.

She licked them, suddenly keenly aware of their generous shape, the extra plumpness of her top lip. "It was…indecent."

A corner of his mouth turned up, humor and something else flashing in his dark eyes. "Indecent?"

Carenza nodded. "Inappropriately suggestive, too." Her brain struggled to maintain clarity as the strong, steady thump of his heartbeat under her palm lured her, called her own heart to match its rhythm. "Who are you?" she whispered, as she leaned even closer into him, as his scent filled her senses, loosened and heated her limbs—made her pliant and longing for something she was somehow certain only he could provide.

Her gaze fell to his lips, to the hard, sculpted lines of them that hinted at a deeply protected, deeply hidden vulnerability. A softness reserved and elusively rare. The paradox of it in contrast to his hard, tough visage captivated her.

Her pulse skipped five fluttering beats as he lowered his mouth over hers, and heat flooded her belly, sinking lower.

His breath brushed her lips, hot and inviting as he leaned even closer and whispered, his tone low and gutter-rough, full of promise, "I'm the bloke sent to bring you home, milady."

A quick intake of breath as his words registered, and in a flash, Carenza's anger roared to life again. She instantly reacted, spurred by the force of it. "I will *not* go!" Recalling the defensive moves Sadie had shown her in case there were ever need, she brought a knee up with as much force and speed as she could muster and connected soundly with the private region situated directly between Mr. Crowe's muscular thighs.

Erupting in a howling whirlwind of swearing and movement, her would-be captor dropped stone-heavy to the ground, his large hands releasing her to cradle his wounded manhood. "Feckin' hell, me ballocks!" tore from his chest, the words shaped with the harsh sound of rookery origins.

Vicious, victorious glee sprang to life alongside guilt in Carenza's chest, and she quickly stepped around his hunkered form, desperation to escape her father's control leading her blindly to the door, pushing her past guilt and into sheer survival. She wrapped her hand around her ugly, ragged cloak on the wall hook by the doorframe and felt the weight of her small satchel inside, stored securely in its inside pocket. "Let that serve as warning should you decide to come for me again, Mr. Crowe," she stated dramatically as she drew the cloak around her shoulders and flung the door open. "I shall not be run aground so easily."

And with that, Carenza dashed quick as a fox down the hallway and out the pub's back door.

Cool night air ripe with the pungent scent of chimney smoke and rookery grime brushed her heated cheeks as she darted down the alleyway separating the Meadowlark Tavern from the seedier, crumbling brick Covent Garden establishments that dominated the next street over. And for many more blocks in every direction after that, each one as ominous and nefarious as the next. Until tonight, there had been no reason for Carenza to wander down any of them.

Tonight, however, she was on the run.

Heart galloping, she cut down a smaller side lane—one that connected to another narrow, winding cobblestoned street that led to yet another nameless, dilapidated alley full of shadows and broken dreams and odd, jutting angles. High above her head, buildings tilted and leaned sadly, protruded rudely into the space above the alley floor, blocking any person's attempt to find sunlight solace during the day.

At night the protrusions loomed overhead, creaking ominously with use and disrepair as Carenza ran down alley upon alley, hoping to stumble upon a hack that could deliver her to a safer portion of the city. Perhaps Crawford's bachelor townhouse in Belgravia. Or Sadie's tiny flat in Cheapside.

Anywhere but home to Mayfair.

Gasping as her foot landed in an old, worn hole where the stone had chipped away, Carenza cried out and tumbled to her knees. Instantly scrambling, she ignored the pain jarring her left ankle and regained her feet, glancing up and down the darkened alley to verify no one was following. Pulse hammering, she listened and heard nothing. Only the faint sound of someone retching in the distance and the scurry of rodents across cold stone as they searched for food. Odd, the rookery streets being so devoid of people.

Relieved, however, that Mr. Crowe seemed to be well behind her, if he was indeed following her at all, Carenza smoothed her skirts and adjusted her cloak until she was fully enclosed within it, hood up and hair covered, before setting off once again, mindful of her tender ankle. With a slight limp she wandered at a slower pace down another winding, narrow lane in search of conveyance. Other nighttime sounds soon filled her ears, along with the more intimate murmurs that occurred between a man and woman. Those she heard coming from a small side alley to her right, and she scampered quite quickly past, rounding yet one more corner. That was not how she wished to discover for the first time the finer, more delicate points of male/female relating. It sounded...

The mixture of curiosity and repulsion brewing in her mind over such scandalous sounds and lewd activities died a fast, brutal death when she caught a glimpse of the sight near the far end of the lane up ahead. Carenza stopped mid-stride and quickly plastered her body against a cold brick wall, praying the dark forms coming from the shadows far up ahead were merely wild figments of her imagination and not something far more sinister. Something she and every London-goer had been much warned about.

Yet it appeared to be them, right down to their attire and the number of them. For good reason, Carenza had memorized their descriptions. She had wanted to be prepared for a moment like this.

The Revivalists.

"This is why proper ladies should remain in the drawing room," she muttered, half regretting her impulsive reaction to run from Mr. Crowe. Compared to the nightmares solidifying in front of her very eyes, he seemed almost sweet and innocent, and she would very much prefer to be standing back in her dressing room with him at this particular juncture in time. Instead, she watched as a gang of men described by the *Gazette* as "the devil's own helpers" made their way down the narrow street toward her.

With trembling hands, Carenza fumbled with her tiny satchel, reaching inside to latch on to the only bit of protection she possessed. As she closed her fist around the small letter opener, a wave of gratitude for its deceptively sharp blade washed through her. Small it was, but mighty.

Unable to take her eyes off the gang of large, black-clad and hooded thugs slowly making their way down the street toward her, Carenza finally convinced her feet to move once more and scrambled down the side of the uneven cobbled street and ducked behind a jutting, crumbling building corner, heart in her throat. If she made herself small enough behind this stack of old wooden crates then maybe they would simply walk past, leaving her undetected? Alive?

Unbidden, Mr. Crowe leapt into her mind. Why hadn't she stayed and let him kiss her? Escort her home? At least then she would be safe. In considerable trouble with her father, but still safe. Or rather, *safer*.

Something fell with a loud crash in the alleyway, and Carenza hunkered into an even tighter ball behind the crates, holding the letter opener in an iron grip and at the ready behind her cloak. Male voices ascended in volume, breaking into sinister laughter and crude comments as the gang of abominations jostled one another and knocked over everything in their path. A window smashed, and the tinkling sound of falling bits of glass on stone jangled Carenza's already stretched nerves. Someone swore. Another hollered for the fun to begin.

"I say, where the deuce *is* everyone?" complained a disgruntled aristocratic male voice, the advantage of wealth and too much drink prominent in his tone. Something about it rang familiar to Carenza's ears but was quickly forgotten in her fear when the next person spoke.

"They're hiding from *us*." Twisted satisfaction oiled the voice, and it seeped out with a kind of filmy wetness that threatened to coat her skin like poison.

Shivering inside her cloak, Carenza fought down the urge to flee and held steady, praying the Revivalists would not notice her behind the pile of busted wood crates. So long as the scarlet silk of her gown remained well hidden behind her drab and tattered outerwear, perhaps fortune would be on her side.

"But I want someone to *play* with," whined another, the sound of wood tapping impatiently against an open palm punctuating the childish, drink-slurred words.

A chill ran down Carenza's spine, and she pushed further into the corner behind her, reaching backward for the wall and whimpering helplessly when her fingers scratched dry, splintering wood and tiny bits of it lodged painfully under her nails. Recognizing a door, she searched with trembling fingers for the latch as the Revivalists drew closer. Impatient with blood lust and too many spirits, they heckled one another, stopping occasionally to vandalize and break.

"Please, please open," she begged under her breath. "I don't want to die."

Finding the doorknob, Carenza nearly wept in relief and then despair when it refused to turn. "No, no, no!" she whispered, clawing at it. "Don't be locked!"

"Did you hear that?" a vaguely familiar voice said. "I think I heard someone." And then, quite a bit more excitedly, "I think there's someone hiding from us!"

Bile leapt into Carenza's throat, and she gagged.

"Come out, come out, wherever you are!" singsonged the oily voice, close enough now she could make out a man's silhouette in the faint moonlight just ahead on the worn cobblestones.

"I'm bored!" wailed another. "There's nothing here. Let's go somewhere else."

"I tell you, I heard someone hiding!" the strange, familiar voice replied.

"It's merely a rat."

"I'm telling you that this is a waste of time. Let's try the docklands."

"It's not, I promise! I'll find them. Come out, little hider!"

Wishing fervently again to have stayed back in the relative safety of the tavern with the dangerous yet somehow trustworthy Mr. Crowe, Carenza tried the knob once more with no success. Biting her bottom lip until she tasted the metallic tang of blood, she struggled against the tears welling in her eyes and shrank as far into the corner against the rough wood door as she possibly could.

Suddenly the door gave way behind her, and Carenza fell backward into the building's damp, inky interior. Tumbling fast, she barely had time to blink and squeak in surprise before she was scooped up by a pair of strong arms and the door closed once again behind her, cloaking her in near blackness.

"Shh," a rough voice whispered against her ear. "I've got you."

Recognizing him instantly, Carenza slumped in relief, her knees turning to water. "Mr. Crowe," she sighed, inhaling his comforting, exotic scent. "What took you so long?"

"As one would have it, kicking a man in the whirligigs tends to slow him down a bit."

"That's no excuse," she replied, voice unsteady with unshed tears as she buried her head against his chest, seeking the steady strength of his heartbeat.

"My apologies," he murmured against her hair, and she felt the vibrations of his words against her cheek, found comfort in the deep tenor reverberating there.

"Those, those *demons*—" she began, but he cut her off.

"There are demons," he told her, his arms tightening ever so briefly around her waist. "And then there are *monsters*."

She shuddered, agreeing, "Yes, that's what they are. Monsters."

"Even demons have their limits." His words came out so softly that she almost missed them.

Just beyond the door, a voice sounded, angry and belligerent with drink. *"I want to play!"* Crashing came next as another window succumbed to their vandalism, shattering to shards.

Fear split the air around Carenza, sent it scattering.

"We need to leave now." Grabbing her hand, Mr. Crowe began moving through the dark interior of the building, his palm hard and big and reassuring. And she went without protest, following readily and trusting him to know the way.

Why did she trust him?

They made it quickly to the front entrance, Mr. Crowe proving himself quite capable and adept at maneuvering through strange places in the pitch dark. She, on the other hand, proved less so. Once again, Carenza tripped over something made of cold metal, and would have toppled to the ground had not Mr. Crowe possessed such a determined grip on her hand. Instead, he merely raised his arm and kept her upright, his hold on her sure and strong.

"Thank you," she whispered.

"Of course," he responded just as she slipped on a pebble or rock or something round and rolling on the floor. Mr. Crowe simply grunted and locked his grip, keeping her vertical and on course.

"Sorry!"

Another grunt.

"Maybe we should—" she started, but the words dried in her throat when his long, strong arms suddenly wrapped around her and lifted her off the ground. Then she found herself pressed against his chest, head tucked under his chin, with the rich, manly scent of him filling her nose as he gently jostled her into carrying position.

Before she could protest, Mr. Crowe utilized his rather broad shoulder and pushed, opening another door that led them out onto another strangely quiet rookery lane and fresh—rather *fresher*—air. For a moment, he stopped and seemed to listen to the night, his heartbeat sure and steady beneath her cheek. "This way." He set off to the left. "We'll move faster if I carry you."

"Why? Because of my infirm ankle?" she asked, curling a hand into the plush velvet lapels adorning the front of his jacket, and noted his clipped responding nod. "Are you familiar with these streets?"

His jaw visibly tensed at the question. "I know them."

Mr. Crowe said nothing more, and she believed it wise not to push him further, so she settled more comfortably against him as his fit, capable body moved with surprising agility and ease through the rookery. With the Revivalists on the loose, the streets remained bare, shutters closed tight over third-floor flats, lights out. It was a place normally abundant with sounds and people and activity, and the absence of it all created an eerie, almost haunted, forgotten feel to the cobbles of Covent Garden.

Not liking it one bit, Carenza held tight to her rescuer and closed her eyes. "Thank you for helping me in the alley."

Again, he only grunted and kept his clipped pace. Lulled by the heat of his body and his thumping, rhythmic heartbeat, Carenza felt the strain of the day sweep through her, and sleep soon followed. Before she drifted off in the safety of his arms, she thought she heard him speak.

"Don't thank me, *hechicera*," he murmured against her hair as exhaustion overtook her and sleep claimed her. "I'm taking you home."

CHAPTER SEVEN

How *dare* he?

Trustworthy Mr. Crowe. Handsome Mr. Crowe. Helpful Mr. Crowe.

Lies.

Well, except for the handsome bit. That portion was objective truth, blast him. A pox on his arresting countenance. How could he save her and then bring her back to *this*?

"Carenza! Carenza Elizabeth, are you paying attention to me?"

"Hmm?" she answered distractedly from the green velvet chaise near the fireplace, blinking twice to focus her eyes upon her father.

Lord Winslow Castlebury loomed behind the desk in his study and slammed a meaty fist on its glossy surface, sending a stack of papers fluttering to the hardwood floors. "Insubordination!" He slammed his fist again, and this time Carenza jumped. "I will not abide it in my home any longer!"

"Winslow," her mother said from her position near the tightly closed doors, her tone coaxing and calm.

"No!" roared Lord Castlebury, his cheeks mottled purple with rage. "I am finished with this…this *game* she's playing."

That claimed Carenza's attention. She sat up straight, her spine stiffening. "My life is not a game."

"Your *life* is exactly what I say it is," her father sneered. "I am the man of this house, the man of this family!"

Fighting the urge to roll her eyes and cry and scream all at the same time, Carenza held steady and did none of those. Dutifully, she swallowed it down—the anger, the desperation, the sadness. Instead, she employed her woman's weapons. It had long been the only way to deal with Lord Castlebury. "And a fine job you have done with the role of it, Father."

"*You.*" His whole body appeared to shake now as he leveled a finger at her, his finger jutted and trembling in her direction. "Disobedient, reckless girl! I should send you to a remote convent in the far north counties and be rid of you. Do you have any idea what inconvenience you have caused me? How much of this family's reputation you have risked? And for what? To tromp around the unsanitary slums of Covent Garden, risking disease from the poor and thieves alike! What *exactly* were you doing in that place?"

"Did not Mr. Crowe already confess to you all my sins?" Each word Carenza uttered dripped of sarcasm—her usual veil of calm composure, her woman's weapons, was cracking. Steam born from anger seeped through the exposed fissures as she thought on her rescuer-turned-captor and how stealthily he had deposited her home and disappeared. Without ripples or waves or any sort of commotion.

Without even so much as her *knowledge.*

If she had not been soundly asleep in his arms, she would have protested. Most ardently. Violently too, perhaps.

Betrayer. That was what Mr. Crowe was. A betrayer.

"Mr. Crowe said very little at all, in truth," her mother stated while she wrung the fibers loose on the sleeve of her dressing gown and her cheeks burned brightly with emotion. Whether it was in horror at Carenza's near social murder of their family or because she truly experienced overwrought nerves over the safety of her child, it was difficult to tell. Either way, she made a valiant attempt at serene outward composure and mostly succeeded. "That man simply brought you in, deposited you on the chaise in the receiving room where you awoke, and provided a rather concise explanation of where he discovered you—near the Covent Garden market engaging with the locals. Then he left, abruptly."

Carenza could not tell if her mother was serious. "Is that where he said he found me?" she asked. "That is everything he said?"

"Yes, is that incorrect?" her mother replied with narrowing, suspicious blue eyes.

"No!" Carenza replied hurriedly, her mind buzzing with the knowledge that Mr. Crowe had not provided to her parents the whole of the night's events with complete accuracy. "That's exactly where I was and what I was doing. Yes, yes it was."

The intensity of her anger toward Mr. Crowe reduced a notch or two. Why had he lied for her?

"I want a complete explanation." Her father pegged her with an icy-cold stare. "You will tell us everything."

"There's nothing to tell," she instantly countered, heart pounding behind her ribs. Swallowing down every emotion and urge she possessed that wanted nothing more than for her to stand up, fists clenched, and scream until the walls crumbled to the ground around them all, she folded her hands in her lap and affected her most innocent expression, turning big, guileless eyes upon her sire. "I simply wished to discover life outside the comfort of our blessed family fortune, Father, so that I may better understand and assist those less fortunate than myself."

"What say you?" Lord Castlebury demanded, physically taken aback, tucking his chin as one did when avoiding a fist to the face. Or something distasteful.

Her mother simply hmphed and crossed her arms over her pink dressing gown, giving Carenza *the look*.

"It's true!" she protested, gripping the inside fabric of her cloak, holding it close. Panic shot clean through her, straight down to her toes, when she felt the rustle of expensive satin against her legs and realized she still wore a Meadowlark dress.

Quickly tucking her slippers under her, lest the red satin give her away, Carenza went about ensuring her dress remained hidden behind the tattered fabric of her cloak as she perched on the edge of the chaise in her father's study. "There is so much poverty, so much pain and hopelessness there. I thought it an excellent way to cultivate understanding and compassion for those whose lives are lived without the comforts and conveniences and privileges we take so readily for granted."

All of which was absolutely, utterly true. She *did* need to see and understand the world beyond the front steps of her privileged existence. For how could one ever truly appreciate what one had without obtaining personal knowledge of anything else for which to compare it? Furthermore, how could a person truly know if what they *did* have was right for them without that comparison?

"Such blasphemy!" her father bellowed. "I will not have it!" Again, he shook a finger at her, his lip curling with disgust under his thick mustache. "I know not what has come over you, but it will end this minute. Your head is corrupted with nonsense and misguided notions, girl. Ladies of class assist the poor distantly through charitable works. You do not *mingle* in person with them! Deuce it, child. It's time you had a keeper."

Dropping her ruse, Carenza stiffened her spine, and her eyes flashed fire. "I require no such person."

"Oh yes, you most certainly do," her father scoffed in disagreement, crossing his arms. "You're a menace, and I have allowed it to go on for too long."

"Winslow—" her mother tried again, but he silenced her with a single, cutting glance.

Seeing it, witnessing her mother seemingly shrink and become smaller in front of her very eyes—all from the callous treatment of a man with the socially reinforced belief in his superiority and control over others—pushed Carenza beyond her bearing point. "I am no menace!" she shouted. "Not any more than Crawford or Catamount. No more than any person wishing to take an active, participatory role in their lives!" She pushed to her feet, mindless now to the scarlet fabric draping her figure.

"You are my daughter. You have no active role in your life. Not until I deem so." Lord Castlebury reached for a brown leather journal on his desk, his hand shaking with barely restrained anger. Latching on to it, he brought it close, opened its pages.

"What are you doing?" Carenza recognized that bound journal, had stared at its interior mere days before. Her stomach responded, twisting painfully as she shook her head in denial. "I'll not do it." Never ever, in a million years. Beneath her cloak, she clenched her hands together.

"You will. And soon." Lord Castlebury nodded decisively and seemed to settle into an idea, his anger reducing to smoldering cinders as he read over the names written within. "A husband makes the finest of keepers."

A choking sort of sound came unbidden, tearing abruptly from Carenza's throat. "Never!" she cried. "I will not be forced to marry."

"You are and you will, daughter mine." The Earl of Castlebury snapped the journal closed, his tone chilling further as he regained his composure and typically distant demeanor. "As you have expressed dislike for every eligible gentleman written within these pages, I shall have to decide upon one for you."

"You cannot be serious!" Her mother's composure broke, and Lady Castlebury rushed forward, the ruffles on her dressing gown flapping freely about her. "We discussed this, and you promised me she would be in control of whom she married. You said that you would not force her!"

"That was before she forced *me*, Susanna. I'll not have the reckless, foolish actions of a child bring about the ruin of this entire family. Marrying her off is the only way to make certain she does not bring scandal to the entire Castlebury name."

"Marry me off?" Carenza's mouth dropped open as offense and disbelief mixed in the pit of her stomach, brewing into outrage. "Am I that much of a burden to you?"

"At this point in time, yes."

"Winslow!" Lady Castlebury gasped, hand to her chest, clearly taken aback. "You cannot mean that!"

"I do. Disliking the fact does not make it less so. She is three and twenty! By all measures, she should be married and the mother of many children by now. Except she's damn near close to becoming an unmarriable spinster! I'm saving her from herself, Susanna. Mark me."

"Do you care for me so little?" Carenza asked. It hurt, that truth.

"Making you marry has nothing to do with whether or not I care for you. It is the expected role of every aristocrat's daughter."

"It is a death sentence." How could becoming another's property be anything else?

"Know your place, girl!" Lord Castlebury shouted. "By God, you must know your place in this world."

Carenza knew where she belonged. Deep in her heart, away from the doctrine and societal expectations and what was considered acceptable or not, she knew the truth of where she belonged. It was *anywhere* she wanted it to be.

"The more you hold me down," she warned, standing regal as any queen, her words infused with conviction, "the more I am determined to rise."

"Rise to *where?*" Her father threw up his hands in clear exasperation. "Where exactly do you think you can rise to?"

"Wherever I want! That is the entire point!" Tears sprang to her eyes, and she was mindless to them, let them fall.

"Carenza," her mother pleaded, reaching hands out in supplication. "Calm yourself."

"Ahoy! What goes on in here?"

All heads swung to the study entrance.

"Crawford." Her father tipped his chin stiffly, acknowledging his heir. "Now is not the time."

"I beg to differ, Father. Now is exactly the time." Tall and athletic, her eldest brother braced his legs apart in a defensive stance and pointed at the door. "Raised voices were detectable from the entrance, and that is a rather unwelcome and most unbecoming greeting." Squaring off to their father, Crawford asked bluntly, "What were you thinking, bellowing like a drunken sailorman on shore leave? You're an earl, for Christ's sake."

"Crawford," their father warned, his cheeks mottling red with embarrassment and rising temper. "Mind your words, lad. I am still Lord Castlebury."

"Then behave accordingly, instead of like a toddler throwing a tantrum." Her brother was unintimidated, bless him. He glanced at her, his blue eyes a paler version of her own. "Carenza, please excuse us. I believe Nora is awaiting you in the library. I'll be along momentarily."

That was Crawford's signal for her to exit the room immediately. Needing no further encouragement, she silently thanked her brother for his interference and hurried across the room, emotions churning in her gut. Motions jerky and awkward from suppressing so much feeling, she made it to the door.

"Are those red slippers?" Lady Castlebury asked when Carenza's hand touched the doorknob, surprise and confusion in her tone. "I do not remember you owning such a pair."

"They are Nora's," Carenza replied without a backward glance, and quickly slipped from the room, shutting the door firmly behind her. Breath rushed from her body in the silence of the hallway, and her limbs were weak with relief. The feeling was short-lived, however, when male voices clashed behind the door.

Pushing away from the wooden barrier holding the sounds at muffled bay, Carenza strode past the dining room and made her way to the library. As much as she wished to climb out of her window that very moment and disappear into the night, Crawford would be looking for her soon. If she was not in the library, he would try to track her down. And she had quite enough of that nonsense from men already.

Immediately her thoughts returned to Mr. Crowe, provoking

a frown as she twisted the door latch and slipped into the library.

"Oh, thank goodness you're here!" Carenza caught sight of Nora pacing a worn path in the plush antique rug decorating the hardwood floor. "Can you *believe* him? The audacity!"

Exactly Carenza's thoughts as well. "I agree. He had no right to behave that way. No right at all." No, Mr. Crowe had less than no right to decide her choices for her. Yet he had. Oh, he had. And now she was facing her father's wrath and a possible forced marriage because of it.

Why couldn't he have simply left her to run away in peace?

"Thank goodness you understand!" Nora exclaimed. "He had absolutely zero justification to handle me in such a boorish manner! I kicked him in the shins for it, I'll have you know."

"Well, thank you for tha—" Carenza stopped. "Wait, he handled you? Mr. Crowe?"

Nora's long plaited hair brushed over her shoulder as she spun her head to give Carenza a most confused look. "I've no knowledge of who that is, but I daresay he did no such thing. Absolutely not. I'm referring to Rainville."

"Rainville? The duke?" Now Carenza was confused.

"Yes, Rainville, the duke. Boorish brute that he is. I care not if he is a duke. He is a *brute.*"

"Yes, yes, you've mentioned that already." Carenza brought a hand to her temple and pushed with her fingertips against the throbbing that had begun there. Her sister was a veritable whirlwind of energy and emotion, and it was dizzying. "What has Rainville to do with anything?" It was Mr. Crowe they were supposed to be livid with.

"Did you not see him bodily remove me with a crude toss of my person over his shoulder?

Carenza's mouth went slack. "I, ahem, did not witness that."

"Truly?" Her sister tipped her head quizzically. "I had assumed the whole of the tavern watched him throw me about like a sack of flour. What were you engaged with?"

"Well, if you must know the truth, I was hiding from you and the complicated Mr. Crowe."

"You keep mentioning him. Who is he?"

"He is *him*," Carenza replied, her heart speeding up at the thought of those too-knowing eyes.

"*Ooooh.*" Nora seemed to assimilate that information before asking, "Why were you hiding from me?"

"Because you weren't supposed to be there!" The words shot out in a higher pitch and decibel than Carenza had anticipated. "You promised," she added in a quieter tone.

"I couldn't help myself," Nora replied, having at least the good sense to look chagrined. "It seemed so fantastical, and you're so brave, and I simply wished to see you perform for myself." She shuffled her feet on the rug and glanced at Carenza, her gaze open and honest. "You've a really beautiful voice, Car."

That washed the irritation clean out of her. Nora rarely gave such compliments. "Why, thank you." And now she could no longer lecture her sibling on her behavior and choices. "Please refrain from such activities in future."

Well, maybe she could.

"Why did the duke remove you from the tavern?" As glad as Carenza was for Rainville's unexpected assistance, his interference in Nora's activities raised considerable concern. Perhaps his actions were born from nothing more than some misguided notion of honor. Perhaps the duke thought himself duly helping a peer of the realm by corralling his wayward child for him. Or perhaps it was something less benign.

That was the possibility she worried about most.

With a great, heaving sigh, Nora shrugged and made her way across the library toward the richly stained sideboard. "I honestly do not understand his reasoning. He kept muttering under his breath, but I could not decipher him through all his pomp and huffing and puffing and manhandling." Once across, she reached for two snifters and a bottle of their father's finest sherry. "Bollocks with the rules. I'm pouring us spirits, and we're drinking them. After the day we've experienced, I daresay we deserve to indulge, just as the men so often do.”

Instantly Carenza opened her mouth to protest, but snapped it shut instead and held out her hand, taking the offered glass. “I agree, thank you. Why should they always get to have the fun?”

“They shouldn’t,” Nora replied with a force and bite that raised Carenza’s eyebrows in surprise.

“Indeed.” She raised her snifter. “To hell with them.”

“To hell with them,” Nora echoed, raising her own sherry before tossing it back with a single gulp and a smack of her lips.

Carenza briefly debated how to go about it before taking her sister’s cue and swallowing it down in one gulp. Warmth hit and spread throughout her chest, and she inhaled deeply, never having experienced the effects of alcohol before. “Woo!” she declared, unsure whether she enjoyed the nutty, slightly sweet flavor and feel of her father’s finest sherry.

“Knock knock,” came from the other side of the closed door, followed by an actual knock, before her brother strode into the library. He stopped short at the sight before him and slowly looked from Carenza to Nora and back.

“Crawford!” Nora squeaked, her cheeks flushed deep pink.

Their brother shook his head and sighed in his rather resigned big-brother way. “You’re using the wrong glassware.” He pointed to the glossy wood sideboard. “Use that small one there with the stem and pour me some sherry, too.”

“Thank you,” Carenza said to her eldest sibling, referring to his earlier assistance.

Taking the drink from Nora, Crawford turned his pale, intelligent eyes upon her. “Of course. Our father can be harsh, however, as we know, and in this he is resolved, Car. He wants you married. It is a must. I was able to secure you until the end of this Season to choose a suitable husband of your taste. But that is it. If you do not choose by then, he will pick the gentleman for you.”

A chill ran down Carenza’s spine and shattered into ice shards deep in the core of her being.

Marriage.

She. Had. To marry.

Suddenly the sherry revolted in her stomach, and Carenza snatched the small wastebasket in the corner near the shelved biographies and retched mightily into it.

"I say, are you all right?" Crawford inquired, his voice filled with concern.

Carenza straightened and wiped the back of a hand across her lips. "I'm fine," she lied with a trembling smile as her stomach clenched once again. "Thank you for all of your support this evening."

"I'm sorry I could not do more." Crawford's expression shone with sincerity.

"You bought me time," she replied, clamping down on her unruly stomach and every bit of her feelings. "Now if you'll both excuse me, I'm exhausted and wish to retire. It's been a trying day."

"Should I escort you?" her brother asked, still appearing un- convinced of her wellness.

"Thank you, but no," Carenza replied, knowing she could not suppress her emotions for much longer. Walking over, she quickly hugged her siblings. "Have a lovely night. See you on the morrow. Oh—if Mother asks, Nora, you own a pair of red slippers."

With that, she rushed out the library doors and up the stairs to her bedchamber. Once inside, she immediately told her lady's maid, "Leave me, please," and began to shake. Trembles at first, becoming waves of racking tremors that threatened to snap her teeth together.

Marriage.

Chattel.

With those words haunting her, propelling her, she felt inside her cloak for her satchel with shaking hands, found it, and strode directly across the floor.

Then she opened the glass doors to the tiny balcony and

climbed down without a backward glance, forgetting about the dangers lurking out there in the dark, disappearing once again into the blackness of night.

CHAPTER EIGHT

DAMON SET DOWN his newest literary acquisition, swearing under his breath as he tried to unwind that evening in his Fleet Street flat.

"What was that? I could not hear past the whistling teapot heating over the fire."

His one and only manservant could barely hear, period. Mostly out of stubbornness, but also some physical limitations. "Not to fear, Bones," he assured the man, mindful to speak clearly. "I've merely a gripe with this latest collection of Byron's works." His gripe being that he couldn't concentrate on it at all, for a certain goddess with golden hair had taken up residence at the forefront of his mind.

She'd slept like an angel in his arms, all the way back to Mayfair. Warm. Soft. Entirely too tempting.

He'd loathed letting her go.

Damon scowled. "I'll ask at the print shop downstairs what their opinions are about the editing decisions made in this newest volume. I'm certain Jamie will have something to say about it." The printer's apprentice was chock-full of opinions and ideals. Such was the luxury of youth.

Living above the bustle on Fleet Street provided Damon with many benefits, the main one being his finger on the pulse of London life. In-the-moment information. Given his line of occupation, being a part of the Fleet Street information pipeline was instrumental to his success. From the *Daily Courant* to the *Gazette*—it was all right there at his fingertips. And over the years a few critical relationships had formed, ones based upon adjoining and common needs.

But damn, could it be noisy.

"Don't open that window," he snapped at Bones as the stocky man reached for the window latch nearest him, and instantly regretted it. "Apologies." Damon waved a hand. His linen shirt sleeves were carelessly rolled to his elbows, and the bared, corded muscles of his forearms flexed with the movement. "It's simply that I've no wish to listen to the clacking of carts or the haggling from late-night vendors, or any voices other than ours, really. Silence is best observed this evening, I believe."

"Nerves?" Bones asked, turning his shaggy salt-and-pepper-topped head to the side to expose his one good ear for listening as Damon reached for a cigarette on the table next to him.

"Is it that obvious?" He grimaced, lighting the tip, and leaned forward in his chair, elbows on trouser-covered knees.

"What's obvious is that something is needling you," his serv-ant stated in his blunt manner, arms crossed over his thick chest. "You've been grumbling and frowning since you walked through the door." They did not stand on ceremony, the two of them.

"I have not."

"Have too."

Damon glared at Bones. "Remind me why I brought you here to work for me?"

"Because I bake the best damn bread in all of London Town," his man boasted with a grin before turning serious. "And because I lost everything when those feckin' Revivalists burned down my bakery and took my Amelia from me, bless her beautiful soul. You found me in the Garden that night, close to death from smoke inhalation while trying save her, and you gave me another chance."

"Bah." Damon waved him off, refusing any inference of his goodness. "I was a cunning, selfish bastard all the way and simply wanted your bread all to myself. Merely saw an opportunity."

The look Bones gave him suggested he was full of horse shite. "If that's what you need to tell yourself. But you saved my life that night, and we both know it." He shook his head again, the motion at once dismissive and yet somehow scolding. "You're a better man than you let on."

"You take that back." Damon shoved to his feet and began pacing, his shoulders rounded like a boxer before a bout, all prickly ill temperament. "I am no such thing."

Good men didn't do demons' work. Didn't smell of darkness and hellfire. They didn't wear it like a cloak.

And they didn't know what he knew.

"Do you have any idea how many secrets I keep?" He spun to Bones. "Horrible, awful secrets?" The weight of it used to crush him, wreck his mind. Then somewhere, somehow, along the way he'd gone numb to it. All of him numb.

Until Lady Carenza Castlebury.

Her scent still permeated his jacket. With these rediscovered emotions churning around inside him, he'd stripped off his outerwear and vest and removed himself from her allure. Surely once he no longer smelled her, he'd no longer want her.

Wrong.

"Fuck me," he muttered, and took a drag on his cigarette, raising an arm above his head and leaning it against the oversized window of his fifth-floor flat, looking down through the glass. Below him, Fleet Street still hustled along, lanterns lighting people's way up and down the old street. On top of the world he was, here. Watching. *Seeing*.

Christ, sometimes he wished he didn't see.

People were the cruelest of creatures.

"Why do you do it, then, if it's so burdensome?"

"Because I'm searching for something," he muttered, feeling that old familiar rage—the one he'd shoved deep, *deep* down inside until he was numb—unfurl its claws and yawn, teeth ever razor sharp.

"What are you lookin' for?"

"Answers."

They still hadn't come. Sometimes Damon wondered if they would at all. That no matter how far down he dug, how wide, they would forever escape him.

He would never know where he came from.

Never know the name of the man responsible for his life, his mother's death.

"Oft times we believe we need one answer when it's another truth we're actually seeking," Bones remarked, casually going about the sitting room tidying and straightening, the domestic sound oddly comforting.

"Oh no," Damon snarled into the darkness beyond the glass, his eyes hard and glinting in the reflection. "It's rather direct. I'm wanting this answer."

"Careful what you wish for," his servant warned with a soft, serious tone. "Most often, all we discover is a bucket full of dung."

Uncertain what Bones meant, Damon shrugged off the concern and pushed away from the glass window, pressure building in his chest—the kind of restless, driving pressure that made it impossible to sit down, to relax in any way. Instead, his limbs thrummed for activity, for strain and exertion. Running a hand through his wavy hair, he began to pace.

He paced a lot.

Noting the worn path across his faded Turkish rug, he raised his cigarette to his mouth and inhaled, his mind churning thoughts over like a rushing water wheel.

"I've the tea steeping. Have yourself some."

Damon shrugged a broad shoulder and ground out his cigarette in a nearby ashtray. "I'd rather not." Lacing his long fingers above his head, he added, "Thank you, though."

"Bad men don't thank servants for tea," he heard Bones mutter as the stocky man made his way back toward the kitchen with its warm wood paneling and warmer hearth. "I'm sayin'."

"I heard that!" Damon called out, glaring at the kitchen archway to the insolent man beyond.

"Not trying to be silent!" Bones tossed back.

"Perhaps you should try it," Damon grumbled, surly and out of sorts, and dropped his hands, flexed his fingers.

"Perhaps," his servant drawled sarcastically as he clattered about in the kitchen just out of view, "you should go work off this foul mood you're in. Sweat it out."

Carenza flashed before his mind, sweaty and gloriously naked and thoroughly aroused. Every muscle in his body tightened as desire flooded his veins. Part of him wanted nothing more than to *sweat it out* with Lady Carenza Castlebury.

"Never happening," he growled at himself. Ladies didn't bed demons.

That fact did absolutely nothing to quell his rising ardor, however.

Now that his mind had her naked and writhing under him, behind him, on her knees *before* him, his body thrummed with the carnal need to fuck. To *consume*—all of her until she was so thoroughly, intimately his that no corner of her was left unbared, unexposed.

When he took a woman, he took *all* of her.

Mind, body, soul.

Damon couldn't help it. He needed everything of the woman he mated. A demanding, driving lover was he. Too much for most misses, his appetite scared all but the most experienced. He never took an innocent. Never had, never will. And Carenza? Well, that lady was diamond-tier, gilded virgin.

Is she *gilded too? All golden curls and precious sweetness?* Damon thought as his cock went hard and his balls dropped, filled with a heavy ache. Would she unfurl her innocent petals and flower for him?

Would she let him taste her?

"I say, why are you growling over there?" Bones hollered from the kitchen, catching Damon mid-growl.

Because he wanted something. Something he could not have and did not deserve. Would never deserve.

"I'm going to the club," Damon decided, spinning on the heels of his boots and heading toward the entrance hall, heart beating heavy in his chest. Something, anything, to release this maddening feeling inside him.

"Excellent! You'd do well to have Longfellow box some sense into you. Though be cautious with those hooligans on the loose out there." Poking his head around the doorframe, his servant added, "Should you like some tea to take with you?"

Bones and his tea. Always the caretaker. It touched Damon much more than he could admit that this man who had lost everything could still care so much for others.

It was why he put up with his nagging. And fussing. And lecturing. Because Bones had heart.

"Back late. Do not wait up," Damon yelled down the hall as he grabbed his dark gray coat from the rack and slung it over his shoulders.

"No sewing of split lips after half eleven, remember. I need my beauty sleep. You get busted up by Longfellow, you find someone else to fix it or wait till morning."

"Yeah, yeah." Damon waved him off, smoothing his jacket across his broad shoulders. "I know your rules."

His servant's rules. His servant had rules.

And Damon followed them.

"Fuck me sideways." Damon scowled and ripped the door open. "I'm out!"

Slamming the door behind him, he set off to Flatt's Club, eager to punch something.

"STOP THROWING WEAK blows and *hit* me." Damon bobbed left and slammed a short, hard jab into his sparring partner's ribs, satisfied with the sound of breath rushing from Aaron Longfellow's lungs on a harsh spurt of air. Sweat dampened tendrils of Damon's hair as they clung to the nape of his neck, and sweat trickled down his bare, glistening back, soaking the fabric of his trouser waistband. Breathing heavily from exertion, he shuffled his feet, dancing lightly on the balls of them as he circled his oldest—and maybe only—friend.

Flatt's was quiet at this time of night. With the other patrons absent, each blow, each grunt echoed off the stark brick walls and the scarred hardwood floors. Shirtless and sweaty, Damon inhaled and prepared to strike, his body rejoicing at the use as it vibrated with energy.

"Too slow," Aaron declared, and sidestepped Damon's approach, spinning out of reach.

"Bastard," Damon grunted, and he frowned at the way the club's owner chuckled. Like he knew what drove Damon tonight even if Damon himself did not. "You'll swallow that smile, you keep laughing at me." To prove his point, he faked a front jab at Aaron. "Don't care if we've known each other since we were ten."

"Then you know I can take whatever you can give, bruv," replied Aaron around a huge grin. "You also know I can tell something has you perturbed."

"I'm not perturbed." Damon narrowed his eyes on his friend. "You're perturbed." He popped the boxer on the mouth, lightning quick, for good measure.

Fire lit in the depths of Aaron's hazel gaze, and he growled, sidestepped. Then he pivoted and thrust an uppercut into Damon's jaw fast and hard enough that his head snapped back and he saw stars. "That's wot you get for the cheap shot."

The next blow landed in Damon's gut, killing his breath as he absorbed the shock and pain of being punched in the stomach by a big, bad, and mean-as-hell bare-knuckle boxer who was also the closest thing he had to family. Two orphan outcasts who'd grown up together in a ruthless workhouse in the Garden.

Sometimes there was a little extra personal in the punch.

Damon sucked air and retreated a step as he collected himself, one part of him aching with pain, another part of him rejoicing in the sensation, the blood rushing through him suffusing him with energy, vital and pure. Loving the pain itself. Because of it, he felt *alive*.

Carenza.

"Wha—?" Damon started, his mind suddenly flooded with the image of her, his nose with the smell of her—his body with that same vital *alive* energy at the mere thought of her.

Pain exploded in his head. Blinding, debilitating.

Damon dropped to his knees, sightless, and all thought seized as he hit the boxing ring floor.

"Got to control your mind, bruv," came Aaron's voice from somewhere nearby, faint and hovering. "Steady there, now. I got you." Hands were on his shoulder now, stabilizing him as his color and shape began to creep back into his vision. "It's got to be a woman or one of your assignments causing you this much grief and distracting you, because you aren't normally so sloppy. That was sheer bollocks. A real shite performance, Crowe."

"You flatter me," Damon managed with a small, crooked smile as blessed normal function returned to his body. The aches, of which there would be plenty, would not be felt for a few hours yet. For now, his still body hummed with the contentment of hard use. Of physical purge.

"Tell me." Aaron did not even pretend to humor him. Always serious, always honest. Always to the point.

"It's both," Damon heard himself reply, surprise rippling through him over his ready response. "She *is* the assignment."

Damn it, more personal sharing? Who was he these days?

"That sounds interesting," the boxer replied, offering him a hand up.

Clasping it, Damon snapped as he regained his feet, "I don't want to talk about it."

"You're already talking about it."

"I am not."

"Are too."

"Well, I'm not anymore. I'm done."

"Clearly."

"Feck yourself." Damon slid seamlessly into his Garden up-bringing, glaring at his oldest friend.

"If only I could," Aaron joked with a crooked grin.

"Christ." Shoving his fingers into sweat-tangled hair, Damon chuckled despite himself and slowly walked off Aaron's surprise blow. Served him right getting dropped, though, for letting her into his thoughts.

You didn't have a choice, a voice inside him whispered.

Of course he had, he instantly scoffed. Momentarily, he'd been weak. Soft. Unfocused. His guard went down, and she slid in.

She was already there, the voice whispered.

"No." He shook his head, curling tendrils of dark hair slapping against his neck as panic slithered up his spine. *"Hell* no."

"Who the bloomin' hell are you talking to?" came Aaron's gruff voice from the other side of the ring. "Did I rattle your brain about your head with that punch? Blast it, do I need to take you to Doc Stevens? You're acting addled."

"I'm fine," Damon replied automatically. He absolutely was not fine, but no person besides him was going to know that. Not even Aaron.

"Certainly you are," the boxer scoffed, but instead of pressing further, he then asked, "Who is she?"

"Too good for me." The words slipped right out, truth and all. Bollocks to them.

"I said *who,* not wot, is she?" Amusement tinged Aaron's tone as he drank water from a metal jug. The overhead candles reflected off the shiny surface, making it appear aflame. "We both know it's given that she's too good for you."

Damon couldn't even argue with that, so he shrugged and continued his slow walk around the boxing ring. "Daughter of an earl. Beautiful. Bold. Too smart and curious for her own good."

"Yes, definitely too lofty for the likes of you," Aaron said, and gave a low whistle.

But Damon barely heard him. His mind was full of Lady Carenza now, and he kept sputtering like some romantically inclined fool. "Gorgeous eyes full of hope and enthusiasm and determination—so beautiful. Like the lakeshore at dawn before sunrise breaks and reality descends, ruining everything. Blissfully peaceful, laden with joy."

Aaron kept right on whistling.

"Why do you keep doing that?" Damon asked, his brows pulling low over his eyes, annoyance tugging them together.

"Because you sound like those sad, pathetic poets you love to read. You've got it bad, bruv."

Damon suddenly wanted to punch Aaron again. Hard.

"Do not," he snarled.

"Why can't you have her?" Leave it to the boxer to state it plainly. To get straight to the very core of things. Ever since they were lads.

Have her. The words sent a jolt of possessive need through Damon.

He shook it off and cleared his throat. "She is a lady."

"Yeah, so?" Aaron set the water jug down and reached for his shirt draped over one of the ring's corner posts, pulled it on. "You've shagged them before."

"Only widows and only once," Damon instantly corrected him, his back stiffening in defense. "And this one is different."

"How so?"

"Stop asking me these infuriating questions!" Damon ordered Aaron in exasperation, spinning around on his heels. Scowling at his friend, he added, "You're as bad as Bones."

"Why's he called Bones? I've been meaning to ask." The boxer grinned—a wide, obnoxious one.

"Stop asking questions," Damon said between his teeth, contemplating the best angle from which to ambush Aaron with a jab to shut his mouth up. Noting the laughter forming on his friend's lips only made him want to punch it more.

"I haven't seen you this agitated in years," Aaron said, his tone suddenly serious. "Not since the night you decided to hunt down your father when we were lads. You were spun up then. This lady got you spun up now."

"So?" An ill-tempered shrug of a shoulder. But Damon could not look his friend in the eye.

"*So*," Aaron drawled, "wot you going to do about it?" Crossing his arms across his chest, he leaned casually against the ring ropes and waited, one russet eyebrow raised in question.

"Nothing."

"Wot was that?"

Damon cleared his throat. "I said nothing. I'm going to do nothing."

"Why?"

"Damn you and your insistent questions!" After yanking his shirt off a nearby ring post, Damon hastily threw it on and climbed out of the ring, stepping down onto the cold wood-planked floor. "I don't have to answer you."

"Ah, true. But now that the questions have been spoken aloud, you cannot unhear them."

"You really are a bastard."

Aaron laughed outright, his massively muscled shoulders shaking with mirth. "I try, I really do."

"You succeed." Damon scowled, knowing what the boxer said was true. All those questions now burned in his mind. Being him, he would have no choice but to answer them. Feckin' friends.

Padding barefoot across the boxing club, past heavy bags hanging in various sizes, Damon retrieved his belongings, put on his boots, and sloppily tucked his shirt into his trousers. Too warm from the exercise to wear his jacket, he draped it over a shoulder.

"I'm out," he called back to Aaron. "You still attending dinner at the flat Thursday next? Bones wants to know." He didn't, Damon did, but caring about people and letting them know that were two separate things. Was rather good to have someone else to blame it on. Like a fussy, over-nurturing manservant.

"Tell him that aye, I will be there. He's making roast and his bread, yeah?" There was an unmistakable note of eagerness in Aaron's voice.

Damon smiled to himself. "He is."

"Then aye, aye, I will absolutely be at Thursday's dinner."

"Excellent," he replied, secretly pleased. "I will inform Bones."

"Oh, and Damon? One more thing."

"What is that?"

"Beware out there when you leave. The Revivalists are once again on the loose. I know you're tough, but still. Beware."

It was the closet to an acknowledgment of caring that Aaron was ever going to give him.

He would take it.

Him. Accepting caring. What was *happening* to him?

"I will," Damon replied, chest and throat uncharacteristically tight. No use mentioning to Aaron his close encounter with the Revivalists earlier that evening. Would only upset him.

Without any further farewell address beyond a nod, Damon strode through the brick building toward the front and pushed the main door open wide. Inhaling a huge breath of warm night air, he took several steps down the cobbled street before the scent registered in his mind. When it did, he cursed softly under his breath.

The summer breeze rustled tendrils of wavy hair about his cheeks and neck as he put on his jacket and changed direction, weaving his way through the tangle of alleys. Several turns he took until the scent once again drifted on the air. "It can't be," he grumbled under his breath, brows drawing down low over his eyes. "I left her sleeping in her home."

Again, his mind flashed with an image of Lady Carenza, all softness and vulnerability as she lay tucked asleep in his arms. Innocent and sweet.

He caught the scent again, nearby this time.

Not so innocent and sweet, Damon corrected himself as he rounded the end of the alley and came to the back entrance of the Meadowlark Tavern. "She wouldn't dare," he said in disbelief.

She would not defy her father again so soon.

Would she?

Certainly, once the earl had put his foot down, she would do nothing but obey his wishes. That was what all high-bred ladies of station did: give up and give in. Though she showed more courage than most, deep down she must be the same. Mustn't she?

Suddenly movement caught the corner of Damon's eye, and he spun his head, looking down the alley, ever aware of the danger of the Revivalists. A lone cloaked and hooded figure slid out of the darkness and stepped toward him into the lantern light spilling over the tavern's back door. A tendril of golden sun was released from its mooring and tumbled loose beneath the cloak's hood, giving her away. A gasp, feminine and familiar, escaped the hidden figure.

Outrage and disbelief filled Damon as he too stepped toward the ring of lantern light and bellowed, unable to restrain himself, *"How are you even here?"*

After several frustrating moments, a long, drawn-out, put-upon sigh was her only response, and then she raised her hands and slowly removed the cloak's hood, revealing a mass of spun-gold hair and heavenly blue eyes that snapped with devil's fire. "It seems we meet yet again, *Mr. Crowe.*"

CHAPTER NINE

N o.

No, no, no, no, *no.*

Absolutely not.

This was not happening to her again. Not after everything she'd suffered through to get here. Not after everything she had already sacrificed simply for being born a female in this world.

Just *bloody* let her have this.

"Get out of my way," Carenza ground out, jaw clenched tight enough to shatter into a thousand shards.

"Oh no, I'm not moving." The blasted Mr. Crowe growled, all low and menacing. "You were left in Mayfair. Not here. *Mayfair.*"

"Well, as you can see"—Carenza sniffed and plucked a pretend thread from the sleeve of her brown tweed cloak, rather prim and proper—"I did not stay in Mayfair."

"That was not the agreement." His words came out tightly leashed, anger nipping right behind.

"Oh, well, as I was merely a pawn, I can assure you I am unaware of any *agreement.*" And it still rankled. Infuriated her. She sniffed again, brushed at an invisible piece of lint on the other sleeve, and counted to ten, drew slow breaths to ease the race of her heartbeat. Anger merely blinded, and she needed calm reason. Especially when Mr. Crowe was involved. Everything about him scrambled her senses like a French omelet.

"You knew *our* arrangement."

Carenza's eyes flew wide as her poise scattered, and surprise colored her tone. "We had an arrangement?"

Mr. Crowe took a step toward her, his height and broad shoulders consuming all her vision as he loomed over her, his dark charcoal jacket nearly black in the dim light. "We absolutely, utterly, clearly, and irrevocably had an agreement. One which you broke being here right now, this very moment. Good Christ, woman, you do try my patience." He leaned down even further until she could see the heat in his molten chocolate gaze. "*A. Lot.*"

Excellent. At least that made two of them.

"If you'll excuse me, I have an engagement to attend." Straightening her back and squaring her shoulders, Carenza attempted to march past the formidable Mr. Crowe as if she had not a care in the world.

His iron arm halted her. Came down like a felled tree, blocking her way.

"The only place you are attending this evening is your residence in Mayfair, posthaste."

She snorted inelegantly. "You sound snooty."

"Do not."

"Do too. *Posthaste*," she mocked, unable to help herself. He was standing between her and her freedom, and if he didn't move soon then she was going to kick him. Speaking of which… "How are your delicates faring this evening, Mr. Crowe? I must inquire."

The look in his dark eyes turned downright murderous.

Carenza retreated a step, rethinking her strategy. After all, she truly did not know Mr. Crowe that well. Better, yes, than some married couples before their nuptials. That was true. God, perhaps better than she might well know her future, forced-upon-her husband. At least she and Mr. Crowe had spoken.

He must have misinterpreted the panic in her eyes and the sudden shallowness of her breathing, because his voice went soft, low as he said, "I will never hurt you."

Simple words, nothing more. Yet it was all the reassurance Carenza didn't realize she needed. Her breath eased.

Until he added, voice filled with rookery harshness, "But you can bet your sweet arse, milady, that I'll take you back to your gilded cage and collect me blunt."

Carenza gasped, shocked at his crassness. "I say!" Her hand flew to her breast. "You wouldn't."

"Oh, but I would." The truth of it shone in his dark eyes. "And I will."

"You wouldn't dare lay a hand on my person! I am a lady." Carenza tipped her chin rather regally and glared down her nose at Mr. Crowe. Which was difficult, considering how bloody tall he was. "Now move."

She hated to be so crude—however... Her gaze wandered down his long, strong frame as she finally took in a good appraisal of him. Rumpled, half-tucked shirt, mussed tangle of hair, trousers partly hanging out of riding boots. Bruising on his devilishly appealing face.

She exclaimed, "Mr. Crowe, I daresay you appear to have been in a brawl!" Instantly filled with concern, she reached for him, tracing the lines of his face, noting each and every swell, every bruise. Soothing them with her care.

He grunted but did not pull away from her touch. "Sparring match at the club."

In fact, if she wasn't mistaken, Mr. Crowe seemed to lean into her fingers ever so slightly. Just the slightest fraction. Yes, she felt it.

Carenza rose to her toes, the worn leather of her boot laces straining across her ankles, and traced the strong line of his jaw, noting the bruise blooming there under the bristle of his facial hair. "Does it hurt?" she murmured, lost in the masculine feel of him under her fingertips. Lean cheeks, strong, winged brows. And eyes—goodness, his penetrating, assessing eyes. So guarded. So lonely.

"Not when you're touching me." He whispered the words

like a holy confession, eyelids drifting briefly closed. Like a cat in blissful surrender to a good petting. *Is he even aware of what he is doing?* Carenza wondered.

Tenderness welled inside her when he *did* lean into her touch, hesitant and shy. "Oh, Mr. Crowe," she breathed, inexplicably drawn to him. This dark and brooding man she barely knew.

A rumble sounded in his chest as she continued her gentle ministrations, like the contented purr of a great lion.

Forgetting entirely that they were in a rather dark, rather grim alley behind a Covent Garden tavern renowned for music, ale, and Friday night fights, Carenza trailed the pad of her thumb across his bottom lip—and thrilled at his quick intake of breath.

"You shouldn't be doing that," he murmured against her thumb, his eyes still closed. His breath spilled over her skin, hot and searing. A thrumming started between her thighs, plumping and slickening her folds with need. With *want*.

"Should I stop?" she asked, unconsciously leaning her aching breasts into his solid chest to ease their sudden sensitivity.

"Mmm-mm," he replied with a miniscule shake of his head, the sound so softly spoken that she almost didn't hear it.

"Mr. Crowe," she whispered again, mesmerized by the feel of him.

Just then the tavern door burst open, and West stepped out, gray eyes wide and alarmed, wooden club in hand. Spotting them, he said with surprising calm, given his wild expression, "The Revivalists have struck down near the docks. Word just reached me. Source says they're moving this way, so I'm closing up the Meadowlark and getting everybody home. That includes you." The pub owner turned his gaze to Mr. Crowe and added, "See her home, will you? I've people here that need my help."

Already in motion, Mr. Crowe latched on to Carenza's elbow through her cloak and began pulling her away from the relative comfort of the tavern lantern light and into the darkness beyond. "I'll see to it," he agreed, his voice rough and tense. "Help those that need it."

West spared them not another glance, simply nodded his head and slammed the tavern door shut. The sounds of locks latching could be heard activating through the thick wood door.

"Well—" she started, tugging against him.

"Home," he ground out. *"Now."*

"And how exactly am I supposed to get there so quickly?" Carenza made a display of looking up and down the tiny, empty alley. "I have no conveyance, and I see no hacks." Not that she was inclined to stay and have another close encounter with the Revivalists tonight. One was more than enough to last a lifetime. More, it was that she felt the need to point out the obvious should Mr. Crowe not see it for himself.

"Please stop talking," the infernal man requested quietly, his head turned at such an angle that he could only be…well…*sniffing* something? Like a hound catching a scent.

"What are you doing?" Carenza demanded.

"Tracking," was his enigmatic answer.

"What does that mean? *Tracking?*"

Once again, Carenza found her hand enveloped in his as he released her elbow and led her quickly through a small labyrinth of rookery alleyways and lanes, refusing to answer. For a few minutes more they strode in silence until she suddenly found herself on the edge of the Garden district, a short block away from decency and relative safety. They stopped near a building with a swinging wooden sign over the door that advertised a men's sporting club of sorts. *Flatt's,* the sign read.

Tucking behind the building, Mr. Crowe led them up a flight of outdoor stairs to a small landing and a simple, white-painted door. He began pounding a fist against the wood. Not at all quietly.

"Open up, it's me," he hissed, rapping his knuckles in an impatient rhythm against the door. *"Pssst!"*

After a tense moment, the scratched door swung open. A giant man with a bushy, red-tinged beard and frown as fierce as any Carenza had ever witnessed took one look at her, and then Mr. Crowe, and gruffly said, "Wot?"

"I need to borrow your curricle," Mr. Crowe said, startling her with the familiarity in his tone. How did he know this…this rather imposing beast of a man?

A long pause.

"No."

Mr. Crowe shuffled his feet, rolled his broad shoulders, and heaved a great sigh. "You cannot say no," he said with surprising restraint. "The Revivalists have struck in Wapping and are said to be making their way to the Garden. I walked here this eve and have not my own curricle, and it is imperative she get home. Therefore, I need to borrow *your* curricle. To escort her home."

"Can't," the gruff-looking man with the wild hair and burning glower replied, and crossed huge, muscled arms over an equally hugely muscled chest, haphazardly covered by an untied, open-necked tunic.

"Why ever not?" Mr. Crowe asked in clear exasperation, his dark eyes lighting with frustration.

"Axle's broke on it," the man replied, and began pulling on a pair of scuffed but immaculately cleaned boots. "We'll have to use the other one."

"We?" Mr. Crowe asked, cutting the Viking a suspicious, narrow-eyed look. "What other one?"

"Carriage needs a driver."

Carenza raised a tentative hand from her corner of the landing and inquired, "Cannot Mr. Crowe do that? Drive it, that is?"

The man leveled on her a hard, unyielding stare. "No."

"Excellent!" she squeaked, a little shocked at how intimidated she was by the sheer size and muscle of the auburn-haired man. If he wished to drive, well, that was terrific by her.

"Why do you have a carriage?" Mr. Crowe asked. "Is the club not fiscally sufficient on its own? Are you a driver for hire as well?" Concern etched his tone.

"Won it," was all the large man replied.

"Ahh. Well, then." Mr. Crowe cleared his throat, saying no more.

As she watched, her heart racing, the two men shared a piercing, thorough stare. Until the giant flicked her a glance and said to Mr. Crowe, "I see why."

Mr. Crowe grunted.

Merely…grunted.

"Beg pardon. See what?" she couldn't help but ask from her corner of the landing far, far behind Mr. Crowe. She looked at the stranger. The man really was rather enormous. And very much a scowler.

Why were all the men of her acquaintance of late such scowlers? They were *men*. In life, they had everything.

Before the man could reply, Mr. Crowe snapped, "Time's wasting." Grabbing her hand once again, he began to make his way back down the stairs. "We go now."

Everything over the next several moments became a blur and didn't stop until she was bundled into a dark, single-seated carriage with a rather long-legged Mr. Crowe eating up most of the space beside her. His rich, masculine scent filled the remaining areas, and Carenza found herself quite very thoroughly surrounded by one very bothersome Mr. Crowe.

Although in this case he was assisting her, so…?

"Let us get this done." He rapped his knuckles sharply against the carriage roof, barking orders to the huge man currently outside perched on the driver's bench. "I wish this night to be over."

No, still bothersome.

Quite.

"I wish this night to be over, too," she snapped peevishly, crossing her arms over her ample bosom, and pushing as far across the carriage bench as she could manage. Which wasn't very much, granted. Still, she believed the statement her action made was quite loud. If he wasn't going to address their almost kiss, then neither was she. "In fact, I wish this night had never happened at all!"

"Somehow I doubt that," he growled, his large body happily taking up the space upon the bench her body had vacated. His thighs—so hard and muscular and thick—splayed wide and continued to brush against her. So indecent. Yet she did not complain. Quite the opposite, rather. She secretly enjoyed the heat of him against her, and shifted the tiniest sliver-of-a-fraction closer.

The team of horses began to move, and the carriage rocked into motion as the large, intimidating man of Mr. Crowe's acquaintance directed them down the alley. "Who is this man assisting us this eve? What is his name?" she asked suddenly, whipping her head around in the darkened interior of the carriage toward Mr. Crowe. "Does he know how to navigate us to Mayfair?"

Amusement laced his deep, rough tone when he answered, his features concealed by the dark, "Aaron knows the direction to Mayfair."

"What's so amusing?" Carenza demanded, instantly self-conscious at his laughter. "What have I said that is so funny?" With the curtains drawn over the carriage windows and the light from the lanterns outside barely reaching within, the distance between them was difficult to discern. She leaned forward just the slightest touch and bumped directly into his shoulder. "Beg pardon." Instantly jerking back, she then bumped into the carriage door, startling her further.

"Are you quite finished fussing?" he asked, shifting his weight, causing his thigh to press more fully against her.

"Why must this carriage be so small?" she said by way of response. Which wasn't a response at all, really.

"Given the state of events of this evening, one would think a lady of breeding such as yourself would be overcome with gratitude for the protection and assistance home to safety."

"I *am* grateful." She was, truly.

"Then perhaps you should act like it."

"What exactly is that supposed to mean?" Carenza demand-ed, bracing her feet as the carriage bounced and pitched in the dark. "I act perfectly grateful."

Mr. Crowe snorted. He *snorted*.

"Oh, well, you know what?" she started, feeling riled inside over his rude response. One didn't *snort* at a lady. At least, *he* didn't.

Well, he did. But he wasn't allowed.

"I know many things," he replied into the dark, his gravelly, low voice and masculine scent an intoxicating combination, scrambling her senses. Why did he have to be so much *man*? It made it exceedingly difficult to think.

"Such as?" Her words came out sharp and taunting. "What do you know, Mr. Crowe?"

The carriage interior dropped into silence, save for their breathing, and suddenly Carenza became highly aware that she was alone in the night with a man she barely knew. A dangerous man. A threat to her freedom.

A man she was irrepressibly drawn to, regardless.

The carriage hit a hole, its right wheel dropping into the worn rut. The sudden motion flung Carenza from one side of the interior to the other as she cried out in surprise.

"Hole!" Aaron hollered from his place outside on the carriage seat.

Somehow in the jostling, her boot became caught under the hem of her simple blue linen dress, and as she was tossed about the interior, the heel pulled on her skirt fabric, tugging the whole of her dress down, exposing her breasts, inadequately bound by a too-small half-corset—the only corset she owned that fit smoothly under her maid's borrowed dress. And by borrowed, she meant pilfered. Though bless Gertie's heart for never saying a word or batting an eyelash when it went missing and Carenza gave her coin from her own reticule to purchase herself another.

Now, however, she rather wished she'd used that coin to purchase a dress that fit *her* appropriately.

"Oomph!" she said, landing unceremoniously atop Mr. Crowe, her cloak flinging wide.

Scrambling to untangle her boot and tugging at the bodice of her dress, she failed to notice how much she was sprawled across his body—until his thigh flexed and she felt it intimately between her own legs. "Oh my!" she whispered in sudden, surprising arousal, frozen.

"Something I know," Mr. Crowe murmured against her ear, his voice sharpening with his Garden upbringing, his breath hot against her skin, "is tha' you may dislike me with your brain, but your body feels the opposite." A hard, large hand snaked around her and cupped her buttocks, steadied her against him. "Your body, milady, very much likes me." He flexed his thigh against her again, and she nearly melted.

He wasn't wrong.

Blast him.

"It is of little consequence," she managed to say, almost flippantly, though her breath had gone shallow and unsteady as heat bloomed between her legs.

"Is it?" he asked, boldly rubbing his thigh against her this time as he skimmed his free hand up her back and yanked off her cloak hood, tangling his long fingers in her hair. "Prove it."

Then his mouth was on hers, hot and searching. No easy, gentle kiss. Oh no—Mr. Crowe took her lips, licking them, nipping them, learning their feel and taste.

"Christ, you're delicious." He groaned, squeezing her buttocks before tracing a path up her ribs to her breasts. When he discovered their half-exposed state, a growl of approval ripped from his chest.

Carenza gasped against his firm lips, sensation after dizzying sensation assaulting her. She was drowning. Floating. Flying. Lost in a haze of desire that had appeared so suddenly, so fully, she knew not what to do other than respond. Openly and without restraint.

"Carenza," he rumbled against her lips, his hard fingers finding her taut nipple and pinching lightly.

"Mr. Crowe!" she cried out.

"Damon," he said, low and rough. "When my mouth is on you, it's Damon."

She sighed. "*Damon.*"

"Tha's the way," he said, and took her mouth again, all tongue and lips and consuming heat. "Again," he demanded.

"Damon," she whispered, her hands exploring his chiseled shoulders before diving into his thick mass of silken hair. Her mouth found his once again in the dark, and she groaned, opened readily for him.

He shifted, and suddenly she was straddling his hips with something hard and thick pressing intimately between her legs. "Feck, yes," he growled, and kissed her, stroked his tongue boldly, possessively against hers.

Carenza whimpered against his lips and wiggled in his lap in an attempt to ease the throbbing ache between her thighs. Desire flared even hotter at the motion, and she gasped, knowing not what to do but desperately needing *something.*

She rocked against the hard length between her thighs, pressing against its heat.

Damon dropped his head back against the seat and released a string of curses, gripping her hips tightly through the fabric of her dress. Liking his reaction and the waves of pleasure the movement created, she repeated the motion and cried out at the rush of desire it sent straight to her core.

"*Hechicera.*" He groaned softly and thrust against her, tormenting them both with pleasure.

The carriage suddenly came to an abrupt halt, and Carenza nearly tumbled backward off Damon's lap. A shocked squeak slipped from her lips, but before she could fall, his hands were there, settling her safely on the seat next to him, tugging her bodice back into place and tucking her oh-so-sensitive breasts demurely back inside.

"Look alive, Crowe," came Aaron's harsh whisper through

the carriage roof as he banged a fist upon it. "We've got company."

"Of course we do." Another string of curses as Carenza heard
him moving about in the cramped interior, righting his own
appearance.

"Who coul—?" she started, but he grabbed her by the nape of
her neck and pulled her close for a quick, hard kiss.

As quickly as it began, it ended and he dropped his hand from
her. Quite in time, as well. She ran trembling fingers over her
disheveled hair in an attempt to smooth the strands, and had just
finished when the carriage door nearest her swung wide open.

"*Out,*" the Earl of Castlebury commanded, voice deadly cold.

Dread filled her, suffused every inch of her being, and she
began to shake. Refusing to let her father see how his anger
affected her, Carenza tipped up her chin and replied, "Hello,
Father." Before she could lose courage, she climbed from the
carriage and stood stiffly by his side, eyes forward. Inside, her
stomach quivered sickly.

Carenza felt Damon drop down from the carriage step behind
her, and the urge to lean into his quiet strength nearly consumed
her. It took every ounce of will to continue holding still, to not
collapse into the safety of his arms. He would keep her from her
father's anger. Keep her from a forced marriage. Somehow, she
knew he would protect her.

"You. Your chamber. *Now,*" the earl ordered her, his tone
clipped. She could *feel* the suppressed rage in her father like a
palpable object.

"Yes, Father," she replied. Though every bit of her screamed
to turn around and run—and keep running—she did no such
thing. Squaring her shoulders, she began walking toward the
door, refusing to look over her shoulder at Damon, though she
could feel his eyes heavy upon her.

"I should be off," she heard him say as she stepped farther
away from his reassuring presence. Yes, he should go, and she
should retire to her bedchamber to sleep, and her father should

say nothing, and everyone should forget this day had happened.

"Stay," her father demanded quietly, his tone like iron. "I want a word with you."

Carenza tripped on the front step and nearly toppled forward into the door. A word? What could her father possibly want to talk to Damon about?

Whatever it was, Carenza decided as a waiting footman ushered her through the door and into the tomblike silence of Tipton House, it could not be good.

Not good at all.

CHAPTER TEN

A BALL.

Carenza had to attend a ball the very next evening, one hosted by her parents. With all the excitement of late, she had forgotten the annual ball held at Tipton House.

Perhaps she had not forgotten. Perhaps she had willfully denied the truth.

Tonight, she must search for a husband.

"Why must he force me like this?" she'd asked her mother earlier that day. "How am I to find a suitable gentleman under this extreme pressure? Moreover, why must I find one at all?"

"You'll do what every other woman in your situation has done since time immemorial. You'll adjust your expectations and make do with good enough. Because you must."

"I would rather go without than settle for mediocre, Mother."

"Unfortunate, then. For that is what you shall have regardless of how you feel." And there was sympathy in her mother's tone, in her expression. Sympathy, but also a certain something else. Something steely and resigned. "I suggest you participate enthusiastically in this search, my dear. For it is the rest of your life."

As if she needed *that* reminder.

"And, child, be thankful for the opportunity to secure even such a luxury as mediocrity. Not all are as fortunate."

Hard words, those.

"Stop fidgeting, Car. People are starting to look," Nora now whispered quietly from next to her as they stood on the edge of the dance floor and drank punch, both of them wishing desperately to be anywhere other than where they currently were. "I hate balls," her sister complained. "So sweaty."

Carenza agreed, "And hot."

"And large. Some balls like this one are hideously big."

"Big or small." Carenza sipped tepid punch. "I detest balls. Quite content I would be to never see one again."

A choking, strangling sort of sound came from behind them, and Carenza spun her head around, startled at the noise. A group of bachelor gentlemen huddled nearby, faces blotched red as they appeared to be having fits. They steadfastly avoided looking in her and Nora's direction, so after a good, long stare, she turned back around and dismissed them.

Not before she spotted Damon, however.

"What the blazes is *he* doing here?" she blurted out, shocked at his presence, her body instantly heating, reacting with memory of his touch. She was about to march directly over to him and ask him that very question, but Nora stayed her with a quiet hand on hers. Carenza settled for staring at Damon, all dark and brooding in the corner by the plant alcove. Her heart began to pound, slow and heavy in her chest. Why was he there?

"Make no movement toward him," her sister whispered in her ear. "I count at least nine pairs of eyes upon us at this moment."

"Truly?" Carenza asked in surprise, her attention turned. "But why?"

Nora released a big sigh and rolled her eyes in the way only sisters could. "Obviously because you are especially beautiful tonight. Madame Toussaint does extraordinary work. Even Lottie looks splendid this eve." She pointed to the dance floor, where their youngest sister partook in the quadrille, looking lovely in her rose-colored silk gown as she spun about the floor with a young, handsome suitor.

"It might be you they're noticing," Carenza offered, noting how vibrant Nora appeared in her dress of deep crimson and with her hair pulled up, shimmering copper in the candlelight. "That color on you is divine."

"That's what Madame Toussaint said as well," Nora replied with a satisfied smile. "Interesting that the color of passion makes me appear so angelic, no?"

Passion.

All thoughts poured like water from a vessel in Carenza's mind and filled back up with Damon. In the dark. His hands on her. His *mouth.*

Her nipples began to pucker under the lavender silk bodice of her dress, and she gasped softly, her eyes widening in rekindled arousal as she continued to look across the ballroom at him. She blinked, yet he was still there. Not an apparition. Oh no, he was all virile, broad-shouldered male in his black evening dress, his thighs thick and heavily muscled beneath his breeches. Her lips felt suddenly parched, and she licked them absent-mindedly, unable to take her eyes from him.

As if he could read her mind, one corner of his firm mouth slowly curled in a half-smile, wicked and knowing. His gaze, so dark and intense, burned into her. He nodded, just the tiniest tip of his chin. But the small acknowledgment, shockingly intimate, sent heat spiraling down her spine.

Ripping her gaze away, Carenza broke the silent spell he had on her, and keenly felt the loss of connection. "I think we are referring to your complexion, not the state of your moral character," she said, belatedly responding to her sister.

Rather than be offended, Nora laughed and agreed, "It is a good thing."

Chuckling softly, Carenza tried to peel her eyes off the brooding man in the corner—he was neither a peer nor landed gentry, and had no business there, amongst the elite of the *ton.* Mystified, excited, and unsettled over Damon's presence, she took several calming breaths and scanned the ballroom.

As usual, her parents hosted a grand event. Decadent in gold and ivory, the ballroom glittered under the chandeliers and wall sconces. From wall to wall the *ton* milled about, some dancing, some in the thick of gossip. Though it was still early, the ballroom radiated warmth. Soon it would be stifling.

"I see you are behaving yourself."

Snapping her head around, Carenza masked her surprise and replied quietly, "Yes, Father. I've no wish to do anything else this evening." Especially since this was the first that he had spoken to her since yesterday.

"See that you don't," the Earl of Castlebury stated, cutting her a glance, his ice-blue eyes unreadable.

"I'm behaving as well!" chimed in Nora with a wide, innocent smile. Carenza knew it was all a display for their father, to distract him from his displeasure at her.

He, however, did not. "And it's a good girl you are, too, my Norabell."

Ugh.

"Father?" she said, keeping her tone perfectly neutral and pleasant, though her stomach churned uneasily. Whatever she felt inside at that moment did not show on her face. She made certain of it. "I daresay I see Mr. Crowe across the ballroom. Is there a particular reason he is in attendance this evening?" Did he have connections of which she was unaware?

"He is here to contain you." The earl flicked her a disapproving look. "He and I came to an understanding after your return home last night. For the foreseeable future, until you've a husband to fulfill the position, Mr. Crowe is to be your escort and your guard. I am paying him handsomely to not let you from his sight."

Carenza's jaw dropped, and she began to sputter, outrage and anger and something else—something far more feminine and personal and *excited* at the prospect of having such close proximity to Mr. Crowe—bubbling in her gut. And yet, how *dare* her father do such a thing! She needed no keeper, no watchman, no nursemaid. She was a woman fully grown!

"I see you disapprove of my choice. That is unfortunate. Do remember that this would have been unnecessary had you minded yourself to begin with."

Biting the inside of her cheek to keep from speaking her mind, Carenza forced a smile, her lips tight and unbearably dry. "How will you explain his presence, pray tell? Several members of the *ton* are openly staring at him." She flicked Damon a glance—and felt the power of him like a lightning strike to her heart. "He does not," she started, before stopping to swallow and catch the breath he'd stolen. "That is to say that Mr. Crowe does not exactly blend in."

Her father cast her a pitying glance. "This is why men inherit titles. I have already considered such possibilities." And with that, her father stepped away from her and addressed the crowded ballroom. "Thank you all for attending this evening! What a glorious night to hold a ball. Lady Castlebury and I are so pleased to have you here." Instantly her mother was by his side, smiling demurely, ever the perfect hostess.

The crowd quieted and stilled as all eyes turned to the formidable Earl of Castlebury and his lady. Curiosity rippled through the room. Even the string quartet ceased playing; her father commanded attention from one and all. Though he was paunchy of gut from too much mutton, roast duck, and drink, the earl's station and ancient wealth embedded a certain confidence of air in him.

"What is he doing?" Nora whispered out of the corner of her mouth, barely moving her lips.

"I've no idea," Carenza whispered back, though in truth she most wanted to shout. How could her father hire her a guard? And how in blazes could Mr. Crowe (yes, after this upsetting revelation, he was once again merely, and at a very impersonal distance, Mr. Crowe) agree to the position?

Bloody men.

Fuming, Carenza clutched her gloved hands together behind

her back to keep from doing something she most assuredly should not. Like strangle her father. Or Mr. Crowe.

"It is grave times we find ourselves enduring with those Revivalists out there once again, loose upon London's streets. So I thank you, most enthusiastically from my heart, for your presence this night. And to ensure your safety and to provide another level of protection and comfort, I have hired a private guard to ensure your well-being. Therefore, should you see a gentleman you do not readily recognize, it is he. Pay him no mind." He chuckled good-naturedly and waved a hand over the crowd, sweeping it in Mr. Crowe's direction. "Now, where were we?" the earl said with false joviality. "Ah! Let us once again dance!" With a snap of his fingers, the quartet resumed their playing, picking up exactly where they had stopped.

Polite clapping and a hum of appreciation came from the crowd as several members of the *ton* regained the dance floor, the evening once again progressing in accordance with the schedule.

"Brilliant, my lord! Simply a brilliant execution of caring for our community!"

"Nooooo," Carenza groaned, shoulders slumping. "Not *him*." Of all the blasted, blooming people.

"I'm afraid so," murmured Nora. "Lord Arnold has decided to attend our soiree."

Annoyance mingled with the anger Carenza already felt over the recent news about Mr. Crowe, and blended, stirring uncomfortably in her stomach. Her chest, already tight with emotion, squeezed further. As the Masked Meadowlark, she knew well the type of person Horrid A truly was. Yet, as her identity was secret, she could not allow that knowledge to affect her behavior toward him as Lady Carenza Castlebury. For as the earl's daughter, she would know nothing of smoky taverns and the aristocrats who frequented them. Nor would she know Lord Arnold was a cretin and a groper.

As Masked Meadowlark, she knew and had experienced all those things.

"Such a gorgeous evening for one of your renowned balls, my lord!" Horrid A bowed to her father, his many ruffles and abundant cravat threatening to spring from his person like the wool of a sheep.

"Thank you, Lord Arnold."

"Might I congratulate you on how well your family appears this fine evening?"

Groaning again, Carenza turned from the perturbing scene, latching on to Nora's hand before Lord Arnold spotted her and requested a dance, and led them through a throng of heated bodies with about as much grace as one could muster, given her circumstances. "Excuse me, pardon me," she muttered along the way. "My that's a lovely dress!"

Finally coming to the end of the crush of bodies, Carenza tugged her sister along, and together they stepped from the crowd. The eastern perimeter of the ballroom was blessedly empty.

"Good evening, ladies."

Except, apparently, for Rainville.

"What are you doing here? Who invited you?" snapped Nora with absolutely no pretense as she openly glared up at the towering, golden duke.

"Who *hasn't* invited me, is the better question," the duke replied, arching an imperial bronze brow at her. "And the answer to that is no one."

"Oh, you have such an inflated sense of self!" fumed Nora, fisting her hands at her sides, surprising Carenza. Such an impassioned response to Rainville! Where were her sister's manners? Her decorum?

Then again, he *had* carried Nora over his shoulder from the pub like a stuffed sack.

"I *am* a duke," he replied with a hint of irritation. "Naturally I am entitled."

"Oh-ho, on the contrary, *Your Grace*," Nora whispered furiously, tipping her chin high and turning a few curious heads in their direction. "When a man accosts a lady, he loses the right to any and all sense of superiority, no matter his station!"

"I hardly accosted you," Rainville scoffed, crossing his arms over his finely tailored black tailcoat as he smiled blandly at the onlookers, his silk cravat perfectly knotted at his throat.

Carenza imagined Nora wished to choke him with it.

"You are *extremely* vexing," her sister ground out, also smiling tightly for those watching.

"Odd—you are the first to express that particular sentiment," Rainville murmured from the corner of his mouth.

"Oh!" Nora huffed, appearing on the verge of screaming.

"If you two do not stop this very instant," Carenza interrupted, "then I shall be forced to improvise a rather dramatic fainting spell." She looked each of them directly in the eyes, brows raised. "I am quite serious."

"Why ever would you do such a thing?" Rainville asked, sounding highly offended, yet his expression remained blank for the audience. A duke quibbling with a female provided quite the gossip fodder. By the neutral way he was behaving, it was clear he wished to be neither gossip nor fodder.

"To do whatever is necessary to distract attention from you and my sister before she is wholly scandalized!"

"You worry for *her* reputation?"

"Absolutely I do." Carenza would have nodded if so many pairs of eyes weren't so keen upon her at the moment.

"Yet you have no concerns for mine?"

She nearly laughed at the absurdity. "Your reputation is solidly intact, Your Grace, and in no danger of toppling."

"Perhaps I could surprise you," Rainville replied, and something in his tone reminded her of her encounters with him as Meadowlark. Though he quite clearly did not recognize her, she recalled him with vivid clarity. His persistent attentiveness toward her and his charming determination to have her perform in his theatre had her reassessing what she thought she knew of the duke. "Perhaps it is *my* company you should be running from in great haste," he finished mildly.

"Undoubtedly," Nora muttered.

"Ceranora!" Carenza said, appalled at her sister's behavior. "I do apologize, Your Grace."

"Unnecessary," Rainville replied, sparing her a reassuring glance. "It is your sister from whom the apology should come."

"Me?" Nora slapped a hand over her chest. "I say! *You* were the one who threw me over your shoulder. Not me. *You.* If anyone is entitled to an apology, it is I."

"Not happening."

"Indeed, you two?" Carenza nearly threw her hands up in exasperation.

"Is everything quite all right here?"

Oh, bloody hell.

"Lord Arnold, how good of you to join us this evening!" Nora said around a fake, bright smile. "His Grace and I were just debating the finer points of dancing. Were we not, Your Grace?"

"We were, in fact," replied Rainville evenly, his golden gaze dispassionate upon the viscount. "Quite a heated debate, I confess. Thank you for your concern."

The viscount eyed each of them skeptically, stroking a hand over a rather poofy sideburn before giving Carenza his full attention. His thin lips slid into a smile that made her skin itch uncomfortably. "Anything for Lady Carenza, to keep her from upset."

"How kind of you," she uttered, wanting to vomit. His voice—the whine of it—unsettled her deeply. It reminded her of something.

A movement from the corner of her eye caught her attention, and she turned slightly to see Mr. Crowe making his way around the perimeter of the ballroom toward them. Instantly her distaste for Lord Arnold melted and turned into fascination at the way Mr. Crowe moved—all strength and surprising grace and agility.

His attention was only on her.

Nerves jittered wildly in her abdomen, and her pulse raced at his penetrating gaze. And when Lord Arnold stepped toward her, she could not help the thrill that shot through her at Mr. Crowe's responding scowl. Though she shouldn't, she rather liked that he reacted in that manner. Almost as if he wanted her for himself.

That single thought sent her mind spinning in a dozen directions. *Did* he want her all to himself? Did he merely wish to kiss her again? Did he wish *more*?

What did *she* wish?

Quite suddenly, the heat in the ballroom became unbearable, and Carenza struggled for breath. "Excuse me," she muttered, and turned toward the nearby balcony doors.

"I say, Lady Carenza, are you well?" Lord Arnold reached for her elbow, a gesture meant to offer her stabilization, yet she knew his unwelcome touch and quickly pulled her arm from his reach.

"I'm quite well, thank you. I see my dear mother waving to me from the balcony, and I must go." Curling tendrils clung to her neck and temples as sweat pearled on her brow. Pasting a polite smile upon her face, she turned to rush off.

"I can lend you my arm and take you to her."

"No!" Carenza cried, and stopped her escape, smiling over her shoulder at the viscount. "That is, I can manage on my own, thank you very much."

"I must insist."

"How goes the theatre business, ol' chum?" Rainville interrupted, solidly stepping into Lord Arnold's path, and stopping him from following her outside onto the balcony. "I should enjoy discussing our mutual affection for the performed word."

"Go," whispered Nora, waving her off with a brush of her hand.

Now was her chance, as the viscount wouldn't dare refuse a duke. "Thank you," Carenza mouthed, and ducked out the open balcony door, making her escape.

Though she knew it was wrong, and even though she was angry at him, she secretly hoped Damon would follow.

CHAPTER ELEVEN

DAMON SLIPPED SILENTLY into the gentle moonlight, following Lady Carenza after she dashed through the doors onto the balcony. As he passed by, he murmured a thanks to Rainville for interfering in Lord Arnold's courting attempts. Pathetic as they were.

Rippling with protectiveness and not a little possessiveness, he forcefully ignored his desire to punch Arnold in his foppish face and restrained a growl as he stalked over the cold stones. Anger and jealousy tugged within him, and he disapproved heartily. More bloody feelings? *Yes.* All because of one very aggravating goddess.

He was expecting her to be on the upper balcony, so Damon's brow furrowed even further when he did not spot her shining golden strands or see fabric the color of lavender fields fluttering in the cooling breeze. "What the devil?" he said quietly. "Where did you go, my lady?" Something about the word *my* struck him particularly hard, and he sucked in a breath, momentarily taken aback by the force of it.

Regaining his wits, he glanced around, searching for Carenza to no avail. He knew Lord Arnold could not have absconded with her, for he was still engaged in animated conversation with the duke. Still, he double-checked over his shoulder, peering through the glass double doors within to the ballroom and the pair of gentlemen in conversation beyond. Spotting the viscount there confirmed Damon's rising suspicion that Carenza had left the balcony altogether, taking the dark walk into the gardens.

Alone.

Of their own accord, his feet set off across the balcony stones, his top boots clacking against the flooring. Sconces and torches lit the terrace as a few people milled about, their voices a blended murmur to his ears as he made his way to a set of steps. The air hung heavy with scents, summer flowers vying with colognes and French perfumes and the pungent sharpness of horse manure undoubtedly released by a horse harnessed to a guest's waiting carriage. Jasmine, rose, peonies—those notes saturated the night breeze. Yet they were not the ones he sought.

Tuning out the conversations buzzing around him and the annoyingly energetic performance by the string quartet inside the ballroom, Damon breathed a steadying, calming breath and let his senses heighten, his focus sharpen. "Where did you disappear to, *hechicera?*" he asked the breeze, knowing it would answer and show him the way. It always did, without fail. Over the years he had learned to trust the wind more than people; his mother's Spanish Gitano blood ran true through his veins. Though she had died while he was still a child, her memory and spirit lived on through his ability to track nearly anything—a skill he remembered well her teaching him and now put to very lucrative use.

Lilac and lemons.

The scent filled his nose, and Damon smiled, a sharp turn of his lips that displayed his crooked incisor. A young miss passing him released a small, frightened yelp and hastened her pace, casting him wary glances as she went. He was unoffended—the response rather amused him. Most people reacted to him that way. Fear with a side of distaste.

Chuckling to himself, Damon kept going, taking the stairs at a clipped pace, the telltale scent of Carenza growing stronger as he descended. Telling himself that he was only doing what he was paid to do—which was guard Carenza and protect her from herself (according to her father, though Damon had other thoughts on that matter)—he stepped off the stairs and onto the gravel garden path, crunching his boot heels against the small, smooth rocks.

A flock of young females came by him as he stepped to the side of the path, making way and respectfully inclining his head. Several curious glances came his way—most of the chits were too young to be aware of his reputation. Their mothers and fathers were a different story, however, and tonight several expressions amongst the attendees were not ones of idle curiosity, but rather worry. For it was one thing to employ his assistance in a personal matter. It was quite another to see him at a public function, complete with the awareness that he held damning knowledge of many of them.

But there was only one man he had any desire to bring down, and that was the bastard who'd sired him. A faceless, nameless monster who had attacked his mother one horrible night in Covent Garden before slinking like a shadow off into the midnight blackness, never to be caught. For over a decade, Damon had made hunting him down and making him pay his life's mission.

Lilacs and lemon filled his nose again, and his gut tightened in response, his heart pounded thick and hard in his chest, and emotions, ones he neither asked for nor wanted, stirred. Yet there they were all the same.

"Where are you?" he asked the breeze again, wandering down one meandering path, through the dense topiary arrangements, to another. Tugging at the knot of his cravat, Damon followed the path as he entered a tall hedge maze, his senses alerting to the utter danger of it for a lone female. Thinking of all the potential things that could go wrong or cause her harm had him quickening his pace and his brow furrowing. Anybody touched the lady—his lady—and they paid dearly.

But she wasn't his lady.

Maybe she is, that aggravating inner voice whispered, making him scowl fiercely in denial.

Damon had no lady.

He had no family.

No real attachments.

He had Bones and Aaron, and that was about it.

It doesn't have to be, the voice prodded.

"Stop it," he growled aloud, turning left down a path filled with fragrant summer flowers. Heady though the scents were, they were nothing to his senses compared to the simple combination that comprised Carenza's personal fragrance.

Damon was a lone wolf, and he liked it that way.

Rounding another tall hedge, he stopped short, his heart tumbling roughly in his chest when he spotted her. In the soft glow of the moon, underneath a blanket of shimmering stars, stood Lady Carenza, looking more beautiful than anything he had ever seen.

"How do you do it?" he blurted, his voice gravelly with emotion.

She gasped and spun around to look at him, a hand flying to her generous breasts in surprise—and he had an almost irresistible urge to bury his face between them and breathe her in deep. "Do what?" she managed to say, though the words came out a thready whisper.

He walked to her, slowly and deliberately, like a trainer gentling a skittish young filly. "Make me question everything I thought I knew."

"Oh, well, it is not on purpose, I can promise you that." The look she gave him, her face half shadowed in the moonlight, had need pouring like liquid through his veins, heating him, stirring his desire. The pleasure he saw wash over her at his words punched him in the gut, had him sucking in a sharp intake of air.

"I know," he replied, coming to a stop directly before her and reaching out to touch a loose strand of her silken hair. "That's what makes it so hard to resist."

"I don't understand."

He could tell by her expression that she did not.

Ah, such innocence.

Aaron was right—the lady was too good for him by half.

"You do not try to manipulate."

A frown tugged at her brow. "No, that is my father's forte."

He agreed, but before he could say anything, she added, "Why did you agree to his demand that you watch me like a puppy that is not yet house-trained, watching for the slightest hint that I might misbehave? Do you not see what a prison he has made for me? You are my shackles."

Perhaps he wanted to be her wings.

Damon's chest seized and squeezed tight, and he gripped the golden strands of her hair in a fist, anchoring himself to her like she were a buoy in a tossing, roiling ocean. "I have no wish to be anything of the sort."

"Then why did you agree?" she pressed, looking up at him with wide, questioning eyes.

"Perhaps because it kept me close to you," he answered honestly, yet keeping the other truth unspoken that the earl had learned of his search and offered him a lead on his father—his first real lead in a decade. "We are from different worlds, different classes. You are sunshine and light and goodness. Perhaps I wished to feel your rays on my face. If only for a little while longer."

"You should not say such things," she whispered, a hand covering his fist. "I do not want you to mean them."

"I do not *want* to mean them." Still, he did. And he knew not what to do with that knowledge.

"Then don't," she said, removing her hand from his. "Don't mean it. Don't watch over me. Don't stop me." Stepping away from him with a stern expression just visible in the soft moonlight, she added, "And especially do not kiss me again."

"Why?" The word was out before he even realized he had taken a breath.

"Because," she offered vaguely, crossing her arms over her front and turning from him. "Just...because."

"That is an insufficient reason, my lady." Drawn by an invisible force, he moved closer to her. It seemed as if he was always drawn closer to her. Him, a man accustomed and comfortable with being alone in the world. "Because you dislike me is sufficient. Because you liked my kiss is not."

Her head whipped around. "I did not say I disliked you."

"Ah, so it is because you liked my kiss, then?" he asked softly, pleasure rippling through him at the thought. When was the last time he had felt something as simple as *pleasure*?

Before a certain nobleman's daughter had absconded through the dark of night and he was hired to return her, pleasure had only been found in very small, specific doses. The turn of a poetic phrase by a literary master. The smell of a newly printed book. The first drag of a cigarette after a particularly chatty encounter when his nerves were up.

Tiny traces of pleasure.

But this feeling now? Knowing Carenza liked his kiss?

Pleasure with a capital P.

"What did my father tell you last night?"

"You're evading and changing the topic." He took another step in her direction, noting she did not retreat. "We were talking about you liking my kiss."

"No, *you* were talking about it. I distinctly was not. In fact, I was quite silent on the topic."

"Are you saying you do not like it?" Because he recalled her clinging to him, her hardened nipple between his fingers, small whimpers of desire coming from her as she met his mouth with her own, stroked her velvet tongue boldly against his.

"Perhaps I did not. Perhaps I barely remember it." They both knew that for the lie it was.

"Should I remind you?" he offered, closing the last bit of distance between them. In his head he knew the dangers, knew the game he played. She was a lady, an innocent. If he showed her the true depth of his desire for her, Carenza would run from him.

"I should not let you," she whispered, tipping her face up

toward his. "Men are the ruination of my life."

"But I am not *men*, milady." He brought a hand up and cupped her impossibly soft cheek, marveled at the delicate feel of it. Knew it masked a will of steel underneath. "I am but one man."

"You're all the same," she whispered, that plump upper lip of hers beckoning to him like a siren's song. How long would he be able to resist?

"You know that isn't true." Though in his experience, she was not that far off the reality. "Some of us are acceptable. Some even good."

"What are *you?*" she asked, grasping the front lapels of his jacket.

"I am neither acceptable nor good." He was gutter trash, born and raised. "But I can kiss you like no other man can."

"This is lunacy," she whispered, even as she fisted her hands into the fabric of his jacket and pulled him close. "I should despise you for all you've done. A part of me does. You are working for my father, keeping me chained."

"And yet?" Lowering his head to hers, he breathed against her full, tempting lips, as his shaft swelled with desire.

"I cannot stop wanting your mouth on mine. I know it's wrong—"

Unable to stand any more, Damon claimed her mouth, taking her in a deep, drugging kiss. He slid his hand from her cheek and dove into her luxurious hair, loosening pins and causing several strands to tumble free. Without remorse he reveled in the feel of her lushly curved body pressed fully against him, her hair spilling over his hands—knowing she would need to pin it back up before reentering the ballroom did nothing to alter his movements. He wanted her, needed the feel of her in his hands.

"Damon," she breathed against his lips when they parted, sagging against him.

"I like it when you say my name," he admitted, something primal stirring inside him. Something that wanted to hear her whisper it exactly like this over and over without end.

"Damon," she said again, setting his blood on fire.

"Now you've done it," he growled, his passion rearing up and uncurling like a great, hungry beast.

"Uh-oh," she replied, sounding not at all upset about it.

The beast inside him snapped its mighty jaws, ravenous for her. Against his better judgment, against everything he knew and believed, Damon could not pull away now. Oh no, she awakened him like no other.

Dropping his hand from her hair, he explored the shape of her—the dip of her waist, the generous flare of her hip—before sliding both of his hands up the bodice of her dress and covering her breasts, squeezing them not gently, but not hard, either—with enough pressure to make her small mew of arousal turn his cock to stone. "You like that?" he asked roughly.

"Mmm-hmm," she moaned, and he could not resist tearing his mouth from hers to kiss a wet, open-mouthed path down her neck to the valley between her gorgeous breasts. There he feasted, tasting and licking until she shivered with pleasure. Then he yanked aside the low, snug bodice of her dress, spilling her breasts into the warm night air.

"Feck, you're beautiful," he growled, and took one taut peak into his mouth, flicked his tongue over it. Again and again he teased as she clung to him, digging her fingers into his shoulders.

"We should stop," she protested weakly even as she held him bound against her. "Someone could catch us."

Let them, a part of him declared greedily. The part of him that wanted her all to himself, that wanted her on her back, panting and screaming his name as she came for him. Over and over.

But he could not—*would not*—take her. Too many reasons stood between them. The biggest one being that he was a common-born Garden slug. The only place he deserved to be was under the heel of her slipper as she stepped on him on her way to someone worthy.

Damon Crowe, son of a Covent Garden Gitano seamstress

and unknown defiler of women, deserved nothing and no one. Never had, never would.

But Christ, he *wanted*.

Oh, how he wanted.

"Do you want me to stop?" he murmured against her fragrant, petal-soft skin.

"No," she breathed. "But I should."

"Yes, you should." And his mouth was on her breasts, feasting once more, his hands roaming down her body, reveling in every single luscious curve as he reached for the hem of her silk dress. Finding it, he smiled darkly, and his curved lips brushed her warm, inviting flesh. "If you know wot is good for you, you very much should."

"*This* is good," she replied as he slipped one of his large hands under her skirt and stroked boldly up her shapely leg, skimming featherlight fingers along her sensitive inner thigh. When he reached the apex and found her curls damp with desire, she sighed. "*So* good."

He agreed.

"Tell me wot you want," he demanded before taking her mouth in another hot, thorough kiss. With a long, thick finger he traced her swollen entrance, groaning with satisfaction at the dew he discovered there. "Tell me to stop; tell me to leave you alone. Because I don't want to. I want only to make you cry out in ecstasy from my touch."

"Then do," she ordered him, and dropped her head back, arched her body into him.

Something snapped inside Damon. Something feral and starved for too long. "Take that back," he demanded almost desperately, even as he parted her slick folds and stroked the length of her beautiful womanhood, glorying in the plumpness, her wetness, utterly at her mercy. "Order me to stop." Taking a tightly pearled nipple in his mouth, he sucked, using his tongue and teeth on her as he pushed his finger inside, and her moist heat nearly dropped him to his knees. He found her tight little nub—

her pleasure center—and rubbed with the pad of his thumb, slow circles meant to drive her mad as he felt dark, primitive satisfaction at the generous size of her swollen bud. His cock throbbed with the desire to rub his head over her glorious nub before burying himself deep inside her. "The things I want to do to you," he breathed, circling faster, taking her higher. "You should run away," he warned, raising his head to take her mouth roughly with his, nipping that full top lip of hers so made for sucking him. "Before I fuck you like I want."

She gasped, "Damon!" sounding shocked and scandalized even as she raised her leg and hooked it around his waist, allowing him full access to her. She clung to his shoulders, and her nails bit into his jacket.

Passion blinded him, and the instinct to claim her, to be the first and only to make her come, took control. Stroking his finger deeper inside her, he began moving back and forth, curling the tip as he withdrew to caress that secret spot inside her. She cried out and rocked into him, her body begging for more, so he pressed his thumb more firmly against her sensitive bud. "Now you've got to come for me," he purred darkly, wanting it—*needing* her orgasm. "All over my hand, love. *Scream* for me."

Mindless now, he worked her until her body went taut as a bowstring and she shattered, her climax breaking over her like a tidal wave. Her mouth opened on a scream, and he took her lips, swallowing her cry, stroking her with his tongue and fingers until the last of her tremors subsided, leaving his cock straining in his trousers.

Then he turned his kiss gentle. Though his body thundered for its own release, he denied himself, taking extra care to bring Carenza back to earth slowly. "I should feel guilty," he roughly whispered, reluctantly removing his hand from her and stroking it lightly down her leg as he lowered her skirts back down.

"And yet?" she asked, her voice lazy with sexual gratification.

Smiling tenderly because he simply could not help himself, he replied as he cupped her cheek, "I feel only honored to be the one to show you the joy and pleasure your body can experience."

Killing him, she licked her lips and stared up at him with glazed, satiated eyes. "Will you show me more?"

If he could, he would show her, give her *everything*—

"Carenza! Carenza, are you out here?" her sister Nora whispered loudly. "You've a full dance card, and our parents know it. Lord Arnold whined to Mother that you missed his assigned number, and now she and Father are searching for you."

—but she would never be his to claim.

"Carenza, where are you?"

"Go." He released her, a sharp sense of loss sweeping over him, and clenched his hands into fists, trying to capture the remnants of her heat. "I'll follow behind, as your guard should. Nobody will know."

"I will," she countered, her husky tone setting his blood on fire. "Tonight, this little encounter will fill my dreams."

He watched her walk away, his body raging with unspent need, knowing that for him there would be no sleep.

CHAPTER TWELVE

"WHY ARE YOU so grumpy?"

"I'm not grumpy," Carenza argued, adjusting her shawl around her shoulders as she and Nora made their way down a main path through Hyde Park the next afternoon, the skirts of her belted cream day dress flapping against her ankles. "I've simply better things to do with my time than promenade in the park looking for eligible suitors. I care not at all if they are eligible, or suitors."

"But you intend to *pick* one of them. Remember? A husband you must choose by the end of the Season."

"I recall, blast it," she muttered, feeling...all right, *grumpy*. How was she supposed to be shopping for unattached bachelors when her head was still reeling from last night with Damon? And yes, it was Damon once again. Of course it was, after that wonderfully educational interlude in the gardens that left her awakened with new awareness of herself, her body—and of the deliciousness that existed for discovery between a man and a woman.

Now the sounds she had overheard back in the darkened alley of Covent Garden that night didn't seem quite so appalling, after all.

Eyes widening at her brazen thoughts, Carenza cleared her throat and tried for the thousandth time already that afternoon to *not* look over her shoulder at the man trailing behind the group of

Castlebury females. To *not* ogle Damon like a common strumpet. Especially as she could feel his dark, penetrating eyes on her with every moment, every breath. And it thrilled her—what they had shared. Thrilled her and terrified her all the same.

Every limitation in her life was due in some form or other to a man. But limitation was not at all what she had felt last night in Damon's arms.

It had felt…

Felt…well…

Freeing.

Her brain ached from the irony.

"Where has your mind scuttled to? I know for a fact you have not been listening, for I've been waiting a full two minutes for you to answer my question." Fingers snapped near her ear. "Hello? Car?"

"Hmm?" Carenza replied distantly, blinking slowly as her attention returned to the present. "I'm sorry, Nora, I must have been lost in thought. What was your question?"

Nora smiled wickedly, glancing about them to see who was listening. Afternoon in Hyde Park was the most eventful time of day, and the park enjoyed several patrons this particularly sunny day, strolling the paths, enjoying picnics. And the horses! So many riders and carriages on the Serpentine. If one was given to paranoia, one could almost imagine that word had gotten out about Carenza's quest for a husband and that all of Mayfair attended Hyde Park in part to witness her husband-hunting attempts for themselves.

If one was given to paranoia.

Which she was not.

Thank goodness.

"Shouldn't you like to take that path over there? It appears better shaded, and I could use a moment's break out of the sun." Pointing helpfully in case her sister missed the small path off to the right that meandered into a grove of pretty trees, she added, "I wore an extra petticoat this morning to accommodate the skirt on this new dress Mother insisted I wear, and I'm quite beginning to regret it. Rather warm, it is." Should that path also allow her a few moments' respite from the curious eyes of the *ton*, then so much the better.

"Certainly," Nora readily acquiesced, and they made a small correction, separating from the main path and the jumble of London's peerage enjoying the out of doors. Too many of them for Carenza's taste. So many artificial conversations, so many empty platitudes.

Forced she was to endure mindless conversations with men in which they inquired after her proficiency in painting and needlework and French—and asked nothing of her thoughts on the latest parliamentary rulings or if she had goals and ambitions and saw something for herself and her life beyond motherhood and the management of a vast estate's house servants. Tiresome as those conversations were, they must be endured. That was not a negotiation, though she *was* grumpy about it. The thought of her father choosing the gentleman for her inspired enough motivation to at least *attempt* a polite smile and hello.

She did not have to speak to all the others, however.

"Thank you." Carenza darted a quick glance behind to her mother and Lottie, who shared a curious, confused look over the change in direction, but followed along the new route. Damon would be directly behind them. But she dared not look, guaranteed her expression would tell a thousand tales and her mother would understand in a blink of an eye what had transpired between the two of them. And she could not risk it. Would not.

It was killing her, not looking.

Damon's eyes, were they banked cinders of heat? Because that was how his gaze felt upon her as she walked. The bared skin on the back of her neck between her satin bonnet and the drape of her smoky blue shawl tingled as if a hand were caressing the sensitive flesh. *His* hand.

"You are welcome, but now you must confess the truth to me." Nora grinned mischievously, leaning close enough that their bonnet brims touched. "What transpired last night in the garden? And *if*," she added before Carenza could speak, "you think I will believe that nothing at all happened with you and Mr. Crowe, then you truly do not know me. I have never felt any tension more palpable than that which rolled last night off your Mr. Crowe in drowning, crashing waves."

"He's not my Mr. Crowe—"

"I think he could be, if you wished."

"I do not wish. Please refrain from making such claims."

Preposterous words! Her heart—what was that *squeeze?* Breathe…she needed to breathe.

Damon? *Hers?*

"I think you *do* wish."

"You are a literal pain in my ar—"

"Oh, girls! I daresay that I see the Duke of Somerton strolling this way. Such a commanding presence he possesses! How lovely to enjoy the attention of such an esteemed family. Yes, quite delightful to visit with His Grace." If a cat possessed a voice after swallowing a bird, it would be her mother's. The smug, sly satisfaction in it was almost embarrassing.

"The duke addresses himself with his family name, Mama. He prefers Rainville to Somerton," Lottie pointed out helpfully, walking efficiently beside their mother. Or helpfully, so she believed. Such was Lottie's way. Others appreciated the constant correcting perhaps a tad less than she realized. As it was always done earnestly, no one had the heart to tell her to stop. The one and only time Carenza had implied that no one wanted to be corrected all the time, Lottie cried from hurt feelings for two hours straight. Carenza had felt like a horrible fool and refrained from making such implications ever again.

"How do you know so much about the duke?" Nora shot the question at Lottie, a tight edge to her voice. "Has he engaged with you?" A frown marred the smoothness of her brow, and her green eyes darkened with some emotion.

"Do you care if he has?" Carenza whispered, wondering at

her sister's strange behavior regarding Rainville.

"Absolutely, I care! It would be absurd if I did not, for he is a most loathsome creature," Nora returned, and clasped her gloved hands behind her back, tipped her chin high, and increased her stroll to a vigorous walk, causing Carenza to hasten her gate to keep in stride. "I should care very much if he takes notice of our Lottie."

"It's not as if I've an obsession with him," Lottie replied defensively. "Though I confess that his new theatre venture sounds quite interesting. I only possess this information about the duke because Lady Pillings went on and on at our ball the other night about the great lack of respect she felt it demonstrated he had toward his late father, that he refused to embrace the traditional ducal address."

"A rogue, then," Carenza jested, thinking more about a certain dark-haired man strolling the path behind her in brooding silence than the smiling, golden-haired duke across the grass walking toward them.

Unable to endure any more, her will crumbled and she slid a discreet glance behind her, toward Damon.

He was watching her.

His eyes, so dark, intense, and knowing, instantly stripped her bare—heart and body. In a flash her mind replayed last night, and she was once again half-naked and clinging to him as his mouth and hands gave her the greatest pleasure of her life, pushing her into a new existence filled with sensual understanding of her body, of the fire that could consume at the hands of a man. Being touched by Damon felt like flying.

Again, as if he read her mind, his lips curled into a small, secret smile, and his eyes nearly burned with intensity.

"Good day, ladies!"

Blast. How on earth had Horrid A snuck up on her?

Most likely because she was wholly distracted by one devilishly handsome Mr. Damon Crowe. Quite rightly, she supposed. She should be concerned if their rendezvous in the garden hadn't left her completely addled and her attention preoccupied.

"I say, good afternoon, ladies!"

Now Rainville appeared.

Had the gentlemen coordinated their arrivals? Or was she truly that unfortunate to receive them both at once? Though, granted, the duke was tolerable. Attractive. Charming, even. No, she did not mind Rainville.

Lord Horace Arnold could bugger a sheep.

Might already have, Carenza thought, and released a short, enthusiastic snort of laughter. *Oh my!*

Sliding a glance toward Horrid A as he gained her side and began pacing with her, his face nearly concealed by the fierce ambition of his sideburns and his ungodly, overabounding cravat, she lost her decorum and snickered aloud. How could she not? His sideburns made *him* look like a sheep in good need of its spring shearing.

"I daresay…" She cleared her throat, snickered helplessly a moment more, and then tried again. "I daresay you look well today, Lord Arnold," she croaked, making the mistake of glancing once more out of the corner of her eye at Damon and noting the humor threatening to turn his lips. After the last word spoken, she clamped her lips together and pressed them in a trembling line, clasping her hands tightly behind her back as her eyes pricked with moisture from withholding her amusement. The same amusement Damon appeared to share.

"Excellent of you to notice, Lady Carenza!" Horrid A beamed, his smile making her skin prickle uncomfortably. "And might I say how lovely you are looking today, as well? I must confess that you rival the roses in bloom for the most beautiful thing in the park!" His gaze dropped to her breasts, and for several heartbeats he openly stared, that sly, shifty smile upon his thin lips.

Now her skin itched, the sensation akin to the abrasion of rough wool rubbing across its surface. Unpleasant, yes. Horrid A was even less so.

"My mother would be pleased to hear you say so." Carenza looked around a bit desperately for her mother, only to find her in animated conversation with the duke and Lottie several paces behind them. Her youngest sister, normally observant and reserved with words, appeared quite chatty with the lion-esque aristocrat. "Should you prefer to speak directly with her?"

Next to her, Nora grumbled something under her breath. Turning to her sister, Carenza caught sight of the displeasure in her expression. "I say, you seem rather put out."

"Why wouldn't I be?" her sibling snapped, turning to glare at Rainville over her shoulder, the peach ribbon of her bonnet flapping with the sudden movement. "The brute has taken an interest in our dearest sister."

Looking back to observe, Carenza disagreed, and snuck another discreet glance at Damon, enigmatic and masculine in his subtle, earth-toned garments and unadorned style. *What is he thinking?* she wondered.

Shaking off the thought, she answered Nora, "It appears to me that Lottie is, in fact, the person directing the conversation. Appears to me that she is quite excited about something. The duke's new theatre, perhaps? She does so enjoy a good play. And I've heard it told that his most recent acquisition is a gem." She leaned over conspiratorially, her cheeks warm from the heat of Damon's smoldering gaze. "I have it on good authority that Thatcher Goodrich is Rainville's new writer in residence." She'd heard the duke declare those very words at the Meadowlark Tavern two weeks ago.

"Truly?" Nora looked her way, surprise lighting her green eyes. "His recent play was extraordinary."

"And sharply witty!" called the duke from several feet behind them. Apparently, Rainville had excellent hearing. "Let us not forget."

"Of course," Nora said through gritted teeth. "We shan't forget!" Under her breath she added, *"Ever."*

"What in saint's name happened between the two of you?"

Struggling to hide her vexation, Carenza settled for raising a discreet blond eyebrow, staring directly into her sibling's eyes. "And you say that *I* have been behaving strangely!"

"You have been behaving strangely."

"Do not change the topic. This is about you."

"What about *you?*" Nora demanded, giving her a good glare. "You've yet to confess what occurred between you and Mr. Crowe last eve."

"Because nothing occurred," Carenza lied, and bit her bottom lip, casting a covert glance at Damon. Again (always?), his gaze was upon her. Her stomach did a slow, tumbling roll, and her pulse quickened.

"For nothing supposedly having occurred, you certainly do keep looking at him quite a lot."

"I do not." Was it really that obvious? Had her *mother* seen?

"Lady Carenza, might I escort you for a while?"

No.

Snapping her hands closed and fisting them at her sides so as not to clobber Lord Arnold with them, Carenza took a deep, fortifying breath. "Thank you, no, Viscount Amslee. I am quite content walking with my sister."

"I must insist," the viscount pushed, smiling, his small and narrow-set eyes glinting with something almost sinister that raised the hairs on her arms and clenched her stomach. Determination twisted his unsettling smile further. "We do have so very much in common. And I do so hate to point this out—and I shall as delicately as possible, for I feel the need to speak for all of us when I say this—but lovely as you are, you have got on in years. A bit long in the tooth, ol' gel. The attentions of a generously endowed viscount should be quite suitable for a lady in such a position as yours. Yes, it should."

If only her boot had stone heels.

"Ouch!" Horrid A clapped a hand to the back of his head, startled, his hat tumbling from his head to the ground as he jerked forward. "That hurt!" The viscount looked around, wild-eyed.

"What the deuce just hit me?"

Spinning around, Carenza just caught sight of Damon palming a small rock in his hand before slipping it up his slate-gray coat sleeve, his expression devoid of emotion. Yet his molten chocolate eyes danced with a combination of irritation and amusement when they settled back upon her. She bit her bottom lip to keep from snorting in wicked delight. Damon, a sense of humor?

"Lord Arnold!" her mother cried out, all concern. "Are you well?"

"I most certainly am *not* well, Lady Castlebury!" Horrid A whined, making quite a display of rubbing the sore spot at the back of his head while he retrieved his black beaver hat from the hard-packed path before them. After combing his thin, lanky strands of lackluster brown hair back into place, he resettled his hat with a great huff. "Something accosted me."

"I saw nothing," Carenza inserted quickly. "Nothing at all."

"Me either," offered Nora.

"I'm so sorry, Lord Arnold!" their mother went on, but, curiously, did not leave the duke's side to see to the viscount. Of course she would not and risk Rainville's lost interest. "A strapping gentleman such as yourself surely would not be troubled by such a small mishap, though, would he?"

"Quite right, quite right," Horrid A grumbled, still rubbing his head.

"I believe it may have been a bird, my good man," Rainville called out, and Carenza couldn't help but notice he sounded very close to laughing. "A large one."

"I'm quite certain it was *not* a bird, Your Grace." Horrid A's thin lips puckered sourly.

"My mistake," the duke replied lightly, shrugging his large shoulders. "The wind, then, perhaps."

"Actually," Lottie piped up, ever the one for accuracy, "I believe the assault came from M—"

"There!" Carenza called out, pointing behind them to a thicket of woods that led down to a large, glistening pond beyond. "I saw someone dash that way!"

"What are you all standing there for, then?" Horrid A demanded with a pout, not moving a muscle. "Avenge me!"

"Oh, for f—" Damon muttered, breaking his silence.

"I'll go!" Carenza declared, seizing the opportunity to step away from Lord Arnold's slimy presence. Before anyone could protest, she lifted her skirts and took off across the expanse of green and through the trees, smiling at the pure joy of moving her body so freely. And perhaps of escaping another minute stuck in Horrid A's intolerable company.

"Wait, that is not proper! It is not done!" her mother called after her, but Carenza heard the duke deftly turn Lady Castlebury's attention with a question regarding the availabilities of rental estates near their own family seat in Somerset, and she quite forgot Carenza's poor manners. "You there, Mr. Crowe! See to her!" the countess said, matchmaking-mother enthusiasm raising her voice a full octave in pitch. "Why, as you know, Somerset is *lovely*, Your Grace! Our small village is quite beautiful. Oh, you should visit us!"

Carenza would have rolled her eyes, but the excitement flowing through her at the knowledge her mother had sent Damon to retrieve her sent her speeding through the trees, her feet light, her legs swift. Laughter burst from her chest, and she hitched her skirts higher, jumping clean over a thick, fallen log and landing soundly on the other side. Would he catch her?

Suddenly a shadow fell to her right, alerting her to Damon's approach.

"Never!" she said, laughing. "You can't catch me!"

"Want to bet?" his rough voice called out, close behind her now. So close she could hear him breathing—the deep, steady breaths of a man accustomed to physical exertion.

Carenza squealed in delight, her stomach fluttering as she grasped her slipping bonnet with a hand and ran flat out for all she was worth. For the thrill of it, knowing he would catch her.

Wanting him to catch her.

Wanting him to do so much *more*.

Pulse racing, heart thundering, Carenza tore through the tree grove, knowing she had perhaps a moment at best before Damon laid hands upon her. *Eager* for his hands on her. The last time had been so very enlightening.

Dark laughter rumbled behind her, the sound reverberating in the pit of her belly, heating her there. "You're already caught, milady."

"No!" Laughter ringing out, she turned fast and dashed between two thick trees, trying to outmaneuver him. Joy bubbled in her chest, effervescent and shimmering. Oh, the feeling!

This man. This *man*.

He sent her flying.

"Caught you." Strong arms whipped around her waist and locked, stopping her in her tracks.

"No!" Carenza laughed, readily giving up, her body already melting into his.

"You're mine, milady," he stated, his rough, gravelly voice making her shiver with feminine anticipation.

"I am no one's," she replied defiantly, her body molding to him as he held her securely in his arms.

"You lie," he whispered hotly, fanning his breath across the sensitive skin of her neck. His scent surrounded her, warm and exotically male as he ran his hands up her ribcage and boldly covered her breasts. He molded them, filled his hands with their plump weight. "I know your truth."

Carenza covered his hands with her own and dropped her head back against his chest, moaning softly. "What is my truth?" she asked, wondering briefly if *she* even knew. For so long it had been that men, in general and as a whole, were bad. Marriage was bad.

But this, with Damon…this felt so *right*.

How could that be?

"*Hechicera,*" he growled gently, and squeezed her breasts, his tanned, strong hands a stark contrast to her small, white-gloved ones. "Your body belongs to me."

She...she could not lie. "Maybe," she confessed breathlessly as his hands did magical, wicked things to her body. Teeth nipped the delicate skin of her neck, and she shivered, gasped, "Damon!"

"I know wot you need, milady," he promised darkly, pinching her nipples through her bodice. He pressed into her from behind, and his manhood, swollen and full, pushed against her. A throbbing, pulsing ache bloomed between her thighs, and she shifted, rubbed boldly against him.

"*Hechicera*," he growled again, trailing kisses down her neck. "You play with fire."

Apparently, she quite liked the heat.

"Kiss me," she demanded, shocked at her own boldness. But desire—this wondrous, newly discovered feeling—thrummed in her body, and she wanted his lips on hers again. *Now*. It made her reckless.

Damon swore, flexing his hands on her breasts. And then she was spinning, the forest a blur of green and brown around her as he directed her backward a few paces. Coming up against the wide trunk of a tree, Carenza barely had time to smile at her victory before he claimed her, taking her mouth passionately. Possessively.

Whimpering mindlessly, Carenza flung her arms around Damon's shoulders and met his kiss with reckless abandon. Clinging to him as the storm of his passion swept over her, she burrowed her fingers in his unruly mane and anchored herself there. Moaned for more.

He gave her more, turning the kiss darker, more sensual. His tongue stroked hers, tasted her until she lost all sense of thought and could only *feel*. Could only *want*. Could only hold on to Damon—her anchor and her flight.

He broke the kiss, his breathing ragged. "You," he panted, his chest heaving with the strength of his desire, "are my undoing."

"What do you mean?" she asked, still lost in the haze of their passion.

"You should not want me." He lowered his forehead to hers, his eyes closed. "I should not want you."

"I should not," she agreed, rubbing his hair between her fingers, savoring the silken feel of his curls against her skin. "It goes against everything I believe."

"Which is?" he whispered, the warmth of his forehead against hers intimate and sweet after the heat of their kiss.

"Men ruin *everything*."

"Generally," he replied, startling her with his honesty.

"You agree?" That was unexpected.

Carenza tightened her fingers around his hair, not wanting the closeness they shared to end.

"I know too much, have seen too much to disagree," he answered softly.

"Why do you do it, then? This profession that burdens so heavily?"

Damon chuckled, low and gravelly. "My manservant, Bones, asked me that very same thing."

"Lady Carenza! Lady Carenza, are you down there? I say, is everything all right? Did you avenge me?"

Startled by the sound of Horrid A's voice, Carenza dropped her hands from Damon and began pushing against his shoulders. "He must not see us!" she hissed.

But Damon was already moving away and bent over. He retrieved some grass from the ground and sprinkled it across her bodice, yanked a leaf from the tree she leaned against and tossed it on her bonnet. "Here, pretend a twisted ankle and I'll carry you."

Without giving her a chance to consider his plan, Damon swept her into his arms and began marching back toward the group. "Look injured," he ordered her quietly. "No one will suspect a thing, trust me."

"Oh, there you are!" Horrid A exclaimed as they made their way from the dense cover of trees. "Did you find the fiend?" Then a shocked gasp. "I say, what is this? Gracious, are you infirm?"

"My ankle!" she cried pitifully, happily playing along. "Oh, the agony!"

"Out of my way," Damon snapped as he prowled past Lord Arnold, appearing every bit the protective guard he purported to be. "The lady is injured and needs to return to Tipton House immediately."

And with that, he deftly dispensed of her least favorite person in the world and excused her from further husband hunting. At least for the day.

Carenza ducked her head under Damon's chin, hiding a grin.

Some men, perhaps, were worth something.

CHAPTER THIRTEEN

I F DAMON NEEDED further proof that he and Lady Carenza were not meant to be, he had it. In blazing, ugly reality. She was Grosvenor Square and Bond Street glamour.

He was the slums of Seven Dials.

While Carenza and the other Castlebury ladies spent the afternoon at Madame Toussaint's on Bond Street, picking out and being fitted with the finest silks, he sat in the back corner of a crumbling pub in one of the seediest portions of the city.

Excused by Lady Castlebury from his watch temporarily (for the visit was for ladies' unmentionables, and he was not to look), he had two hours before he must return to Mayfair. To a world that was not his own.

To a woman he rather wished could be.

"Thank you for meeting with me." He slid a piece of folded parchment across the scarred and not quite flat wood table of the Horse and Hound, arguably *the* most notorious tavern in all of London's Seven Dials rookery. Old stench clung to the pub's dark interior, and curious stains seeped permanently into the stone floor, making one wonder whether they were ale spills or blood spills. Given the average clientele, Damon put his money on blood. "These are the details I've collected so far."

Short, shifty-eyed, with a crooked nose the size of a dinner plate, the snitch Castlebury claimed could help and had suggested he meet rolled his ale glass leisurely between his dirty fingers.

"Wot's the rush, eh? Got meself a thirst to quench afore I start talking."

Damon signaled to a barmaid, an exhausted-looking chit with ruddy cheeks and light brown hair poking out from under her cap. "Keep the ales coming."

"Whisky too, an' don' stop!" hollered Castlebury's informer. "Hear me?"

"You payin'?" she asked Damon, a hand on a plump hip.

"I am," he replied.

Satisfied, she left them to retrieve a pitcher of amber liquid and two tall ale glasses, as well as short glasses and a bottle of whisky.

"Where were we?" He turned his attention back to his companion.

"Me name's Mouse, an' I got the name the way it sounds. 'Cause I hear fings." He grinned, showing several black and missing teeth. "An' I hear ye got needs I can help wif." He eyed Damon, taking in his understated attire. "Ye don' seem so fancy as the earl."

"I'm not." Of that much, he was completely certain.

"Ye got the blunt?" The snitch looked skeptical, narrowing his bloodshot eyes greedily on Damon.

"Here's your ale and spirits, gents." The barmaid slapped a tray with the full pitcher, bottle, and assorted glasses on the table and turned to leave.

"I got the blunt," Damon confirmed, his voice low as he kept an eye on the barmaid walking away, certain she was listening. He let just enough of the Garden slip into his speech—a warning to Mouse that he was no gentry, no new money. He was something to take much more seriously.

Slowly, so as not to startle Mouse, he reached into the pocket of his greatcoat—a smoky black number that came to his knees and hid a great many things. Such as the bag of coin he discreetly reached for and slid across the smooth bench seat to the informer. Years of customers imbibing as they sat there had worn two distinct grooves in the wooden surface. His coat also held a short, nasty little knife that he pulled out and began to rudely clean his teeth with. "Mutton to eat," he offered by way of explanation, though he knew Mouse would understand the unspoken message he was truly sending.

"Hmm," Mouse said, eyeing the knife for a beat before pouring the two of them rather full whiskies and sliding one toward Damon. "I hear there's sumthin' ye're lookin' for. A bloke, yeah?"

"Yeah." Though Damon preferred to call his sire every cutting, bloody epitaph he could think besides something as banal as *bloke*. But before they talked about his search, he had another pressing question. Placing the knife back in his pocket, he asked, "Why didn't Castlebury send you on his family errand? Why me?"

"Bah." Mouse waved him off and took a long pull of his whisky, drinking until it spilled from the corners of his mouth and slid in tiny rivulets down his skinny throat, seemingly oblivious to the accompanying burn strong spirits provided. "I'm a snitch, no' a bloody Bow Street Runner. Castlebury had wont for sumthin' I don' do."

It made sense, actually.

"'Sides," Mouse added, tossing a vague wave Damon's way, "ye be the tracker. I heard all 'bout Demon, the bloke wot knows and hides fings for a fee."

A fight broke out at the bar, sending thick wooden stools suddenly flying through the air as drunken locals deep in their cups yelled slurred insults up and down the long, narrow pub. Damon slid a glance to his right as a stool whipped by his vision, several inches from his face. Unflinching, he merely raised his voice to be heard over the brawling. "I've appreciation for your skills," he said rather loudly. "Take a look at the parchment I gave you. I think you should have no problem discerning my notes. If you've heard anything of use, tell me."

The snitch unfolded the paper and gave it a long look, and then gulped down another glass of whisky, barely stopping for breath. Slamming it on the tabletop, he replied around a belch, "I may ha' heard sumthin"." He eyed Damon's coat pockets openly. "Then again, maybe no'."

Fighting impatience and irritation, Damon reached into a different coat pocket, pulled out a cigarette, and lit it, took a long, *long* drag. As if he was contemplating something important, he kept quiet for several moments before casually reaching into his coat pocket again and retrieving another small coin bag. As he did with the earlier one, he slid it quietly across the bench seat. "Perhaps this will shake your memory loose."

Mouse narrowed his blue eyes on Damon, assessing, before scooping up the bag and tucking it into the shaft of his scuffed, old boot. "How old is ye? Six, maybe seven and twenty?"

He was eight and twenty. "About that, yes. Why?"

"Eh," the snitch said, pouring yet another glass of spirits and leaning sideways in his seat, resting one elbow casually on the table. Damon figured if drink loosened his tongue and got him talking then it was worth dealing with a completely pissed street rat. "Sumthin' naggin' me brain, is all."

"If that nagging feeling has anything to do with this conversation and the money I'm paying you, then it behooves you to share with me. Now." The words came out perfectly amiably, but the look Damon shot the informer glinted hard with warning. He took another pull on his cigarette, waiting.

"Don' rush me," Mouse snapped, his sunken cheeks flushed from too much drink too quickly. Snatching up his glass, he sloshed some amber liquid over the side onto his hand and licked it off, his movements uncoordinated and awkward. "Finkin' sumthin'."

Though he had seen many things over the years, Damon still had to force himself to keep his disgust hidden at the snitch's snakelike tongue. "*Fink* away," he replied a tad sarcastically, holding his cigarette between his fingers simply for the comfort it provided. The familiarity of action. "Inform me if you discover anything."

"Tha' an insult?" Mouse puffed his bony chest out belligerent-ly. The rough fabric of his tunic was threadbare in places.

"Absolutely not," Damon lied.

"Fine." The snitch sniffed and swiped the back of his hand under his nose. "Might be I recall sumthin' from when I was young. Me mum yapping 'bout a tosser wot liked to harass the other doxies an' her when they was doin' their business in Covent Garden."

"That's where my mother was located."

"Yeah, yeah, I read yer sheet," Mouse boasted with a black-toothed smile. "Me mum was a whore, but she learned me to read."

Having spent the last ten years of his life searching for infor-mation, *any* information about the man who had attacked his mother, without success, Damon asked, "Is there anything you might have heard? Anything at all?" Smashing his cigarette out in a tray on the table—a thin plume of smoke rose from the dying ember, curling into the stale air—he added, "I'll pay." Money was, ironically, not an issue for Damon. Not anymore. Nobles paid bloody handsomely for secrets.

Mouse slouched in his seat, eyes too bright from drink, and slurred, "Finkin' the bloke wot made 'is rounds wif the lightskirts was a bloomin' toff. Me mum said he talked fancy."

A *toff*.

Everything inside Damon chilled, went very still.

"Are you certain of that?" he asked after several steadying breaths, his mind reeling with the possibilities. An aristocrat—such a person could be traced. *Found.*

Finally, Damon had a lead!

"Me finks, yeah." The informer's eyelids were starting to droop heavily, his slump getting progressively lower as the drink caught up to him.

"Thank you," Damon murmured, his mind racing now. "Drink up," he added distractedly, reaching out to pour the snitch another glass.

Mouse hiccupped and sloppily flung out a hand for the drink. "Castlebury pinches 'is purse when we meet. Only one drink. This is nice."

"How did you two meet, you and the earl?" Damon had been wondering. Idle curiosity, nothing more. Too many years in this business had taught him not to be shocked by such things as a peer employing a snitch. In truth, they often employed much worse things. They merely had the money to hide it.

Mouse hiccupped again, his chin nearly to his chest now. "Me cuzzin," he slurred terribly, raising a hand and circling it in the air as if he was writing. "He wrote sumthin' important. Sumthin' wot paid gobs of blunt."

Every instinct in Damon leapt to alertness, screaming that this was somehow important. "Do you know what it was?" He leaned forward and emptied the rest of the bottle into Mouse's whisky glass, his pulse beating rapidly. On the outside he appeared calm and detached.

"Nah." The informer swatted a hand in front of him, pulling a drunken, uninterested face, slumping almost horizontally now on the bench seat. "Long time ago. Earl pays me now, all I care."

Fair enough.

Buzzing with new information, Damon tossed coin on the tabletop as Mouse succumbed to his drunken slumber. "Rest well," he murmured, and slid from his seat, stretching to his full height and turning several curious heads his direction. He met their stares with a steely one of his own, and they turned their heads right back around and left him be. Exactly as he expected them to do.

Adjusting the collar of his jacket and shaking his hair loose of it, Damon strode toward the door, ready for any of them just in case.

The barmaid stepped in his path, blocking him with a coy, willing expression on her face and a suggestive smile on her lips. "Want to take me home, handsome? I please cheap, especially for a gent with yer blunt." She ran two fingers up the chest of his coat. "I can tell ye're a fine ride."

Carenza flashed across his mind, naked and riding him like a prized stallion, and his chest squeezed tight with need. "Afraid not," he replied gently but firmly. Removing his hands from the front of his jacket, he sidestepped and reached once again inside his coat, retrieving a few more coins. Damon pressed them into her hand. "For the disappointment."

"Feelin' better already," the barmaid chirped, displaying a charming dimple in her right cheek when she smiled. "Come 'round again, handsome. I'll make it worth your while."

Reaching for the door, Damon stopped when he heard a commotion from the table where Mouse lay inebriated. He spun in time to see the snitch bolt upright on the bench seat, eyes glassy with whisky as he hollered, "Forgery!" Then his eyes rolled back in his head, and he slumped once more unconscious in his seat.

"Don't mind him," the barmaid said. "He spouts all kinds of crazy things."

Crazy or not, Damon thought as he pulled the tavern door open and squinted against the sunlight greeting him outside, the word was important. And though he'd come seeking information on his father, it appeared he had found something potentially as juicy.

For it was about the Earl of Castlebury.

Resisting the urge to slam the door behind him, Damon stepped outside and noted the position of the sun in the sky. Was it really that late on?

More importantly, was Castlebury all he claimed to be?

Or was he merely a liar and a bully to his family?

And his own sire—could he truly be of the aristocracy?

As Damon made his way back across town, his mind turned over and over all the information he had received, his blood boiling. Careless it was in hindsight, really, of Castlebury to send Damon to his hired man. For he would always discover more than he should.

Forgery.

Unable to sit still, Damon kicked a booted foot restlessly, mindless to the buildings passing by and all the people bustling along as a hired hack returned him to Mayfair. He could not stop a question from circling in his head, over and over. What had the good earl forged?

A deed?

A legal document?

A horse pedigree?

Damon knew not the answer, only that he would discover it eventually. Probably as soon as he tracked down Mouse's cousin, the forger.

Sighing, he adjusted once more in his seat, barely containing his energy, and asked himself another question as the horse pulling him clopped along the cobbled streets. After all this time of searching, why wasn't he more focused on the new information about his father? His sire might very well have been a member of the peerage. It was a lead—a real lead after all these years! Shouldn't he be more consumed by that?

Damon frowned. Yes, yes he should. So why wasn't he?

He didn't like the answer that rose within him, and he swore under his breath.

Castlebury had a secret. And secrets tended to hurt people.

And anything that could hurt Carenza took precedence over everything else.

Everything else.

"Fuck me."

That truth was very, very telling.

CHAPTER FOURTEEN

"I'M GOING OUT tonight, and no one is going to stop me." Carenza flung the oversized windows wide and stepped onto her tiny balcony, knowing Damon was out there somewhere watching. "Do you hear me down there? I. Am. Leaving."

Fully expecting an argument, a confrontation—something— she was greatly surprised to be greeted by silence. Crickets chirping. The lone hoot of an owl.

But no Damon Crowe.

"Odd," Carenza muttered, and adjusted her cloak about her shoulders so that it would not tangle on the tree branch she had been using as her escape route for over a year now. "Curious he's not here." The pang of disappointment around her heart over his absence sent her frowning down the mighty oak tree. "How is this adventure so easy?"

Not that it had not been easy before, because it had. Until her father had hired one Mr. Damon Crowe to see her behaving and corralled accordingly. Though, truth be told, he had done very little in the way of containing her. Except for the night in the carriage that had landed her a personal guard.

Carenza shook her head and dropped lightly from the tree to the ground. Her father had unknowingly placed in her way the one person she was genuinely at risk from. For something about the dark and brooding man spoke to her heart. And anything affecting her heart was a very, *very* big risk.

"Where is he?" Looking around the extravagantly designed grounds of Tipton House and seeing nothing, she swallowed her disappointment and straightened her shoulders. If Damon did not wish to guard her this night, that was a good thing. It meant she was free.

Where the deuce *was* he?

Had he changed his mind? Decided he did not want her father's money?

Was he gone because of their kisses?

"Blast it, Carenza, stop being a ninny." After serving herself the stern lecture, she glanced back up to her darkened chamber window and waited a heartbeat. Still nothing. Sighing, she settled the cloak around her, ensuring it wrapped and lay appropriately, concealing her within its plain brown fabric. Her reticule jangled softly against her thigh as she quickly made her way through the gardens toward the mews. Her usual path took her past the stabled horses and down the alley.

Carenza rounded a corner and ran smack into Damon.

"Oof!" The wind was sucked from her body, and the hood of her cloak tumbled down, but his hands—his hard, competent hands—steadied her as she caught her breath.

"I've got you," he said, his rough-edged voice low and reassuring. "Easy there."

"Where did you go?" Carenza asked when she regained her wits, having the strongest urge to kick him in the shins for making her think he had abandoned her. Resisting the childish impulse, she slapped him on the arm instead. Much more mature, really. "I thought you had left me!"

Damon was silent a moment. "Never," he finally replied. Something about the way he said it sent butterflies fluttering wildly in her stomach. "I've been waiting for you here, knowing you would try to leave."

"You're not going to try to stop me, are you? Because I warn you," she said, her determination rising, "I will *not* be stopped."

"I've no wish to hinder you this eve," he replied easily. "Quite the opposite. I've a curricle readied and waiting a few streets over."

"Why?" she blurted, confused. "You're being paid to keep me under lock and key."

"Perhaps I've had a change of heart." The way he said it had her breath hitching.

"What would compel someone such as you to have a change of heart?"

"Someone such as I?"

"Yes, such as you."

"Information."

"Information?" Truly? Not her beguiling wit? Or the fact that no one deserved to be a kept possession?

"Truth. Fact. Information. I've learned to rely on these things."

"Not your feelings?" Her gaze dropped to his firm, unsmiling mouth, and she had the strangest urge to lean into him and kiss him until that severe mouth of his softened. Until it gave.

He shook his head—the slightest movement—and his thick, wavy hair rustled about the collar of his jacket. "Feelings are easily manipulated," Damon murmured, and slowly reached out, tucked a stray strand of loose hair behind her ear. "That is why I generally have none."

"You don't have *any* feelings?" Carenza whispered, having quite a lot of them at the moment herself.

"Mmm." He appeared to think on it, squinted an eye in thought, his rugged face shadowed in the dark of night. When he spoke, his tone was deep and rough and warm with suggestion. "Not until recently."

The way he said it warmed her from the inside out.

Carenza was on her tiptoes, rising to the balls of her booted feet before another thought had space to enter her mind, leaning in to kiss this dark and dangerous man proclaiming to possess few feelings. Wanting to give him rather *big* feelings. The kind that he gave her. It seemed only fair.

A loud, crashing sort of sound echoed down the empty alley-way, jolting the two of them apart. "We should go, if you're still wanting to." He reached for her hand—a ready movement he employed much of the time with her.

Carenza bit her lip to keep from smiling, sliding her hand easily into his large, hard one, loving its solid warmth. Loving…well…

Just loving *something*.

"Follow me." Damon tugged her hand, leading her away from the crashing sound.

"Perhaps that was a rat or a stray cat?" she guessed, following closely behind him. Close enough to smell his masculine scent. She found great comfort there.

Damon, for all his dark and danger and grumbling, made her feel safe and sheltered in his presence. Protected. Like she was something precious and valued.

"It's an animal," he agreed after briefly lifting his face to the night sky. "Smells like a cat."

"Explain that," Carenza ordered him as they made their way to the curricle. "What you're doing. It fully appears as if you are sniffing the wind." Which was bizarre, yes?

"That is precisely what I'm doing."

"Smelling the wind."

"Yes. Precisely."

"How? Why?" And then a thought occurred to her. "Good God, can you smell *me?*"

Damon grunted. Simply…grunted.

"Oh, deuce and damn, you *can* smell me." Was it awful? Did she smell terrible? She promised that she practiced good personal cleaning!

"Lilac and lemons," he said, voice low and rough with a hint of something in his tone that reached right inside her and wrapped warm and tender around her heart, squeezing gently. "You know, for a lady, you swear rather a lot."

"Thank you," she replied proudly. "I've been practicing."

"Odd, base endeavor for an earl's daughter."

"Precisely."

He released a short, surprised laugh. "You're one of a kind, milady." There was a hint of admiration, of *affection* in his tone.

Interesting for a man who possessed no feelings.

"I've made it my life's aim to endeavor to be anything at all besides a proper Mayfair lady. I confess I take pride in being a sort of ill match. Rather a Mayfair misfit, if you will, in many ways. Knowing that, understanding who I am, helped me discover the courage to break free of the constraints laid out by *proper* society. Such as learning several colorful profanities."

"Is that so?" Damon murmured, humor lacing his rough, masculine tone.

"It is," she said primly.

"What other secret talents do you possess?" he asked when they reached the curricle and he assisted her up, sending a spiral of heat up her spine at the touch of his hand upon her. "For we've already tallied singing and cursing."

"I can ride a horse like a man, I'm a crack shot, and I can defend myself physically if ever the need should arise," Carenza boasted as she settled on the curricle seat, breathing deeply of the fragrant night air. And if her brothers knew any of this, they would undoubtedly scold her terribly. Especially Crawford, who as the eldest Castlebury sibling was most concerned with propriety. That was why she had learned privately from Sadie—the shooting and the physical defense. The horse-riding split saddle she had learned as a child. It was far easier than sidesaddle—and quite a bit more enjoyable, to her way of thinking.

"Good," was all Damon said as he settled himself and began driving. Then he added drolly, "And me ballocks well remember."

They fell into an easy silence on the way to the Meadowlark Tavern, only once breaking it to speak. "Thank you," she offered sincerely. "I know you should not be helping me."

He fell quiet a moment and then replied, "I see your father's aim, and I'm not him. I realize I have no right to constrain you. Keeping you safe is the most important thing, beyond what I should or should not do."

"He'll likely fire you for this if he finds out, you know."

"I do," Damon said. "But the Revivalists are out there somewhere, and I will continue to do my part. Not to stop you. But protect you."

"Why?" Why would he say, *do* such a thing?

"Because…" He flicked the reins and set the curricle rolling down a cobbled lane at the edge of the Garden district. "Because…" He growled and swore under his breath. "Fuck. Because," he burst out, "I'll not be the one to keep you bound. If you want to fly, then I say, god damn it, let yourself fly. Touch the stars if you wish."

Tears welled in Carenza's eyes, and she drew in a sharp breath. Such passion in his words! As if…as if… "D-do you mean it?" she stammered in disbelief.

"I really fucking do, milady," Damon answered, his voice harsh and vehement—and it touched Carenza in a way nothing ever had before. It touched her *heart*, made it swell with emotion and stutter—and stumble. Stumble dangerously close to the precipice of love. A place she never thought to be.

Damon drew the curricle to a stop. "We're here," he said roughly.

He moved so quickly that Carenza had no warning. And then he was there, wrapping her in his strong arms and kissing her like he was a man drowning and she was his lifeline. "Carenza," Damon groaned—*pleaded*—and kissed her with raw, ragged-edged desire until everything melted into blinding, driving need.

"Damon," she gasped, tearing her mouth away, emotions storming her internal castle walls, blowing holes in her armor, her *beliefs*. Crashing, tearing them to the ground, destroying everything she thought she believed. "You should not say such things!"

"I know." And he kissed her again, hard and consuming.

"Now," he ordered her, his breathing ragged. "Go to it, Meadow-lark. Your audience is inside waiting."

While Carenza blinked and breathed her way back to reality, Damon climbed nimbly down from the curricle. "Take my hand." He offered it to her, and it somehow felt rather significant when she *did* take it. As if it was somehow more than a mere climb down from a carriage. Rather, it felt a bit more like an act of deep, profound trust.

Somehow, it felt less like agreeing to put her hand in his—and more like her heart.

How, she wondered a little frantically, *does that not change everything?*

"Oh, there you are! Good Christ, Meadowlark, you sure do know how to keep them waiting." The tavern door banged wide open against the stone walls, bounced twice before settling.

Reeling inside, Carenza somehow managed a bright, playful smile. "It is true, I do," she agreed, jesting with West. Reluctantly, she stepped away from Damon—and felt his fingers brush, tangle ever so briefly with hers as she went. The jolt of pure light that shot up her arm had her gasping—and promptly coughing to hide it from West.

"You all right?" the American asked, his gray eyes narrowing on her. "Your voice okay to sing?" He crossed beefy arms over his broad chest and frowned. "We adore having you here and all, but your health in the most important thing."

That was, well, surprisingly thoughtful and sweet. Almost brotherly.

"I am quite well," Carenza assured him, and brushed politely past West. "I'll be ready in fifteen minutes."

The pub owner nodded in acknowledgment. "Crowe, hold up," West said over her shoulder as she stepped over the Meadowlark Tavern's threshold. "I've a question for you about Longfellow's upcoming bout against the Spaniard."

Hearing West, Carenza knew Damon would be waylaid and not directly behind her when she turned a corner down the narrow hall and came to a startled, abrupt stop.

"What are you doing here?"

Catamount, her other brother, lounged against the wall, his long, dark coat tattered, his boots dusty. "Crawford told me what you've been up to."

Traitor.

Getting her back up, Carenza stiffened. "And you've come to put a stop to it, have you?"

Catamount yawned and shook his shaggy brown-blond head, his green eyes red-rimmed from lack of sleep. "You know me better than that." Pushing away from the wall, he explained, "My Runners and I are working nonstop down at Bow Street trying to piece together any leads on the Revivalists' return. So far, we know very little. Only that there's about ten of them in total. Ten aristocratic madmen who could be anyone of our—*your*—acquaintance. And they appear to most frequent the rookeries. Less patrol there, and less chance of getting caught. The poor are less trusting of Runners and the Metro Police, and so less gets reported."

He raked a hand through his unkempt hair. The dark smudges of exhaustion under his eyes were rather concerning. Carenza knew her brother had personal reasons for catching the Revivalists, for feeling so determined, and it wasn't simply because he was captain of the Bow Street Runners. Because of them, he'd lost somebody.

"I'm worried for you," he went on. "We've been tracking the movement and location of their attacks, and I think they're going to hit the Garden again soon."

Though the thought sent a chill down her spine, Carenza replied calmly, knowing his personal loss undoubtedly amplified his worry. "I appreciate your concern." Hugging Catamount, she confessed, "Whatever your reasons, it's good to see you. You don't come by Tipton House often enough."

"Father lives there."

And that said everything.

West spoke up from behind her, finally catching up. "Captain, what brings you by?"

"Just passing through." Catamount released Carenza, ending their hug, and his cool, assessing green gaze settled over her shoulder. "Crowe," he said, nodding in greeting.

"Captain," Damon replied, returning the nod.

"You two know each other?" she asked. Of course they did. They were men. They all knew each other. Like members of a club.

"Meadowlark! Meadowlark!" rang out, the chant reaching down the hall to the back of the tavern.

Satisfaction filled Carenza. Goodness, it was nice to be wanted! Unbidden, her gaze swept behind her to Damon. *Oh yes,* she thought, biting back a smile. *It feels very, very good.*

But enough of that. She had an audience waiting.

"You should know," her brother said, halting her, "when I say that I think the Revivalists will target the Garden district again soon, it's because I mean it. With the tracking, we know that Covent Garden is due. I know what you're doing here, Car, and I know why. I'm not out to stop you. But I want you safe. This whole goddamn city isn't safe."

If the entirety of London wasn't safe, then wasn't she better off with the one man whom she truly felt safe with? Carenza glanced at Damon again.

"Can't stop people from wanting to live their lives, though, captain," West observed pointedly. "People don't want to live afraid."

"Afraid keeps them alive," Catamount stated flatly.

Just then, Sadie poked her head through the door and hollered down the hall, "Things are getting rowdy out here, West! You might want to get out here."

"Damn it." West immediately left them and rushed down the hall and into the heart of the pub, shouting, "Break anything in here and I break you!"

Looking from her brother to Damon, Carenza said, "I've got

to ready myself. Excuse me."

"You're not leaving?" Catamount asked, eyebrows rising in surprise.

"This might be my last time here if you're correct about the Revivalists," Carenza replied with a painful little hitch in her chest at the idea of never singing in the tavern again. "I'm going to see this through."

Though his brows drew together in clear displeasure, Catamount wasted no breath arguing. He merely turned to Damon. "You'll see to her?"

"I will," Damon replied gravely. Somehow his vow of protection did not seem suffocating. Rather, it felt greatly reassuring.

After saying goodnight to Catamount, Carenza entered her dressing room and was changed moments later into the Masked Meadowlark, once again ready to pluck the heartstrings of the pub's patrons through song. In a shimmering pale gold dress this time, and a gold sequined mask decorated with peacock feathers, Carenza stepped back into the hall and strode toward her side entry door, opened it, and quietly slipped through.

Entering the rowdy pub from behind the hanging curtain, she spotted Damon straight away. Her heart skipped a beat. And then another as it teetered near that scary precipice of love. "Bloody ill timing," Carenza muttered to herself, mildly panicking. Love? She wasn't ready for that.

Suddenly the curtain shook, and Rainville was there. "Please forgive my intrusion," he said, stepping beside her, his voice low and easy. "But there is something imperative I must tell you."

Unease skittered through her, and she glanced at the duke, uncertain of what he might have to tell her. "We barely know each other," she pointed out.

"We know each other better than you admit." Rainville bent down and leaned in close, whispering, *Lady Carenza.*"

White-hot shock speared through her body, and she jerked, unable to keep from outwardly reacting.

"Easy," the duke murmured. "I've no wish to shout out your

secret. Quite the opposite, actually." His golden eyes held only sincerity. "Count me as a confidant."

"How long have you known?" Carenza asked though gritted teeth, caught between panic and the desire to trust him. She glanced through the curtains at Damon conversing with West at the bar, wishing at that moment that he was by her side and not so far away.

Rainville smirked, every bit the aristocrat in his finely tailored red velvet jacket. "Ever since the night your immensely aggravating younger sister came poorly disguised to the tavern. As I was performing a gentleman's duty and attending her home, she muttered something under her breath not meant for my ears." He grinned then, handsome and charming. "But hear her I did. She said, and I quote, 'I only wanted to see my sister sing.' Lovely, loyal sentiment, that."

Nora.

Before she could get her ire up, Rainville held out a supplicating hand. "I'm not sure if you're aware, but I've been trying to earn your good favor. I've interfered as often as I could with Lord Arnold's courtship attempts. We both know how he really is, and I wished to prove to you that I am trustworthy. If you come sing in my theatre, I will endeavor to protect your secret as if it were my own. I promise."

Carenza looked up at the duke, saw only honesty there. "I believe you." And she actually did.

Could she do it? Carenza wondered, pulse quickening with nervous excitement. Could she sing at Rhodes Theatre in front of such a crowd? *So* many people. Was it truly a dream she could bring into reality? Did she have the courage?

"I'll consider it." She would. Because what if she *could* actually live her dream?

"Meadowlark! Meadowlark!"

Carenza could not stop the grin that spread across her countenance. A sudden thought occurred to her, and she turned to Rainville. "I say, Horrid A—I *mean*, Lord Arnold appears not to be here this evening. That is a relief." Having one night without his disgusting overtures would be a blessing.

"I do believe you are correct," murmured the duke agreeably. "Aren't we fortunate?"

Suddenly the front door to the Meadowlark Tavern was flung wide open, slamming against the wall and reverberating. A bone-thin young lad of about twelve years, wearing threadbare, tattered clothes shouted, his voice cracking terribly, "The Revivalists are coming! They've entered the Garden district off Newton Street!"

Chaos erupted in the pub, people shouting all at once and scrambling for the door. Pushing and shoving, people panicked, trying to flee.

Terror gripped Carenza, but then Damon was there by her side, his presence strong, protective, and reassuring. "Come," he ordered her.

"My carriage is directly outside," Rainville yelled over the screaming crowd. "It's closest, and my men are armed. Trust me, come with me."

Carenza took Damon's hand and squeezed tightly, nodded. "Lead the way."

Going back through the small stage door behind them, they avoided the crush and were safely ensconced in Rainville's plush carriage in moments. Squished tightly between an oversized duke and Damon's hard, tough body, she focused on breathing while the duke barked orders.

"We made it," she said as the carriage lurched into motion and she realized that between two capable men was not a bad place to be. "We're safe." Carenza slumped in relief and gratitude.

And she had a realization.

Some men, perhaps, weren't merely worth *something*.

She slid a glance at Damon, her heart stuttering.

Perhaps some men were worth *everything*.

Then another thought—one much less profound and earth-shattering, one much more selfish—occurred to her: she never even got to sing.

Blasted Revivalists.

CHAPTER FIFTEEN

"I CANNOT BELIEVE I must be forced to endure this. It's unconscionable!"

"I am sorry, Carenza, I truly am. But in this you must obey your father. He is the Earl of Castlebury. When it comes to it, we have no choice but to obey. We are but women within his household. He is in control."

"Ugh!" Carenza threw up her hands and cut her mother an incredulous look. "Are you truly telling me that you believe that…that boorish nonsense? It is drivel designed to keep women from believing in their own importance, their own inherent rights as crucial members of society!"

"Carenza, *enough!*" Lady Castlebury exploded, her composure crumbling, exposing a furious, tormented woman. One full of grief. Her face contorted with the weight of it. "*Stop it!* Just stop it!"

Stunned, Carenza fell into silence, chest heaving, emotions swirling like a furious wind behind her ribcage. She clenched and unclenched her hands at her sides as she and her mother squared off like pugilists in the drawing room of Tipton House. With Lottie and Nora entertained elsewhere for the moment, it was only the two of them.

The way Lady Castlebury had designed it when she informed Carenza of the news.

She was to be escorted today by Lord Arnold on an outing to

the Royal Academy exhibition at Somerset House.

Across the expanse of plush blue carpeting, mother and daughter stared, breathing heavily.

"I—" Carenza started.

"*No,*" her mother cut in, slicing her hand through the air in front of her, her eyes bright with anguish. "I have had *enough* of your disobedience, your belligerence. You are the daughter of an earl, a member of the aristocracy. It matters not at all—*at all*—what you wish, want, or believe. What makes you think you are any different than the rest of us? Why are *you* so special? You have pushed your father too far. Lord Arnold is perfectly respectable. He has approached us about courting you, and your father gave his consent. Give the viscount a chance, daughter. I'm quite certain he is not so terrible as you seem to think."

"He is worse," Carenza stated flatly.

"Be that as it may," her mother said, patting loose strands of hair back into place, regaining her composure to a degree, "it matters not. You are attending with Lord Arnold as escort. Please ready yourself. He will be arriving shortly."

Seeing the futility of further arguing, Carenza swallowed her anger and asked, "May I at least bring Nora along?"

"Your lady's maid will be quite enough chaperone for the day."

Everything inside Carenza froze. "What about Mr. Crowe? Will not he be attending?" Dread sank low in her belly as she recalled her return home last evening. She had arrived without detection, she was sure of it. No one had stirred, most especially not her loyal servants who were the most responsible for helping keep her secret. Had someone exposed her? Surely last night was not the reason why Damon wasn't attending?

"Mr. Crowe's services will no longer be needed. Your father relieved him of duty early this morning."

No.

No, no, no.

"Why? I do not understand." *Bring him back!* her heart

screamed. Where was he?

"Your father had his reasons." Tipping her head slightly, her mother studied her closely. "Is this news of Mr. Crowe upsetting?"

Yes.

"No, Mother," Carenza choked out, fighting for composure, her throat tight with unshed tears. Damon gone? Without word or warning? No! It could not be. It was not fair.

"Good. For your father has hopes the viscount will make his intentions clear rather shortly. Therefore, there is no need of Mr. Crowe any longer." Her mother spoke the words so carelessly, so casually, as if they didn't shatter Carenza's entire world. "The viscount is a fine match, daughter. Not a single bad mark on his character or reputation, no ill financial dealings—nothing untoward at all! Regardless of whatever nonsense you seem bent on believing. I suggest you discard those silly notions and accept the inevitable. You can make the most of this, you know, and be quite happy. Or if not happy, then content."

A world without Damon? Carenza shuddered inside. It was one she refused to contemplate.

"I am taking Nora," she called out as her mother began to leave, her muslin skirts rustling.

"*No, you are not!*" Lady Castlebury cried, rounding on Carenza, her eyes blazing with fury. "Good God, child! If you knew, if you only *knew* what was at stake, you would not be so hasty to dismiss this man! You would *run* to the altar to marry Lord Arnold!" Visibly shaking, her mother flung the drawing room doors open and swept through, calling behind her, "Franny will be awaiting you. The least you can do is try to enjoy the outing."

When her mother left, Carenza threw herself back onto the nearest settee, her heart lodged in her chest.

No Damon?

No steady presence, no comfort, excitement, safety?

No more of the one person she could not get enough of?

That was…that was simply *wrong*.

Instead, there was Lord Horace Arnold. And the Royal Academy exhibition. And several hours of grueling endurance.

"Oh, stuff it," she muttered aloud, her emotions a complete muddle. "How bad could a few hours with him really be, out in public amongst members of the peerage? He's bound to behave with a modicum of respectability."

If she must endure it, she decided, pushing up from the settee, then it was better to dive in and get it over with.

CARENZA STOOD IN the Royal Academy exhibition hall at Somerset House, staring at the elaborate portrait of King George III portrayed as a Roman emperor, and silently screamed. Time spent with Lord Arnold was much worse in actuality than one could even imagine. The cuts, the snide remarks, the lewd looks. It was exhausting.

"It boggles the mind that the Royal Academy considers this *art*. Why, it's merely juvenile scribbling! They'll simply let anyone in these days, won't they?" Lord Arnold sneered as he pointed at the same portrait Carenza had been studying, his bright blue jacket and spring-green waistcoat making him stand out amongst the *ton* like the dandy he was.

She glanced down at his overly polished shoes and highly creased trousers and wondered how much time it took his valet to dress him.

Poor valet.

"Your cravat is slipping." It wasn't, but Carenza could only stand so much, and she was quite quickly reaching the end of her tolerance.

The things a woman was forced to endure.

Anger's flame sparked in her chest, but she kept it banked through sheer force of will, knowing it would do her no good. Only clear thinking and strategy would relieve her of this mess.

"Goodness me!" the viscount exclaimed, and immediately attended his ridiculous cravat, fussing and cooing at it as if it was an infant in need of coddling. "There, is it snug once more? Do tell me it is!"

Biting back a smile at his dramatic response, Carenza glanced around the exhibition hall and tugged at the satin ribbon of her bonnet. No matter how she tried, or how many times she retied it, the ribbons were too tight. Almost choking. She cut her company a look.

Much like her companion.

Many members of the *ton* milled about Somerset House today; the exhibition hall was a crush of lavishly dressed people discussing the latest impasto technique and the canon of classical masterpieces. For most of the outing, Carenza had avoided Lord Arnold's unwelcome advances, though the viscount had tried repeatedly to touch her without consent. The first attempt had been to the small of her back—which she had avoided by quickly turning to the couple next to her and commenting on the painting they were observing. After that there had been several elbow grabs, one hip brush she had somehow sidestepped—and a neck graze with his fingers that the viscount had blamed on an invisible gnat.

The only touch she wished to feel was Damon's.

Reflexively, Carenza glanced behind her, expecting him to be just there out of reach, watching, guarding, a strong, virile presence. Only Franny was there instead of him, looking demure in front of a wall covered in gilt-framed paintings.

Damon's absence, the loss of him, had her aching deep inside.

"Look, there's Lord Barnes over by the poorly done marble of Dionysus." Horrid A snickered and leaned close. "Rumor is he's gambled away all his family's money and is so overextended that his tailor will no longer offer him credit." His small eyes danced with mean merriment at the poor gentleman's misfortune, turning Carenza's stomach.

"One should feel compassion for Lord Barnes, I should

think," she offered while steadfastly avoiding the viscount's hands. They were everywhere, like octopus tentacles. "For not everyone has the luxury of endless wealth."

"True, true." Lord Arnold brushed her off, laughing cruelly. "More's the pity for them."

Breathing in a long, steady breath meant to inspire patience and fortitude, Carenza wandered the exhibition hall, Franny trailing discreetly behind, pretending great interest in the art pieces around her. She would, in truth, much prefer to be at the Meadowlark Tavern searching for Damon. What must he be feeling? Thinking? Was he experiencing this odd, empty feeling too?

Perhaps that was just her.

"You look radiant today, by the by. Quite the proper lady." The hideous yellow walking dress with the high neckline had been her attempt to cover as much of her figure from Horrid A's view as possible. "Very befitting for the elevated station of an earl's daughter. Or perhaps," he added with a lascivious waggle of his thick, bushy eyebrows, "the future wife of a very respectable viscount."

"What say you?" Carenza jerked backward, bumping into someone directly behind her. "I'm so sorry!" she blurted, alarm rising within her.

Wife of a very respectable viscount.

Oh, dear God, no.

"None's the harm," the matron she had bumped replied with a warm, kind smile. "It is a jumble in here."

"Thank you for understanding." With her heart racing, Carenza looked all around the great hall inside Somerset House, seeking anywhere that she might hide and find a moment's reprieve.

"You needn't act so skittish," Lord Arnold whispered in her ear, having somehow managed to regain her side. His white-gloved hand firmly gripped her elbow.

"Lord Arnold," she protested, yanking her elbow away, but

he held steady with a near-painful grip.

"Nor should you stand on such formality," he said with a sly smile. "For we shall become well and intimately acquainted before long."

"I'm quite certain I know not what you mean." Panic welled inside her, constricting her throat. Carenza was well and truly afraid that she understood *exactly* what the viscount meant. "Excuse me."

Taking her leave, Carenza pushed quickly through the throng of art admirers in the exhibition hall, her gaze darting here and there, searching for a place to hide, some privacy.

"Lady Carenza!" the viscount called out behind her, turning several curious heads in her direction.

Fervently she wished for Damon.

Just…Damon.

Shoving through the crowd, Carenza spotted a large silk printed standing screen set up in a far corner surrounded by potted palm plants. Turning toward it, she caught a blur of motion out of the corner of her eye and gasped. Damon? Could it be?

Heart leaping with hope, she focused across the large hall, but the brief glimpse of dark hair and familiar broad shoulders that she thought she'd seen was gone. A figment of her imagination.

Crestfallen, she rushed to the trifold screen and dashed behind it, thankful for the momentary bit of privacy when she found it empty. Carenza dropped unceremoniously to the red-cushioned bench with a great, heaving sigh. For a blessed moment, until her lady's maid and Horrid A caught up with her, she could breathe.

Why Lord Arnold? The viscount was a worm—a spineless, slimy worm. Of all the gentlemen her father could have picked for her! It rather seemed he'd chosen the worst of the lot out of sheer spite.

"There you are!"

Inwardly, Carenza groaned. "Here I am!" she replied with

fake brightness, and stared down at Lord Arnold's overly polished shoes. It was better than looking at his weasel-like countenance, and his giant, ridiculous sideburns. *Go away.*

But, of course, he did not. Oh no, Horrid A dropped to the bench beside her, purposely crowding her, pressing his unwelcome thigh to hers. "I confess I'm rather glad for this moment of privacy—"

"Where's Fanny? I do not see her. Shouldn't we go look?"

"—for there is something of great import I've been wanting to ask you."

"No!" Carenza protested, shooting to her feet, panic clawing at her throat. *He cannot do it!* she thought frantically.

Lord Arnold rose with her, a smug, self-indulgent smile turning his thin lips. "I understand it is typical of your fairer and more delicate sex to proclaim disinterest toward a suitor when the opposite is your true feeling. I am prepared for your affected resistance." The viscount lashed out an arm, gripped her hard at the waist, and pulled her close. "Do not fight me," he ordered her with a hard glint in his eye. "For it shall be my lawful right very soon."

"No!" Carenza cried again, this time pushing against Horrid A.

"You needn't play the coquette, Carenza. Do not be coy. I know your true feelings for me. You demonstrated them clear enough in Hyde Park when you so valiantly came to my defense. I knew then that you held great affection for me." With a fierce, painful grip, he pulled her closer, held her captive.

"I did not give you leave to call me so familiarly!" Shoving at his hands, prying, she tried ineffectually to get away from him. But Lord Arnold held her in a vise grip, a mocking, taunting humor entering his gaze.

"As you are to be my wife, I most certainly may dispense of the formal address." Suddenly his eyes went hard as obsidian. "*Whatever* I want," he sneered with a faint whine in his tone that nagged at her, terrorized her with its familiarity. "You will *not* deny me."

Shock doused her, turned her instantly cold. Carenza shook her head in denial, began slapping at his hands. "I'll never marry you!" she spat. "Unhand me this instant!"

"You *are* to marry me," Lord Arnold insisted, drawing so close she could smell the staleness of his breath, see the tiny black pinpricks of his pupils. "Terms were settled with your father just this afternoon. In thirty days or less, if I can arrange a special license, you shall become Lady Carenza, Viscountess of Amslee. Now kiss me—I can wait no longer."

His lips were on hers, slimy and cold like a dead snake. His tongue, his *tongue*, darted out and licked the seam of her lips, tried to force entry. He groped her breast and squeezed viciously. "Stop pretending you don't want this."

At those awful words, her fear melted under the sudden heat of her fury. Recalling Sadie's training, Carenza raised her knee and slammed it into Lord Arnold's ballocks as hard as she possibly could. "I *don't* want this," she seethed as he released her, squealing and shrieking, sounding quite like a pig. "I will *never* want this."

The viscount crumbled to his knees, his face contorted in pain and outrage. "*You*," he panted, glaring at her with an expression very close to hatred. "Once you and I are wed and I own you, I will teach you your place."

Loathing those words, Carenza straightened her gaudy walking dress and stepped around the viscount crumpled weakly on the floor. "I will *never* marry you."

"Your father consented!" Lord Arnold said. "It is binding!"

"Eh." Carenza shrugged, determination rising inside her. "We'll see."

She stepped around the silk screen, leaving a sniveling viscount whimpering on his knees.

CHAPTER SIXTEEN

S HE'D KNEED THE bastard in his ballocks.

Good.

Damon had watched the whole thing from a distance, through a narrow slice of space between the trifold screen. It had taken every ounce of control not to flatten the shit-sack. Even now, hours later, he seethed with leashed fury.

He could no longer see Carenza.

Since the earl had gutted him with the news that morning, it was all he could think. All he could *feel*.

Damon needed to hit something. Anything. Stalking through the doors to Flatt's, he spotted Aaron ahead amongst the weekly fight-night crowd, patrons from every walk and station come for the exhilaration of watching a good boxing match. Several cheered when they spotted him, calling out to him in greeting.

"I'm here to fight," he growled, pointing around the large, open room.

"You're in luck then, bruv." Aaron smirked. "It's wot we do here. But there's no mill tonight, only regulars for sparring bouts."

"Who's listed?" Aaron kept a blackboard that men signed up for a session on. It was most often hung on the brick wall to the left of the boxing ring. Damon didn't want to look; his mind was filled with one crucial thing: no more Lady Carenza Castlebury.

She was to marry the Viscount of Amslee, the slimy sod, Lord

Arnold. The very bastard she had kneed in the ballocks for accosting her at the Royal Academy's exhibition at Somerset House. Cad. Spineless, worthless cad.

How could Damon protect her now?

The Earl of Castlebury was handing his daughter to a lecher. And he did not care at all.

Damon had stood in the earl's study, fuming, wanting to strangle the earl for his callousness, his lack of regard for his child. The only thing of concern for the earl was how quickly the wedding could be arranged, the banns read.

"I care not for her feelings in this matter. Do you?" the earl had asked with a raised white brow.

"I care when anyone is forced against their will," Damon replied, his heart thumping a heavy, devastated beat.

"She'll get over it." Castlebury waved Damon's words off, uncaring. "They all do."

Not Carenza.

Though his palms itched to strangle the Earl of Castlebury, he did nothing more than stand silently while the aristocrat paid him for services rendered.

"I trust that between this and the lead I provided, we owe each other nothing. Carenza will marry Lord Arnold, and it shall be his responsibility to keep her in hand. No one needs to be the wiser about her late-night outings, as they've come to an end. Scandal averted."

And just like that, the wall inside him crumbled, and Damon was flooded with feeling. So much feeling, every bit that he had locked way down deep. It rose like a mighty wave, threatening to take him under.

Never, *never* had he felt this way.

He'd left the Earl of Castlebury's study, his heart twisting painfully, his payment from the nobleman untouched on the desk. For an hour Damon walked around London, a hollow thrum in his chest, until he had looked up to see the Viscount of Amslee escort Carenza across the street to the grounds of

Somerset House directly in front of him. Possessiveness, primal and fierce, ripped through him, followed by a need to protect her that was consuming.

"Fuck the earl," he swore, crossing the street, his powerful stride eating up the distance. "His daughter deserves protecting."

And so he had watched Lord Arnold's pathetic attempts, maintaining distance with great reluctance. Only when he heard Carenza cry out from behind the screen had he moved to interfere.

Now his mood was black, and he wanted to hit something. *Someone.*

Ripping off his jacket and waistcoat, Damon pushed his way through the crowd of spectators eyeing him with open interest.

"I'll put two shillings on Crowe. He looks to be in a foul mood."

And that started the round of betting that wasn't supposed to happen for fights that were not strictly legal, while Damon divested himself of his attire. "Who wants me?" he called out to the crowd, greedy for someone to hit, for somewhere to put this awful, desperate feeling.

Circling the boxing ring like a caged beast, Damon scanned the crowd, noting a few ladies. His chest tightened until he realized none were Carenza—*his* Carenza. Who belonged to another man. A cowardly lecher with oversized sideburns.

"Come on!" he angrily called out, throwing his hands up, pacing the ring in low-slung trousers, bare chest glistening under the candlelit chandeliers.

"I'll do it." A burly Irishman stepped forward, a grin lighting his blunt features.

The crowd cheered, and Aaron stood at the side of the ring, arms crossed over his chest. "You need this, bruv?"

Damon nodded once, sharply—decisively. "I do." He rolled his shoulder muscles, loosened his neck.

"All right, then." The bare-knuckle champion nodded back. "Wot's your name?" he asked the Irishman as he entered the boxing ring, arrogance dripping from him.

"Name's Duffy," the thickly muscled young man replied, removing his shirt and tossing it to the wood-plank floor just outside the ropes.

Dark, ugly hunger tore through Damon, and he toed the line, eager to strike. As soon as the Irishman stepped to the line, starting the match, he whipped out an arm, connecting solidly with his opponent's jaw.

It was over before it began.

Duffy dropped unconscious to the mat, eyes rolling back in his head.

Damon's chest heaved, and he paced away from the fallen Irishman, the corded muscles in his abdomen flexing with the movement. "I need another bloke," he panted to Aaron.

"Wot's got you so fired up tonight?" Aaron helped the amateur boxer from the ring while the club buzzed with new wagers. "Good show, mate," he offered to the felled boxer, patting him on the shoulder as he climbed down from the ring. "Off you go now. Puke in that bucket there if you've the need."

Riled now, blood flowing, heart pounding, Damon fed the hunger and turned to the crowd to call for his next opponent. And there he was, directly in the center of the crowd gathered around the boxing ring.

Lord Horace Arnold.

Something inside Damon snapped, something furious and hurting, and he leapt over the ring ropes, stalked toward the viscount, his muscles rippling.

"I say, what is your issue?" Lord Arnold tugged at a sideburn awkwardly and glanced nervously around him, finding no one willing to assist him. "Do you see this heathen? *I* am not asking to box with him. See how he stalks me?" he appealed to the crowd. "Call this brute off me. I only came to spectate."

"*You touched her,*" Damon snarled, advancing on the viscount.

"I had the right!" Lord Arnold replied belligerently, his chest puffing indignantly beneath his waistcoat. "She is my intended."

A sound started in Damon's chest, deep inside where his demon lived, and it grew before releasing itself on a sound so wholly inhuman that Lord Arnold's eyes nearly popped from his head. Moving swiftly, his arm a blur, he latched on to the viscount's extravagant cravat and yanked him to the toes of his top boots, bringing him close.

"She belongs to no one," he stated very clearly and slowly for the toff to understand.

A flash of something mean and predatory traveled through Lord Arnold's gaze. "She will belong to me. And I will do with her whatever I wish, and no one will stop me," the viscount said. "Especially not street scum such as you who fancies a shag with her himself."

Damon's fist collided with the viscount's nose. Blood erupted, pouring in small rivers over his mouth and down his weak chin. "*Never* speak of her that way." His voice was low, deadly.

"Or what?" Lord Arnold spat red and glared at him as he collected blood in cupped hands before him. "You think you have any say?"

"I think I just proved that I do." Damon's gaze flicked briefly to the viscount's broken nose. "There's more of that if necessary."

Hatred flared bright in Lord Arnold's eyes. He sneered, his teeth smeared red with his own blood. "You've no idea whom you are dealing with. But you will, you'll see." Straightening stiffly, the viscount notched his chin, wiping at the blood with a jacket sleeve, trying desperately to affect an air of superiority. "You will regret crossing me."

"Unlikely," Damon replied, knowing for a fact that he would not.

"*Fight, fight!*" The chant broke out amongst the crowd, along with some good-natured heckling.

Anger still raging, Damon shifted his gaze briefly to look over the crowd. From the corner of his eye he saw the viscount's face twist into something dark with loathing, watched him move to attack. Spinning lightly on the balls of his feet, Damon sidestepped Lord Arnold's lunge. He slammed a fist into the viscount's gut, brought him to an abrupt halt.

Bent over and groaning, Lord Arnold swore.

"Every fancy knows of Richmond's training. Light of feet, fast of body. You missed his lessons, clearly," Damon said, referring to bare-knuckle legend Bill Richmond, who revolutionized boxing, demonstrated how to *move*. A technique Damon had learned and employed well.

"Into the ring." Lord Arnold straightened and spat, sending blood and saliva to the scarred wood floors. Yanking at his cravat and panting, the aristocrat waved a shaky path to the ring ropes and climbed through. "I'll not tolerate my honor being impugned this way."

"You have no honor." Greedy to meet the viscount, Damon prowled his way through the eager crowd, his sights only on the bastard toff. "You have no decency."

"What? Says you? A commoner with no pedigree?" Lord Arnold laughed harshly. "Who's ever going to believe *you*?"

"I am!" yelled Aaron, his arms crossed over his massive chest.

"Me too!" called out another.

And then another and another. Until the viscount's eyes bulged in disbelief.

"I see 'im gropes our Masked Meadowlark, I 'ave!" declared someone from the back.

"He did *wot*?" hollered another in response, and a murmur ran through the crowd.

"Not our Masked Meadowlark!"

"She's an angel, tha' one! How you gonna grope an angel?"

"Teach him a lesson, Crowe!"

"Stop it!" screamed the viscount as he rushed the ropes, pushed against them while he snarled at the spectators. "The Masked Meadowlark is a whore! Nothing more than a worthless whore who can sing. How *dare* you defend her over me?" His eyes blazed with indignant fury. "She is *nothing. I* am a viscount, a righteous member of the nobility!" And he hissed—he hissed very like the snake he was.

Damon saw red, blazing anger when the viscount called Carenza a whore. "Watch what you say about the Meadowlark here," he warned Lord Arnold.

"I'll not censor myself for a common whore."

"Wrong answer." Protective rage swallowed him, and when someone from the crowd shoved the viscount through the ropes and sent him spinning in his direction, Damon was ready.

Lord Arnold's face pinched angrily, and he swung, though his punch glanced off Damon's bare shoulder. Spinning out of the way, Damon rounded, came up beside the viscount, and sent a searing jab to his ribs. The jolt of impact slammed into him and reverberated up his arm. He grunted with the effort, teeth bared, his crooked incisor visible. His left arm came across, and he connected with Lord Arnold's eye; the harsh smacking sound of flesh on bone echoed through the club.

The lord's head snapped up and around, and he spun like a corkscrew before dropping to the mat.

"Get up." Damon danced lightly on the balls of his feet, sweat streaming down his temples, his blood thundering. "Get up, you coward."

The Viscount of Amslee looked up at him, hatred in his eyes. "You'll pay for this."

"I will take the chance." Damon held his fists in front of him defensively, at the ready.

"Finish 'im off!" someone called out.

The viscount lay writhing on the mat.

"He can't talk about our Meadowlark that way!"

"Yeah, she's a right lady!"

Damon paced around the ring, his body glistening with sweat, his muscles straining from use. When he circled around and came to Lord Arnold, he stopped, crouched down in front of him. "You would not make such comments about your future wife."

"Lady Carenza is not a whore," the viscount argued, eyes

narrowing, blood crusting dry on his thin upper lip. "At least, not yet. I will ride and train her accordingly."

Damon lashed out and slammed his fist into the viscount's nose again, causing a fresh round of blood to gush from it—and Lord Arnold to howl with pain.

"My nose!" Cradling it, he scrambled backward to his feet. "You broke my fucking nose!"

"A small price to pay for a lady's honor," Damon snarled.

"Devil it, take Meadowlark. She's a trollop anyway."

"She's taken." The words were ripped out of Damon's chest—unbidden, raw, agonizing truth.

"Well, you certainly can't have Lady Carenza! She's my intended, and you're nothing but common gutter trash."

Damon shrugged, a roll of powerful shoulder muscles. "I don't disagree."

"Even if she *did* want you, there's nothing you can offer her." The viscount swiped at his nose.

Love.

Damon could offer her love.

Something he had never given *anybody.*

"C'mon, knock him out!"

And the full truth of it took the fight out of him. "We're done here," he growled, cutting the viscount a hard look. "Take your things and leave."

"We're not done," Lord Arnold said as he dabbed at his bloody, misshapen nose. "You haven't seen the last of me!"

"Yes, I have," Damon replied, climbing from the ring, knowing that all the punching, all the fighting, would never make Carenza his. He walked away, done.

She was gone. *Gone.*

And Damon was in agony.

CHAPTER SEVENTEEN

"I AM HERE for Mr. Crowe. May I speak with him, please?" Carenza asked the stocky, gray-haired servant who opened the door of Damon's fifth-floor flat on Fleet Street after her fourth (fourth!) hard knock. Impatience hammered at her breast.

For the past few hours, she had anxiously searched London, trying to locate Damon, finally finding fortune with the giant boxer whose flat was above that club. Aaron was his name.

"Mr. Longfellow gave me the address. I'm certain it's correct," she offered as encouragement, for the poor servant seemed quite dumbfounded by her appearance.

Although…

"I do realize that a call this late in the evening is rather unorthodox." Carenza noted the servant's hastily donned clothing, and concluded the four knocks were the consequence of calling upon Damon at a time when most servants were asleep. She leaned toward the servant, clutching her brown tweed cloak closed in front of her, and whispered, "I'm so sorry!" And then she added with an earnest nod, "But it is rather pressing."

"Who is it, Bones? What bloody person is calling this late?"

"Damon!" Carenza gasped, her heart rejoicing at the sound of his tough, gravelly voice.

"You must be what's causing him such grief lately. Come inside." The servant finally found his voice and regained motion, shuffling to the side to let Carenza pass through.

"Thank you." Stepping past him into the entry, she was immediately enveloped in Damon's scent. It clung to the finely tailored jackets hung up tidily to her right; it floated on the air.

She paused a moment and breathed it in deep.

Damon's home.

A surprisingly nice, comfortable space, with golden oak floors and green-papered walls the color of forest leaves. Carenza gave the man—Bones—her cloak with a quiet word of thanks.

"Right this way." Bones waved her straight down the hall. "He's probably still in his chair in the parlor, reading."

"Bones? Can you hear me? I asked who's at the bloody door." Irritation colored Damon's tone, along with weariness and a heaviness that tugged at Carenza's heart.

"You go on," Bones gently encouraged her with a tip of his chin. "I'll put the kettle on for tea."

"I shan't...I shan't need tea..." she whispered, trailing off when she realized she was already alone. Alone. In Damon's home.

"Damn it, Bones. Why aren't you answering?"

With Damon.

Knowing she was in for quite a bit of walking when she set out in search of Damon, she'd worn her most comfortable boots, plain and brown and so very comfortable—they made little sound as she trod lightly down the printed carpet runner toward the back of the flat. Itching to touch and take in what was his, she ran featherlight fingertips across the surface of a sturdy side table, the gilded edge of an oval mirror, the corner of a painting that depicted a darkened, stormy sea and a lone figure on a breaking raft, his body and countenance twisted and hideous like a demon, but a single shaft of light falling through the clouds on a small, startlingly white pair of wings protruding from his back.

Tears sprang to her eyes for the creative man, and she marveled at the artistry. Then she was there, stepping through the archway into the heart of Damon's home. And he was there, sitting in his chair reading, beautiful and perfect and anguished, his eyes dark with pain.

"Carenza," he breathed, his eyes widening in disbelief at her unexpected appearance.

And just like that, she fell. All the way over that precipice, tumbling down—way, way down—into the endless depths of love. *So* much love. It flooded her from her toes to her hair, tearing an overwhelmed cry from her lips.

Instantly, Damon moved to rise from his leather chair, and she held out a hand to stay him. "Please don't get up on my account."

"Don't be ridiculous—"

"Bones is making tea." At a loss with so much feeling, she stepped into the warm candle- and fire-lit room, and noted the comfortably plush settee and matching chairs, the low-burning fire in the fireplace, the large expanse of oversized windows lining the far wall. Heavy brocade curtains of a rich mahogany and gold thread framed the windows and had not been closed. Drawn to them, Carenza stepped to the glass and marveled at London, spread out, glittering below. "It's beautiful," she whispered.

"Why are you here, Carenza?" Damon shook his head. "You should not be here."

"Could, should. I care not," Carenza declared, anger at the injustice rising. "I'm so tired of being dictated to! As if I have no desires, no rights, or choice." She spun around to him, ripping off her cloak, for now its weight was so very constricting. Mindlessly, she dropped it to the floor and stood before Damon, chest heaving, in nothing but her lace-up boots and plain cream nightgown, her hair tumbling loose over her shoulders down to her waist.

"Wotcha wearing there, Carenza?" Damon asked, his voice suddenly gutter-rough and seductive as silk. The sound of it brushed over her skin like a caress, warming her. He did not rise, however. He leaned back in his chair, his thick, muscular thighs spread, his tunic open at the front nearly to his waist. Dark chest hair was just visible, and she wanted to touch the springy softness, learn its texture. She wanted to fill her senses with Damon.

Only Damon.

She glanced down self-consciously at her nightgown. "It was a spontaneous escape tonight. I hadn't the time to dress properly, only to grab the correct boots."

"Ah," he replied, his rich chocolate gaze heating as he took a very thorough perusal of her body. "Makes sense."

"It did!" Carenza threw her hands up, startled when Damon groaned. "Are you all right?" she asked, suddenly concerned.

"Quite." He grunted, shifting in his chair. "Your silhouette is rather lovely."

"Tea?"

Carenza and Damon's attention spun to the archway at the sound of Bones's voice.

"No," Damon rumbled. "Rather busy here."

"Oh!" the servant squeaked when he peeked to the right and glimpsed Carenza standing there in her shift. "Well, um, yes. Very good." He blushed clean to the roots of his hair and clapped his hands briskly, quite flummoxed. "Carry on, carry on. I shall be off." Bones turned to leave, and disappeared briefly before his head popped back in. "Goodnight."

She thought Bones had retreated, until he appeared once more in the archway and cleared his throat, looked up at the ceiling, hands clasped behind his back. "Might I add that you seem lovely, my lady. It's…" He cleared his throat again, blinking decidedly wet-looking eyes. "It is excellent that you are here. He is a good man at heart. Now, ahem, I bid you goodnight." Bones spun around and slid the pocket doors to the parlor closed, and this time his retreat echoed down the hall.

"A good man?" Carenza questioned into the sudden silence, raising a brow tartly.

"So he keeps insisting," Damon grumbled, waving a hand lazily in front of him. "He's hopelessly optimistic."

"Is he?" She moved quietly across the rug toward him. "What

about you?"

"I'm terribly pessimistic." He reached for a cigarette on the small table next to him.

"Nasty habit, those," she commented, glancing at his cigarette. "You should think about quitting."

"Is that so?" he murmured, tilting his head in question, his dark brown waves tumbling sensually around the collar of his tunic.

"It is." She nodded, stepping to him and sliding it free from his fingers. Leaning to the side, she set it down on the table and paused, catching sight of a handwritten poem titled "An Ode to Lady Carenza" on parchment nearby. She snatched it up and started reading.

> *Carenza, a lady without compare*
> *With radiant sunlight hair, whose heart has shown*
> *That love, once long gone, has found a new home*
> *To bloom and grow and thrive*
> *A heart once shriveled now beats renewed*
> *With love for the Lady Carenza*

"Did...did you write this?" she whispered, setting it down as her own heart began a fast, hopeful beat.

A pause. "I did."

"You write poetry." Her mind was spinning. This man? This tough, capable man?

"Poorly." He grimaced, his dark eyes watchful on her.

"Don't tell Lottie," she jested lamely. "For she will hound you mercilessly. She loves all forms of the written word."

"Noted," he answered softly.

"You, um..." Carenza realized how close she was standing next to him, that his hand rested on the chair mere inches from her thigh. "You... Well, you wrote here that you love me." Her throat constricted with emotion.

"It's merely poetry."

"So, you don't, then. You don't love me?" It was suddenly imperative she know his truth. It changed nothing. Not why she had come this night, not that she must marry the despicable Lord Arnold (confirmed by her father quite harshly), and not that the two of them had a future of any kind.

But if he *loved* her?

That...*that* was something to hold on to during the lonely nights ahead.

"Why have you come here tonight, Carenza?" Damon reached out a hand and clasped hers, sending sparks of heat shooting up her arm. He stared up at her, his eyes swimming with emotion. "You are to marry another."

"I don't want him!" Carenza burst out, jerking her hand away and pacing away from him back to the window. The fireplace glow was reflected in the windows, dancing flames and shadow. "I never wanted *anybody!*" she shouted. "Until *you!*"

Her body burst with renewed energy, and she rounded on him, emotions spilling over. "I was perfectly content with the spinster's life, you know. Yes, I was. I had pictured a lovely little stone cottage in the country where I would spin wool into blankets and clothing and sell it for money and consider myself blessed that a man did not *own* me."

Oh, she was wound up now. She stood before the windows, her legs planted wide under her nightgown, and released every bit of feeling she had been forced to swallow over the years. Because she knew this man, this *man* could withstand the ferocity of her storm. Needed him to.

"Carenza," he said quietly, leaning forward in his masculine leather chair, his skin nearly bronze in the firelight.

"But then..." She threw up her hands. "But *then,*" she said, and balled her hands into fists, scrunched her face. "You came along, you intrigued me, and you listened to me, and you didn't judge me, and you allowed me to be, well, *me.*"

"Carenza."

Her hands were on her hips now as she went on. "And you

claim to be awful and know awful things—and I do believe you do—but I've seen you be kind, and...and with you I feel not chained at all, but rather exhilaratingly, extraordinarily free."

"*Carenza.*"

"Oh!" She closed her eyes, which stung now with unshed tears, and bit her bottom lip, worried it with her teeth. "You've gone and tumbled everything I thought I believed, and...and you are just, just *bloody* wonderful. And if you *loved* me? Oh—"

"Carenza!"

Startled, she opened her eyes in time to see Damon leap from the chair and rush toward her, his dark eyes blazing.

"For the love of God, shut up."

He kissed her, took her mouth with a kind of sizzling hunger that shook her, buckled her knees. And his hands were on her, everywhere, stroking, *branding*. One of them was anchored in her hair, fisted there. The other explored her body with an impatient possessiveness—rather like a need to know her shape immediately.

To claim what was his.

She opened for him, ready and willing, and he took the kiss deep to a place of rich sensuality, drugging her with his taste, moving his tongue in a rhythm that started a responding pulsing—a luxurious, erotic ache—in the glorious space between her legs. Instantly, she wanted his hands on her again, rubbing her there, taking her to places filled only with wondrous sensation and bursting, liquid light.

As if he could read her mind, Damon gripped her hip, fisting a handful of nightgown, and pushed her backward, guiding her until she encountered the hard window glass. She gasped at the cold against her shoulder blades and clung to his hard, muscular shoulders, gripping him through the fine weave of his tunic.

He tore his lips from hers. "I'm going to make you come, milady," he promised, his voice low and harsh with rookery, and kissed her neck, her jaw.

"*Please.*"

A growl rumbled in his chest, and he released his hold on her hair, ripped the bodice of her nightgown, thrilling and a bit frightening in the best way. Then he swore a string of curses, and his mouth was on her breast, tonguing her puckered nipple. Crying out, Carenza drove her fingers into Damon's thick, silky hair and held him to her. He kept up his gentle assault while he raised the hem of her nightgown and found her slick and ready underneath.

"Christ, you're wet." He groaned against her nipple, bit it between his teeth, and flicked his tongue over the tip, back and forth until she writhed against him.

"Damon!" she whimpered, head back against the window glass, her body burning with ecstasy.

"Tell me to make you come," he whispered darkly, flicking her most sensitive place with a strong, sure finger. Tendrils of intense, exquisite sensation unfurled and wove throughout her body, binding her to him like an invisible rope.

He kissed her hard, thoroughly, and then pulled back, watched her intently, his eyes nearly black with passion.

"Make me come," she breathed.

"Fuck," Damon growled. *"Fuck."* He spread her, stroked a finger deep inside her, his thumb rubbing her bud now in a driving, demanding rhythm. "That's it, love," he encouraged her, bringing his free hand up to cup her jaw, rubbing his thumb across her cheek before he kissed her with open-mouthed, carnal need. "Come," he commanded.

And she did.

Carenza broke apart, splintering into shimmering, golden beams of light.

Yet Damon gave her no relief.

"Oh no," he said, "you're not done. *Again.*" He flicked his thumb, and her body thrummed.

"Again," she sighed. "Give me *everything.*"

DAMON COLLECTED A pliant, satisfied Carenza against him and laid her gently, tenderly on the plush rug before the fireplace, though his body raged for release, to *take*. Leaning over her, he nipped her jaw, cupped a full breast.

"More," she purred softly, arching into him.

He laughed low, his cock full and heavy between his thighs. "Quite the greedy li'l minx, aren't we?" Damon gave her what she wanted, feeding her another long, thorough kiss. Satisfaction, primal and male, filled him at her sighs, her lush, gloriously curved body wiggling under his.

"You make me feel—" she whispered, before mewling and writhing when he set his mouth to her torso, licking and nipping the petal-soft skin exposed when he tore her nightgown further apart. "I feel so…so…*hungry*. But not for food," she added, spreading her legs wide as he traced a path lower. "For *you*."

"Me?" The word rumbled in his chest.

"Yes," she said. "*You*."

Damon knew he should go slow, knew he should be gentle. He didn't want to hurt her on her first time. But never in his life had he felt so connected, so close to another person—so *wanted*.

It undid him.

Raising himself on his arms, he bunched the fabric of her nightgown and tore it the rest of the way down, exposing her to him; her body glowed, alabaster perfection in the firelight. "Beautiful," he whispered roughly, his hands on her long, shapely thighs, caressing, working their way to the curls at the apex between her legs. "*La mas bonita, hechicera.*"

He quickly removed his clothes, smiling wickedly when she looked him over, gasping, her gorgeous, passion-glazed eyes going round at the sight of him.

"You're so big," she whispered, licking her lips as she openly stared at his cock. "Will it… Will we fit?"

"Here." He kneeled between her spread legs, placed her hand on him, closed her fingers around his shaft. "Don't be afraid." Through hooded eyes he watched her, this incredible lady, as she slowly, tentatively began to stroke him.

Damon groaned as her soft, innocently exploring hand brought him quickly to the brink. He reached down and stayed her hand, breathing harshly.

"I'm sorry!" Carenza tried to tug her hand away, but he shook his head, held her still on him.

"Never apologize for your touch." He cupped his hand around hers, showed her how to move, helping her slowly stroke his shaft, tormenting him. He closed his eyes, dropping his head back in surrender, letting her explore his body. Tonight, it was hers. *He* was hers.

When he could stand no more, he removed her hand and bent at the waist, nibbled a path down over her gorgeously full, round hip to her blonde curls and her perfect, beautifully powerful cunt. "Let me taste you."

Languid from two climaxes already, Carenza opened eagerly for him, and he spread her slick, plump folds and licked her, devoured her, his hunger demanding satiation. Release.

Damon lapped at her, sucking her swollen clit between his lips, flicking his tongue over it. Slow and leisurely at first, and then faster and harder as she began to pant and thrust her hips into him. "That's it," he growled when she fisted her hands in his hair and raised her knees, braced the bottoms of her feet on his wide, strong shoulders.

"Damon," she moaned, her head rolling back and forth.

"Come on my tongue, love. *Come.*"

And she did.

Carenza screamed his name, and he rose over her, braced his hands on either side of her face. "Look at me," he demanded, pushing his cock impatiently at her hot, wet entrance.

Her eyes fluttered open, and Carenza dazedly looked at him. "Mmm?"

"You're mine," he growled, and drove into her, burying his shaft deep inside her in one long thrust.

She gasped. "Yours," she agreed, raising her knees and taking him deeper. "Yours."

Damon lost himself then, gave over to the need raging through him. Dropping his forehead to hers, he thrust—hard, long strokes—until he felt her velvet sheath tighten around him, signaling her impending release, and he buried his cock deep. So deep he knew not where he ended and she began; their bodies and souls fused, entwining invisibly.

On a mighty cry he came, clenching tight as the wave washed over him like a typhoon, wrecking him.

As his world shattered, he held on to Carenza.

His lady.

His one and only love.

Oh God, his *love*.

CHAPTER EIGHTEEN

S HE WAS LEAVING.

Not just Damon's bed—which she had done quite early that morning while he was still sleeping, her heart aching fiercely. And she was not merely leaving Mayfair, or even the whole of London. Carenza was leaving *England*.

Anything to avoid marriage to Lord Arnold.

Snake.

Weasel.

Fiancé.

"Ugh!" Carenza pulled a face and stepped through the back door of the Meadowlark Tavern before closing it with a soft click behind her. Although it was probably unwise, she'd simply *had* to come. How could she leave without saying goodbye to West? Sadie? The two people who had supported her the most as Meadowlark.

She could not risk her sisters accidentally ruining her escape, and so she had hugged them supremely hard and long before retiring for bed, and settled for leaving them each notes promising to write once she was settled in Scotland. Perhaps, in time and if she was fortunate, they could come for a visit. That would— well, that would be quite lovely.

If her father did not completely disown her.

"Rather *disowned* by one's own family than be *owned* by another," Carenza muttered, hefting her extremely full travel bag down the tavern hall. As the plan was to never return to Tipton House, she had gathered all essential items and placed them in her bag. The peacock-blue carriage dress that she wore had been selected for being the newest of her traveling dresses. For it may be quite some time before she could afford a new wardrobe. A home, carriage, food—those were the essentials, the first items to procure with her earnings as the Masked Meadowlark. While not a fortune, she had saved a tidy sum. Enough to live her quiet spinster life.

Damon.

Her heart squeezed painfully, and she choked back a cry. Now that she knew him so intimately, the spinster's life held little appeal. Still, it was far, *far* better than a life lived as Lord Arnold's wife. His *property.*

Now that she knew Damon's touch, no other's touch would do.

Now that she knew his heart, no other's heart would do.

No other *man.*

Rather a life alone than spent with the wrong one.

"Meadowlark, is that you?"

Carenza placed her bag in her dressing room, replying, "It is!" Briskly, she strode down the hall and through the door to the bar, the heels of her boots clicking on the hardwood floors. She pitched her voice low. "I have not come to sing, however."

West looked up from pouring ales, a white towel slung over his broad shoulder, and frowned in concern. "You feeling all right?"

Noting several interested customers glancing at her, Carenza reached the bar and leaned far over the glossy wood top. "We need to talk." She lowered her voice even further, smiling casually like her whole world hadn't turned upside down, that it was not ending. As if she had not fallen in love with a man—the *perfect* man for her—only to be forced to marry another. "Sadie, too." Carenza signaled to her friend farther down the bar helping herself to a pint.

Without looking to see if they were following, Carenza tucked a stray blonde curl back under her wide-brimmed bonnet and spun on the heels of her boots. She took a long, thorough look around the cozy tavern, with its huge open fireplace, thick-beamed ceiling, and simple wooden tables and chair sets scattered about, her chest hitching with the knowledge that she may never see the place again. May never again sing there.

So much change, so fast! How was she to keep up with it all while her heart was breaking?

Wiping at the tears that insisted on falling, against her strict orders for them to do the opposite, Carenza noted one last time the velvet curtains and the small center stage at the front of the pub. Oh, how cruel life was!

"What's wrong, Carenza?" Sadie asked the moment the three of them stepped through the door separating the pub from the back storage areas.

"You seem bothered," West added, his thick brows pulling low. "Like something mighty bad is chewing at you."

"I'm leaving!"

And with that said, Carenza burst into tears. Hot, grief-fueled tears that poured down her cheeks and spattered like raindrops across the decorative embellished bodice of her carriage dress.

"Oh, darling!" Sadie reached for her and wrapped her tightly in a hug. "Whatever for?"

"Did Crowe cause this?" West scowled. "I know he has been sniffing around you like a hunting dog on a fox scent."

"He did not." Carenza shook her head, still hugging her friend close. The comfort felt nice. Who knew when she would once again experience the comfort of a hug? "Damon only made me love him."

Sadie gasped.

"*You?*" West asked, clearly shaken. "He did *what* to you?"

"Oh, Carenza." Sadie squeezed her tight. "That is tough."

"It is." Love, it turned out, *was* rather tough.

"Do I need to beat him?" West demanded, suddenly seeming

to recover from his shock. "Surely he deserves it."

"No." Carenza sniffed and straightened from Sadie's embrace. "You could pummel Lord Horace Arnold, Viscount of Amslee, however. *He* is the reason I am leaving."

"Do not tell me—" Sadie started.

"My father engaged me to him! *He* is my intended. Without thought to my feelings or desires. Without thought to the agreed terms of letting *me* pick by the end of the Season. Oh no, Father settled terms with the viscount yesterday. Without *me*. Without considering me *at all*. It's *my* life!"

"That's awful!"

"*That* rat-faced toff? You're engaged to *him*?" West asked.

"Yes, and yes. But I will not be yoked to such a person."

"Carenza, you can't run away. Your family—" West started.

"Of course she can!" Sadie tossed an arm around Carenza's shoulder protectively. "A woman can do whatever she needs to do to protect and care for herself. No man can judge what a woman does until his own life and all choice have been taken from him by another. Controlled by another." Sadie glared at West. "Have yours?"

"Well…no."

"All right, then."

"Thank you," Carenza said. It felt wonderful to have her friends' support.

"But what about Damon?" asked West.

Carenza stepped away from Sadie and hugged herself. "What about him?"

She wanted him, loved him—and could not have him. There was not much left to say. She was bound to another.

Emotion welled in her chest, and Carenza's shoulders began to shake. At that moment, it was all too much—simply too much. How could life be so unfair?

"Are you going to cry?" The pub owner looked at her, a bit panicked. "I'm not so good with the crying."

"I'm not"—Carenza sniffed, tears welling—"crying. You're

crying."

"I'm going to get you something for your nose." West glanced up and down the empty hall frantically. "Damn it," he muttered when he saw nothing.

"Where will you go?" Sadie asked quietly, pulling a small linen square from her peach-hued dress sleeve and handing it to Carenza. "You know I will do anything I possibly can to help you."

Carenza took the delicately embroidered linen square and dabbed her watery eyes, a part of her noting the fineness of the fabric and precision needlework. "Thank you." And then she burst out, emotions swelling like the tide. "Thank you both so much for everything!" Overwhelmed, she broke down crying.

"There, there," West said, patting her shoulder awkwardly, before hooking a thumb over his shoulder and turning his head toward the door to the main part of the pub. "I, um, need to get back out front, though."

At that moment, the back door of the tavern was flung wide open, splintering as it slammed against the wall.

"Hey now!" West hollered, spinning his head back around. "Who the hell are you?"

Several men dressed all in black with matching black face coverings rushed through the door, shouting obscenities.

"The Revivalists!" Sadie cried.

Terror welled in Carenza, and she froze, shocked still by the mob of monsters coming full speed at her. "No!" she screamed, jumping and shrinking against the wall. But there was nowhere, no place to go in the hall, no way to hide, and Carenza watched in horror as one of the Revivalists turned their wild, menacing gaze her way.

"That one," he said, pointing a black-gloved finger at her. "I want her."

"The hell you do!" shouted West, bunching his fists.

"Carenza!" Sadie screamed, and threw herself at the madmen trying to get to her. "Run!"

Carenza turned, but a hand latched on to her dress sleeve. Blindly, she struck out, connecting solidly with one of their faces. Her attacker swore, and his voice was so familiar that she halted momentarily.

"Little bitch!" the Revivalist snarled, grabbing her viciously around the waist.

"Don't hurt her!" Sadie screamed, but was silenced with a blow to her head and dropped like a stone to the floor.

West was next—the glint of a knife blade flashed before the bartender grunted and doubled over, blood blooming across the belly of his tunic.

"*You*," the monster with the familiar voice said, reaching for her once again, grabbing her painfully and drawing her so close that she could see the whites of his beady eyes.

And that was when it struck her, like lightning from the sky, why this monster's voice was so familiar.

Carenza gasped, terrified. "*You!*"

Pain exploded in her head, her temple throbbed, and her world went black.

How could he let Carenza marry the Viscount of Amslee?

"I can't," Damon said, kicking at a pebble with his Wellington as he strode down Fleet Street, making his way back to his flat after an afternoon searching St. Giles and Wapping for a forger who—it turned out—had died three years ago in a drowning accident in the Strand. Though Damon had his doubts about it being an "accident," given the forger's line of work. "But what choice do I have?"

None.

He had none.

"Fuck me." His chest hurt; his heart was sore as hell. Damon raised a fist and rubbed there, pressing the heel of his palm against his sternum. "Was easier when I felt nothing."

But then Carenza had come along, as bright as the sun itself, and thawed him from the inside out. Made him feel. Made him *love.*

"Bloody hurts."

"Wot's tha', mate?" a man in a tan hat questioned as Damon walked along the bustling street. Curricles and hacks and single riders on horseback hurrying somewhere moved along Fleet Street, ever in a rush.

Damon ignored the man, reached into the breast pocket of his dove-gray waistcoat for a cigarette, and recalled Carenza's gentle admonishment at his habit. He checked the time on his pocket watch instead, eager to refresh himself at his flat before making his way to the Meadowlark Tavern. Surely Carenza would be there. Of course she would be there. She would not stop living for herself, no matter what.

Though he knew not what could be done about her engagement to Lord Arnold, he knew that staying away from her was impossible.

The way she had given herself to him last eve still devastated him. So open, so giving. So incredibly passionate. Damon's heart squeezed, and his cock swelled. He coughed, off-kilter at the opposing sensations happening right there in the open on Fleet Street.

"There you are!"

In mid-stride, Damon froze and spun on his heels. When he saw who hailed him, his shoulders eased and a friendly smile softened his mouth. "Jamie, good to see you. How do you fare this afternoon?"

Jamie, the young printer's apprentice, returned his greeting and shrugged his shoulders—thin now but hinting at the width and strength to come. "Oh, I'm well as can be expected, I suppose, Mr. Crowe." The kid tipped back his tweed cap, his fingertips black with ink, the haphazardly rolled-up tunic smudged with spots of the black liquid. "We just got the latest edition of that rumor rag you despise printed up and shipped out. I'm about to call it a day and close up shop. Cleeve says I can. Sure is a rare thing, finishing before the sun is down. Goin' to enjoy while I can."

"Absolutely." Youths. So enthusiastic, so…young. "Have a grand night, then." Damon smiled again, sending the lad on his way.

"Oh! I near forgot." The printer's apprentice held up a finger. "Hold a moment. I got something inside the shop for you. It came only a bit ago, but I got distracted helping Mr. Lowe load his cart." Jamie dashed down two doors into the printer's and returned a moment later with a folded piece of parchment.

Damon eyed the parchment warily. "Who gave this to you?" Suspicion crept up his spine, narrowed his dark eyes.

Jamie pointed down Fleet Street, his young face honest and guileless. "Can't say that I know him, Mr. Crowe. But he gave me that parchment and took off at a fast pace down the street that way."

"Thank you, lad. Do you remember what he looked like, this person who gave you the parchment? Can you describe him to me?"

Jamie pushed his tweed hat further up his head and scratched his temple, scrunched his freckled face in thought. "Small fellow. *Huge* nose."

Castlebury's snitch.

Though he wanted to snatch it from the kid's hands, Damon took the parchment from Jamie with forced casualness and patted him on the shoulder. "Got it. Excellent job, thank you."

"You're welcome, Mr. Crowe. Have a good night."

Mumbling something in the vein of a farewell, Damon dismissed the printer's apprentice, his pulse beating rapidly as he unfolded the parchment and looked over what was inside.

His life came to a grinding, shattering halt.

"It can't be," he breathed. After all this time. After all the failed searches, after digging through all the secrets and filth of the aristocracy, his efforts had finally, *finally* borne fruit. His vision blurred, and his breath hitched, and his mother—his kind, loving mother—swam before his eyes.

For years she had carried the shame, the guilt of having been violated by a man, of bearing him a child. Damon. A child she could have refused and abandoned, but whom she had loved dearly until her dying breath—when the pain of her violation had become too much to further bear, propelling her to take her own life. Leaving Damon an orphan. Alone. Afraid. Unloved.

Now he knew the bastard's name.

With hands trembling from the emotion coursing through him, Damon read the name—the single, incriminating name—beneath a sketch of the perpetrator's family ring: *Amslee*.

The bastard who had raped his mother was the late Viscount of Amslee. Fucking *Amslee*. Lord Arnold's father.

Damon's father.

All the effort, all the searching, the weight of other people's sins on his conscience, and now he *knew*.

Damon gulped air like a drowning man and leaned against the nearest building, bent over at the waist, paper clenched in his hand. Grief swarmed him, surrounded him, settled *inside* him. All the grief he had held back about his mother all these years. This bastard, this no-longer-faceless, now-named bastard broke her, drove her past the last vestiges of her endurance. And because she was nobody—a poor Spanish seamstress in the rookery—nothing to society, the son of a bitch had gotten away with it until his dying day. Taking his horrible, awful secret to the grave.

But now Damon knew.

And a part of him, the little child inside who lost his mother far too early, wanted to cry. Just cry.

"Oof." He released a gust of air, straightened, and looked down at the folded parchment in his hand. Frowning at it, he narrowed his eyes and noticed the small, terribly scribbled handwriting shoved in a corner margin like an afterthought. It read: *Cuzzin rote wot made the Castlebury gel a proper lady. More ale pleez?*

"Fucking Christ," growled Damon, ignoring the drunkard snitch's plea for more free drink. *"Castlebury."*

The earl was a liar and a hypocrite.

Goddamn nobility.

Suddenly it all made sense to Damon; the pieces were falling into perfect place. "So *that's* why he's forcing her to marry the Viscount of Amslee." Or should he call him Lord Arnold, his half-blood brother?

What in bloody hell was he supposed to do with *that* information?

"There you are, thank God!"

Damon glanced at the frantically calling brunette running down the street toward him and recognized her from the Meadowlark Tavern. She was Carenza's friend, Sadie.

Oh hell, *Carenza.*

"Where is she?" Damon demanded, somehow knowing something was wrong.

Screeching to a halt before him, the petite woman panted and stammered terribly, "Th-th-the Revivalists!"

His blood ran cold. "*Where is she?*" he demanded again, grabbing the small woman by the shoulders, shaking her none too gently. "Where is Carenza?"

"Th-they *took* her!" Sadie wailed, her brown hair tangling wildly about her face, her eyes huge and glistening with fear. "The Revivalists kidnapped her from the tavern! Oh God, Carenza." Tears overflowed and streamed down her face as she openly wept. "They, they got her!"

His mind churning with fear for Carenza, he had the presence of mind to ask, "Is everyone else alive? Where's West?" And then, "Do you know where they took her?"

"No." Sadie shook her head, swiped a forearm under her dripping nose. "I don't know wh-where they t-took her. West is injured." Her gaze went distant and unfocused. "Maybe he's dead. The blood, oh God, the blood." She sobbed, hugging herself tight.

But then her head popped up and she slapped him on the chest, over and over, as if trying to remember something important. "Oooh. Oh! O-one of the Revivalists!" Her head shook back and forth, and she kept patting his chest rapidly. "He, he's…we know him! Ooh, what is it? What is his name? Th-the one who took Carenza?" And then she stopped, went utterly still as her eyes went round and she stared unseeing up at him. "It's… He's…Amslee." She gasped, her eyes refocusing. "It's Lord Arnold!"

"Fuck!" Damon swore, his insides freezing with worry. *"Fuck!"*

"Where is she?" Sadie shook. "Oh, God."

"I need you to listen to me very carefully." Damon gripped the woman's shoulders and held her steady, fear for Carenza screaming through him like an Irish banshee. "This is very important. Can you hear me? Do you understand what I am saying?"

Sadie nodded, her eyes terrified but clearing.

"Good. Now, go directly to the Bow Street Runners' headquarters on Bow Street and get Carenza's brother, Catamount. Tell him what happened, everything you know."

"Bow Street. Catamount. Right."

Damon released his grip and fought to quiet the terror ripping through him for Carenza. "Good. Go now."

Sadie nodded and spun around on her worn boots, took several steps, and spun back around. "What will you do?" she called out, walking down the sidewalk backward as she waited for his response.

Closing his eyes, Damon took several steadying, calming breaths and turned his nose to the air, his ears to the wind. Listening. *Smelling.* Trusting them to lead the way. He caught a hint, a tug of the slightest something at the edges of his consciousness (lilacs and lemons, perhaps?) and pressed his lips in a grim, determined line. "I'm going to find her."

Amslee was a Revivalist.

Lord Arnold.

The worthless toff who was obsessed with Meadowlark.

Damon's eyes shot open. And he knew. He *knew*.

"I know where she is!" Crumpling the parchment into his trouser pocket, no longer concerned about his sire in the face of this horrible reality, Damon pushed his panic down and set off at a run down Fleet Street, calling out the location for Sadie to relate to Bow Street.

He knew where to find her.

Damon only prayed it was not too late.

CHAPTER NINETEEN

CARENZA WOKE TO a pounding headache and the feel of rope binding her wrists behind her back. "Wh-what happened?" Oh, her head throbbed! Her shoulder too. Fiery pain seared a path down her left arm, and she cried out helplessly.

"Wakey-wakey, li'l bird!" A voice broke through her pain, called to her. "That's it. Just like that Masked Meadowlark. Or perhaps I should call you by your given name, *Lady Carenza.*"

Blinking rapidly against the tears burning her eyes, Carenza tugged against the bindings, found they held steady. The voice, the monster's voice, was so familiar. "D-do I know you?" Another thought. "Where are the others?"

Suddenly a masked face appeared directly before her, and beady, wild eyes hard as glass glared at her. "Boo!"

Carenza screamed and jolted, tried to jerk away. Where was she? Was anyone looking for her? She remembered the rush of black-clad men into the back of the tavern, recalled West falling limp to the ground from a stab wound to his stomach. "Oh, West!" Carenza cried.

"Eh, I don't think he's dead," her captor sneered. "He didn't smell dead. And I know that smell. I like that smell."

As she yanked at her ropes again, Carenza's vision cleared enough for her to see her surroundings, to recognize where she was. The cold, smoothly polished floor beneath her as she sat, shivering and terrified, helped place her somewhere familiar.

A theatre.

And suddenly Carenza pieced it all together, knew who was behind the plain black mask and all the horrible, gruesome attacks. Knew who was a Revivalist.

"Lord Arnold," Carenza whispered, her voice raspy with fear and disgust. "I-it's *you!*"

"That's correct!" Lord Arnold exclaimed excitedly, clapping his black-gloved hands together. "Oh, how lovely for my name to precede me!"

Memory tumbled through her aching brain, and Carenza looked around desperately for anyone, anything to help. But to no avail. It appeared she was alone in the big, ornate theatre with Lord Horace Arnold: a Revivalist and her fiancé.

"And you!" he declared, standing in the center of the stage all in black, and her stomach lurched greasily. "It seems as though we have *both* been keeping secrets. And really, is that any proper way to start a marriage?" Somehow, he had a dagger, a sharp-tipped thing, and he pointed it at her. "Tsk, tsk, my lady. That will not do. A lady must reveal all things to her future husband."

Scooting back, shoving with the heels of her boots, Carenza pushed herself on her bum across the stage, her mind screaming for help, for a way out of this. "I won't marry you!" Shaking her head, Carenza kept her attention on her crazed fiancé, and saw his eyes glowing with a sickness, a kind of unholy madness.

How was she to survive this?

Keep him talking! the voice in her head screamed. *Keep him talking and give someone, anyone, time to find and help you.*

"You will marry me!" Lord Arnold shouted, spittle spraying out. He rushed her from across the stage, slapped her hard across the cheek. "Whore that you are!" He backed up a step, nodded his black-masked head. "Oh yes, I will teach you your place."

"My place?" Blast it all, she was sick and tired of hearing about her *place*.

"Whore!" Lord Arnold rushed back to her and slapped her again, snapping her head back and clattering her teeth. But she refused to cry out.

"If I'm such a whore"—Carenza straightened, spat blood from the lip he'd split, and glared at the viscount, as her anger now vied for space alongside her fear—"why do you want to marry me?"

"You *were* perfect," Lord Arnold snarled. "The perfect young lady from the perfectly established, ancient family. No scandals, no marks. It would have done so much to elevate me in Society, our marriage." The viscount spun on his heels, stalking across the stage with a sharp rapping of his boots on the stage floor. "No one would dare question me then. I would have been above reproach!"

"But you're a murderer!"

"Well, when you say it like *that*," the mad aristocrat said, playing with the blade of the dagger he had plucked from a small side table of prop weapons. "We prefer to call it cutting out what is unnecessary." He nicked his thumb with the dagger blade and grinned happily. "Oh, this is sharp!"

"I *heard* you." Carenza remembered that night. Terror and disgust filled her for this monster of a human. "I *heard* all of you Revivalists in Covent Garden. And you, *you*...oh, you sounded *gleeful*." How? How could anyone delight in another's torture? Get so much joy in another person's pain? "I hid and I *heard*—I listened in that alley."

"*You*." The viscount's eyes cut to her, glinting bright with madness under the theatre lights. "I *knew* someone had been hiding! You li'l sneak, you." He slapped her once more, and Carenza cried out this time, unable to hold it in as she lost vision from the force of it. "Ah, but no matter. We can finish what I wanted to start that night."

Carenza struggled backward across the floor, yanking feverishly at the ropes. "All those people you killed; all those lives you destroyed! Why? How could you do it?"

"You question me?" Lord Arnold rounded on her, held the small, pointed dagger aloft. He aimed it at her heart, stepped in her direction, his whiny voice echoing, reverberating in the big, empty theatre. "You, who has been whoring about with that gutter scum, that…that Damon Crowe." He waggled the dagger at her. "Oh, I saw. I witnessed firsthand the way you two behaved when you were in the same room as one another. You, like a bitch in full heat." His small eyes scrunched up in fury behind his mask. "And *him*. Sniffing around *you*, a pathetic mutt with no pedigree wanting a hump with a lady." The viscount hissed between his teeth and came at her, held the dagger blade to her cheek. "And when I put one and one together yesterday after my little run-in with your mongrel cock and realized in devastation that *my* virtuous fiancée was nothing more than a common whore who could sing pleasantly—who has been spreading her legs for rookery trash—well I, of course, had to make you pay dearly. I mean, it *is* only fitting."

Lord Arnold crouched next to her, and Carenza flinched, but held her gaze steady as he reached out a long, bony finger and gently wiped the blood from her split, swelling, and bruised lip. Then he put his blood-covered finger in his mouth and slowly, thoroughly licked it clean. "Mmm, tasty."

Carenza's stomach lurched, and she gagged.

"Do you know," he said conversationally, rising to his feet as he continued to lick the very last drops of her blood from his finger with a demented smile, "that there has always been an Amslee viscount doing his societal duty to rid the world of waste, of the ones who do nothing, are nothing? Who drag the whole of society down simply by their mere presence? Oh yes, there has always been a Viscount of Amslee at the helm. There was the Fourth Viscount of Amslee—my personal hero—whom I quite take after, actually. He was a member of the Mohocks, the band of brave noblemen we Revivalists emulate."

"And there's you," Carenza whispered, glancing about for something, *anything* she might use to aid her escape. "A Revivalist."

"A traditionalist, yes, through and through." The mad aristocrat beamed proudly, puffing out his chest.

Good God, where is someone?

Closing her eyes, shutting them tightly, Carenza sent out a wish, hoping beyond hope that Damon would find her.

"Do you know how furious I was to discover that my fiancée, *my* intended, was the very same slut singer who refused to perform in my theatre?" Lord Arnold flung his arms wide, motioning to the theatre seats behind him, the gold and red brocade, and their intricately carved wooden backs. Posh, so very posh the theatre appeared in the dim candelabra lining the silk screen walls. "So much elegance and beauty. Apparently too much for the Masked Meadowlark slut."

Carenza's brain ached as she tried to keep up with the swift changes in the viscount's mood and topics. It was so very dizzying.

"I have never felt so shunned, so scorned, so…humiliated before in my life. It shall not be borne!" Rage twisted his lips, and they pulled back from his gums in a snarl, baring strong white teeth. He raised the dagger, gripped it with both hands above his head, and barreled toward her, his eyes blazing. *"Whore!"*

Suddenly a motion, a blur, came from off stage to her left, and went directly at the viscount. A flash of dark, unruly hair, broad shoulders, and a tall, powerful body. A rumbling roar echoed off the theatre walls, the sound bone-chilling with its fury.

"Damon!" Oh, thank God, *Damon.*

DAMON FLEW AT the mad nobleman and tackled him. He lifted him off his feet and slammed him to the ground before hitting him, roaring all the while in blind, consuming rage. The smacking, raw, and vicious sound of flesh on flesh, flesh on bone, filled the theatre.

Damon kept at it, hammering the madman—the *murderer*—over and over, not stopping or slowing when the sound of bones breaking under his knuckles rang out with a snap, and blood sprayed out from the viscount's nose.

"You"—Damon swung, connected with a grunt—"sick bastard."

"My nose!" Lord Arnold shrieked. "My fucking nose!"

"Here, let me help," Damon snarled, and slammed his fist into the viscount's nose again, ruthlessly, until the Revivalist dropped limp and unconscious to the floor.

Heart hammering, blood racing, fueled by fear and a desperate need to find Carenza, Damon spun from the knocked-out viscount and rose, prowled the stage to his love, his one and only love, and dropped to his knees before her, breathing heavily. He cupped her cheeks gently, tenderly, his hands bruised and battered and bloody.

"Oh, thank God, Carenza!" He kissed her, hard and brief. "Are you hurt?" he asked, his chest heaving from exertion and so very much emotion. "Oh fuck, oh Christ, I thought I had lost you." He stroked her face, her shoulders, looking for signs of injury.

"My hands," she rasped, her golden hair tangled in clumps before her face, her top lip cut at the right corner, swollen and bruised. "They're still tied."

"Did Arnold do that?" His voice was low, deadly as he looked at his love, knew there had been pain for her. He stilled inside until there was one simple truth. "I'll kill him for hurting you." He reached behind Carenza and made quick work of the rope restraining her.

"I am well. I will be all right." Her eyes grew round and filled with tears. "But West. He…he—" She pressed her lips together, wincing in discomfort.

Anger rumbled in his chest, and Damon began to rise to his feet, the rope from Carenza's wrists in hand. "Where are the other Revivalists? Sadie said there were more." He looked around the theatre, but saw no one.

"Gone," she replied as he helped her to her feet. "Before I regained consciousness. He was the only one here."

Because she was alive, because she was safe, because he could not help it…because he *loved* her, Damon swept her into his arms and kissed her once more. "When we are done here, I am going to tell you that I love you and that I will do whatever it takes to convince you to have me. I am a rich man, Carenza. You will want for nothing." He looked up and over his shoulder as Lord Arnold began to whimper and stir. "Remind me," he said, striding to the viscount.

"I'll remind you," she called out. "Remind me to tell you that I love you too!"

His heart shifted inside his chest, expanded wide, full with Carenza. Only Carenza. *Ever* Carenza.

His *love*.

Damon would see them safely home so that he could demonstrate his love for her over and over, until the early hours of dawn. And then he was holding her close and never letting her go.

A step or two from the prone viscount, Damon had glanced back at Carenza, his mind needing yet one more assurance that she was, indeed, alive, and relatively unharmed, when it happened. Lord Arnold opened his eyes and rolled, swift and unexpected, swiping at Damon's ankles. The connection caught him off guard, and he stumbled, fell forward toward the stage floor, hitting his temple hard on the corner of a wooden stage prop crate.

"Damon!" he heard Carenza scream as he went down, twisting as he fell, taking the blow to his head.

Lord Arnold released a sound so high-pitched and eerie it threatened to shatter their eardrums, and then he slithered, rocked sideways, and regained his feet, raising the dagger above him, about to strike Damon in the heart.

"Drop your weapon, Lord Arnold! *Now!*"

The powerful call came with a crash of thunder as Catamount and his Runners burst into the theatre, pouring down the aisles in long coats, double-barrel pistols aimed and at the ready. "We *will* shoot!"

The viscount twisted around, searching for an escape, and finding none as more and more Bow Street Runners filled the theatre, fanning out to surround Lord Arnold, pistols levelled on his chest. He snarled and bared his teeth like a wild, trapped animal, his eyes wide and white-rimmed.

"Where are the other Revivalists, Amslee? We know you did not kidnap Lady Carenza alone," Captain Catamount Castlebury said, his voice devoid of emotion, completely composed even though Carenza was his family. "Tell us who and where they are and you will be spared."

"Give my brothers' names over to you? Surely you jest."

Damon watched from his prone position, his mind dizzy and slow from the crate to his temple.

"I never jest," the captain of the Bow Street Runners replied, sounding utterly sincere. He raised his pistol, sighted on Amslee.

"I will *never* betray a brother. Never! It is tradition!" Lord Arnold shifted, moved his arm holding the dagger—and the Runners prepared to shoot.

"Carenza, stay down!"

"You will never find them!" Lord Arnold declared, and laughed maniacally, raising the hairs on Damon's forearms.

And in one swift motion, Lord Arnold brought the dagger to his throat and slit it wide, laughing still as blood gushed from his wound and he dropped lifeless to the ground, his laughter dying in a wet, popping gurgle.

"Carenza!" Damon called out, leaping to his feet.

She was there, in his arms, kissing his cheek, his lips. "Oh, Damon!" she cried, burying her face in his chest as he wrapped her in a tight, protective embrace.

"Carenza, my love." The pain in his head receded under her healing kisses. "I love you." It felt so good to say it! "I love you," he repeated as she looked up at him, her gorgeous, big blue eyes glistening with emotion. "I love you."

"I love *you*," she whispered, and kissed him, filled him with warmth and hope and promise. Christ, he wanted to promise her everything.

Bow Street Runners burst onto the stage then, barking orders and surrounding the very much dead Lord Arnold, Revivalist member.

"Damn it," Catamount swore as he pushed through his men, looking tired and grim and determined in his long coat, his face unshaven. "Now we're back to no Revivalist leads. I needed that canary to sing." The captain turned to Carenza, reached out a hand, and placed it on her shoulder as Damon held her tight. He refused to ever let her go. "I'm thankful you're safe, sis." Catamount flicked his tired green gaze down to the viscount. "At least now you don't have to marry him."

Damon tensed as that truth washed over him. That truth and the other closely related fact—his newly discovered one.

Around him, Runners talked in low murmurs, lowered their pistols, and placed them discreetly away.

"What should we do with the Viscount of Amslee?" one Runner asked, nudging the lifeless body with the toe of his boot.

"Throw him in the Thames," Damon muttered, his heart thundering as he realized all of life's new possibilities. Possibilities of a way in the world that he had never dared dream of.

He released his hold on Carenza and slid a hand into his pocket, found the parchment there. "You don't, um…" He cleared his throat, found the words that he most wanted to say. "You don't have to marry *that* Viscount of Amslee." Damon unfolded the parchment and held it out for Carenza to see, his heart, his everything, right out there on display for her and all the world to see. Christ, he felt vulnerable. But he wanted her more than he wanted air—this creative, independent woman.

"What is this?" she asked. "I do not understand."

"I did not either, until a few hours ago." Damon grasped her hand and laced his fingers with hers as he pointed with his free hand to the drawing of the ring. The exact rendering of the one currently resting on the dead Amslee's pinky finger. "You don't have to marry that Viscount of Amslee," he repeated, "but you could marry *me.*" His heart pounded fiercely. He was so much in love it hurt. "I am the real and true Viscount of Amslee."

"I don't understand," Carenza said, her brow furrowing. "Wait, are you saying what I think you're saying?" The hope he saw in her incredible blue eyes lifted him high, made him feel like he could fly.

"That's right, milady." He cracked a smile, a full, wide-open grin that displayed his crooked incisor as he laughed and let his rookery show. "This damn bloke is the son of the late Viscount of Amslee, just discovered. Believe me, it's a very long story."

"Oh, is it?" Carenza asked, sliding back into his embrace. "I like stories. Especially long ones."

"I like *you,*" he murmured, wrapping her in his arms and kissing the tip of her nose.

"I like you," she replied, and rose on her toes to kiss him soundly on his mouth.

"So you'll marry me, then?"

His heart rejoiced when she nodded.

"I will," she agreed, making his whole life, his whole *world.* "But first, I must hear this long story. And perhaps an explanation about the scribbles in the corner of the parchment that undoubtedly involve me."

"Fair enough," Damon agreed. He lowered his forehead to hers and thanked his lucky stars for this miracle—this incredible woman to love. "The story begins with a young Gitano girl in Spain who traveled to London to become a famous dressmaker."

"Oh, this is going to be long story." She tucked herself into his arms, fitting perfectly. "Perhaps we should go elsewhere?"

"I know a place." He led her down the stage steps and through the theatre aisle to the exit.

"Oh, really?"

"It's true, I do. The manservant there is rather pushy about his tea, however."

"That's only because he cares."

"I love you, *hechicera.*"

"I love you too, Damon Crowe, newly titled Viscount of Amslee."

Damon grimaced over the address but figured he would get used to it.

He kissed the top of Carenza's golden head, gave thanks.

A stuffy title was a small price to pay for the incredible gift of her love.

EPILOGUE

Six weeks later
Rhodes Theatre
London

"**I**T'S MARVELOUS," CARENZA whispered, staring out at the audience of Rhodes Theatre from backstage. The most opulent theatre she had ever seen, the place captivated her with its elaborate balconies and gorgeous seating arrangements.

"Why, yes, it is. I agree," Damon replied softly from behind her, sliding his hands up the bodice of her sapphire-blue silk and satin dress and squeezing her breasts through the expensive fabric. Instantly, they plumped and grew sensitive, heavy, wanting his touch. Aching for it. "Simply marvelous," he purred.

"Stop it," she said, slapping halfheartedly at his strong, clever fingers even as she arched into him, craving his touch. *Always* craving. Would it ever end? Would the hunger ever ease?

She hoped not, most fervently.

"Every night you come for me. On my tongue, on my hands, on my cock." He kissed her neck, trailed his tongue along the sensitive curve of her ear, his hot breath making her shiver with anticipation. "Every single night you come for me. But it's not enough. It's *never* enough." He pressed into her from behind, fit her to his erection, and heat pooled low in her belly. His manhood, so full and ready. For her, Damon was always ready. Another thing she hoped would never change. For she had discovered quickly just how much she enjoyed his manhood. She adored caressing it, kissing it…licking it. Oh, so many delicious things. Quite the discovery it was, her unending fascination with his body. It was simply so *hard*, so, well, manly.

"You do wicked things to me, *hechicera*." He sank his teeth into the nape of her neck, and she sucked in a quick breath, excited by the sting. "It's why I had no choice but to marry you."

"Very clever of you, Viscount Amslee."

For two glorious weeks they had been wed already. Two weeks filled with loving this complex, wonderful man. A man who turned out to actually be the legitimate heir to the Amslee viscountcy—older than Lord Arnold had been by two years.

"You know, I've got a rather lot of heavy lifting to do to clean the smudge off that family legacy. Amslees. Lot of buggers, madmen, and thieves."

"And you," Carenza pointed out, tilting her head to the side to provide him better access. "You are absolutely none of those things."

"True," he agreed lightly, tracing his fingers along the low-cut line of her bodice. "Merely a demon redeemed by the love of one extraordinary woman."

"Which reminds me," she started, but stopped when she felt a draft slither up her skirt behind her. "What are you doing?"

"Helping you relax before your big debut. That's wot I'm doing, love."

"Stop it—someone will see us!"

Oh, but she didn't want him to stop. His hands did wondrous, delicious things to her body. And when one of them slid under her skirt and touched her, a thick, long finger slipping between her folds to stroke her just where she desired him the most, Carenza forgot entirely that she was backstage at Rainville's Rhodes Theatre, about to perform there for the first time as the Masked Meadowlark, with a full audience already seated and waiting.

"Oh, don't stop." She melted against him. "Keep going."

"Whatever you desire, viscountess." Damon's voice, his rough, rookery-edged voice, softened and went warm with love. Love for her. This tough, dark, and dangerous man. It was amazing.

She could not deny this man anything, because his touch sent her flying, his love sent her soaring on wings of possibility and trust so beautiful and precious that she often wondered how it was that a girl such as her could experience such a gift, such a blessing.

For several minutes there was only the sound of silk rustling and shallow, rapid breathing as Damon sent her to the stars once more. When she came back down, she knew his love was a precious, unique blessing. "Thank you for seeing me." She spun slowly in his arms and kissed his beautifully sculpted mouth. "For truly, really seeing me."

"You do the same for me," Damon replied, setting her dress to rights, one corner of his mouth hitching up in a crooked smile. "You even tolerate my desperately bad poetry."

"The attempts are admirable." She kissed his stubbled chin, let her love for him show in her eyes. "Severely flawed, but admirable."

"Carenza, Carenza..." He flung up his hand and declared theatrically, "With your long and most beauteous hair—"

"I'm going to have to halt you right there, Shakespeare."

Carenza and Damon looked over, chuckling as Rainville approached, appearing every bit the duke in his red velvet jacket and gold-threaded waistcoat, his tawny hair glistening in the low theatre glow. Quite honestly, the duke rivaled her Meadowlark gown for showmanship.

"There is a rather full house out there, I'm quite pleased to say. Your talent is known and adored far and wide, Meadowlark," Rainville said. "Thank you, from the bottom of my heart, for allowing me the opportunity to showcase you in my theatre."

Excitement burst in tiny bubbles in her chest. "Thank you for keeping my secret."

"Of course." The duke inclined his head regally. "When you are ready—*if* you are ever ready—you will tell me."

"Exactly." Carenza nodded her agreement and smoothed the fabric of her gown. "And thank you for giving my family the best seats in the theatre." Even her father was in attendance. When one got a direct, personal invitation from a duke, well, one did not tend to refuse.

After the night Lord Arnold took her, she had spoken out in full with her truth, to her family. Her father had balked and raged until Damon took him into his study for several quiet minutes. The Earl of Castlebury had emerged a *much* more amiable gentleman—one inclined to let his daughter do whatever she pleased.

Bless Damon and his ways with a good secret.

"I do not know if you're aware, but West and Miss Sadie have excellent seats in the balcony as well," the duke continued. "I have been tasked to tell you that they wish you well and are proud of you."

"We all are." Damon reached for her hand, squeezed it gently. "There is nothing you have proven that you cannot achieve." Bringing her gloved hand to his lips, he kissed her knuckles, his dark eyes warm on her and filled with so much love. "I worship you, goddess of my heart."

"Oh, please." Rainville groaned. "Not this again. You are no bloody Byron. I keep telling you."

"But I could be."

"No, you can't."

And so the two bickered until Carenza squared her shoulders and made her decision. "It's time."

Strength. Resiliency. Courage. *Hope.*

The woman's weapons she cherished the most. The ones that she held the closest, that she protected the most fiercely.

Because of them, she was *here.*

"I love you, *hechicera.*" He grabbed her, pulled her close, and kissed her, lingering. When he was done, he pulled back and said with total confidence, "You can do this. You can do this, and I'm right here watching, cheering you on."

She *could* do this.

Carenza tied her mask into place, took a big breath, and stepped onto the stage and into the spotlight. The force of it was blinding. Exhilarating. *Powerful.* The crowd erupted in applause, and the sound of it was everything she'd dreamt.

She glanced to the side, just off stage at Damon, and smiled wide, ready to take on anything.

She could do this, because love had given her *wings*.

The End

About the Author

Jennifer Seasons started her career writing contemporary romances for Avon and is the author of several popular contemporary and Regency historical romances. Born in California, Jennifer has lived all over the West and now resides in the mountains of Massachusetts with her husband and their children. A dog and several cats keep them company. A lover of autumn, cozy cardigans, and coffee, Jennifer can often be found writing her novels by hand in notebooks, bundled in said cardigan with a steaming mug of dark roast nearby. When she's not writing, Jennifer enjoys running, hiking with her family, gardening, and lounging in a comfy spot with a good book and a homemade chocolate chip cookie or two.

Amazon – https://www.amazon.com/stores/Jennifer-Seasons/author/B00D8GZ5EE
Twitter – https://twitter.com/JenniferSeasons